LAKE OF URINE

A LOVE STORY

GUILLERMO STITCH

Sagging
Meniscus

Printed in Great Britain and the United States of America.
Set in Janson with LaTeX.

ISBN: 978-1-944697-94-5 (paperback)
ISBN: 978-1-944697-96-9 (ebook)
Library of Congress Control Number: 2019952593

Sagging Meniscus Press
Montclair, New Jersey
saggingmeniscus.com

For K

Acknowledgements

My deepest thanks go to Matt Dennison, without whose support and encouragement in the early stages I might not have gone ahead, to Christopher Allen for his insight and to Katherine Graham for hers, to Sally Houtman who is no longer with us and whose contribution to this work cannot be overestimated, and to John Patrick Higgins who is as culpable for the final shape of the thing as I am and whose participation I made sure, every step of the way, was torturous. Above all to Katja Spindler, whose minor and major corrections have been many, on and off the page.

Contents

Lake
of
Urine

Part One

Seiler

IF ANYBODY TELLS YOU this story isn't true they are lying. It is a true story; I am lying if it isn't, and I don't lie.

It's the story of me and Ms Emma Wakeling, and the winter I was holed up with her and her two girls, Noranbole and Urine.

What a winter! It was the deepest we had ever known, and I am uniquely qualified to say this because I know exactly how deep it was—I measured it with a piece of string and there hasn't been as deep a winter since.

That winter was so bitingly cold and full of wolves that we could only get so far from the house without freezing or getting picked off. You see that house down there by the river? The Fleming house. That's as far as any of us got.

That other house a little further along the bank was unreachable from November till early March. There was that one time Noranbole did an overnight in the Fleming house and then went on to that other house, where the Maypoles live, the next day. But that was unscientific of her, brave as she was.

Poor soul.

This is the piece of string, and if you were to stand on the Wakelings' back porch and hold it while I took the other end and walked, I would be able to touch the Flemings' front door and go no further. It would have to be you on the porch as I am no longer welcome there. Interestingly, there are no other landmarks of any kind along the circumference that the string's tip describes around the Wakeling house which correspond exactly with its length. So the Fleming house is a very exact measurement.

Useful comparisons have been made possible by this ingenious, if you'll excuse me, use of string. I have been able to demonstrate by attaching a small weight to one end—such as a stone or metal implement—that that winter was far deeper for example than the creek down where the little copse of trees is behind the Bennetts' house. However, the lake up by Swan Hill, about which we have all wondered, turns out to be even deeper than the winter string. Icy cold, black and very, very deep.

A number of winters have passed since that one and I have strings for all of them, but this one is the original. The yardstick, if you will. The root, the seed, the get go, whatever you like.

The first.

They are all different lengths, or depths as I like to term it.

Measuring this last winter was a particular challenge; it was unusually mild and I was able on one occasion to get as far as town, over seven miles away. I had to stop every hundred yards—the length of my longest spools— and tie another on. I suppose I might have gone even further since town provided the chance to rest and reprovision but Lepidopter, my mule, had run out of patience and wouldn't budge.

※

There isn't a nice way to say this: I never liked Urine. Always sniffing around, poking her nose in where it wasn't wanted. Ms Emma thought her wistful and sensitive and said so often; truth be told she was the favorite. Morose and secretive, I'd have called her. No company for anyone except that stupid pup of hers. She wasn't at all like Noranbole.

Noranbole! What a creature! How she brightened up the tool shed when she brought me down my milk!

Her beauty however was of no consequence to Ms Emma, who mistreated and made a scullery maid of her. Poor Noranbole! To be so exquisite and so overlooked! And not just by Ms Emma but by all the local snotnoses, any number of whom spent their time lurking round the place, hoping to catch a glimpse of her dreadful sister while Noranbole toiled in the dirt and debris of the household, and no one troubled themselves about her. Both girls were of marrying age and Ms Emma had a time of it keeping her eye on them, and not so much on them as on the lads who hovered round them like flies, and not so much round them as round Urine, the awful one.

※

"Here's your milk."

"Ah, Noranbole! There you are. I noticed you weren't around this morning. For several hours. Couldn't see you anywhere! Off drudging somewhere, I expect. Were you drudging? Of course you were! You're always drudging. I've spoken to Ms Emma about it but she won't listen to me, will she?"

"No."

"No. Nope. Where's that sister of yours? I can't imagine she shared any of the drudgery with you, did she? Hm? Oh the injustice! Basking, I imagine, is where she is . . . mind you I sometimes feel as if she's nearby . . . watching . . . but that's neither here nor there. Basking, in the leering attention of local bucks. She should mind out, you know—they may be young but they're not all innocent!"

"I know."

"Still, not so much of an issue for yourself, is it? Hm? Not so much a concern. Although for the life of . . . tell you what—I'll have another chat with Ms Emma this evening. For all the good it will do. You make yourself scarce. Well you always are in the evening, aren't you? After the dinner things are cleared. Scarce that is. Such a quiet, unassuming girl. You deserve so much better, Noranbole!"

"Anyway, there's your milk."

✻

We were sitting under the lean-to at the side of the house that evening, Ms Emma and I, out there for a bit of privacy. Noranbole was nowhere to be seen but that horrendous girl Urine was lurking around the place as per usual.

"Shift up. Move your bum."

We were wrapped in every threadbare blanket that could be found in the house, to keep the cold at bay. It was difficult at the best of times to have a sensible conversation with the woman but I was determined to bring up the Noranbole question. To resolve matters once and for all for the girl.

"It seems to me . . . Ms Emma, that the, eh, load is unequally . . . um, eh-eh-encumbered upon the girls . . . if you see what I . . ."

"Turn over."

"Like so? . . . and that . . . if perhaps the chores could be more equally divi-i-i-ided . . ."

"Do stop going on—this is tricky enough as it is and you're making it trickier with your prattle. Concentrate!"

"Yes of course. Don't think I don't, eh . . . it's just that, what with the cold this year . . . there's quite a b-b-b-bit to be done around the place. I'm bound to observe, Ms Wakeling tha-tha-that U-U-Uriiiiine!"

"Good. Now run along and fetch me my pipe."

She was right there, right outside the lean-to when I went to fetch Ms Emma's pipe: the wretched thing and her creepy little dog. I wouldn't be surprised if she'd been there all along.

"You called?"

✳

Noranbole and Paul Bennett. Boathouse by the creek.

"I don't know, Boley. It isn't easy to admit but I think the courtship might have gone off the boil. She isn't very big on signals at the best of times; she hasn't as much as glanced in my direction in three years nor has she ever said a word to me in all the time I've known her. I tell you, a less tenacious suitor . . . but lately her indifference seems more . . . pointed, if you see what I mean. A more virulent, committed apathy.

"Oh that I might have offended her! The very thought impales me! That I might have unwittingly, cloddishly, foolishly, inadvertently, tragically and/or stupidly said or done something or omitted to say something or forgotten to do something. Both, perhaps? I don't know, Boley; I miss her previous, less ferocious neglect. *That* I could work with. Careful with your teeth."

Noranbole taking more care.

"Oh the loneliness! The heart-wrenching, dreadful loneliness of her ignorance! The terrible, gut-heaving solitude of her basic unawareness! The isolation! And the cold! The biting, stinging cold! And the dark! The deep dead cold in the dark shadow of her lack of attention or regard!

"That said, I'm optimistic. I wouldn't have stuck it this far if I wasn't an optimist. I can see it going places; all it needs is that spark, you know? If only there were . . . maybe if . . . she's your sister, Boley—you wouldn't have any pearls would you? A morsel of comfort for me? Hm? An encouraging snippet?"

" . . . "

"A shred of hope, perhaps? A sliver? A pinch of pepper to spice it up a bit?"

" . . . "

"Dollop of sauce? A jot, even?"

" . . . "

"An iota?"

Noranbole lifts her head to shake it.

"Nope."

We have all wondered about the lake up at Swan Hill. The black mass of water between it and Henry Mason's farm. The children aren't allowed up there; we have demonized Mr Mason and made a bogeyman of him to keep them away. He's actually a really nice guy.

The stories we tell about it are manifold and without favorable conclusion, happy ending or hope. In our imaginings we see the lake bed littered with the dead. It is certainly the darkest place in our world, but is it the deepest?

History is peppered with accounts of our attempts at answering the question—the cave paintings in the Swan Hill Crevice, of diving tribesmen, the tantalizing gnosticism of the Swan Hill Scrolls, and so on.

However, not one instance of a successful plumbing has been handed down. Countless lives they say, have been lost to the venture, but the surface remains an opaque singularity. By the time my parents pitched our trailer at the lake's edge, the measuring of its depth had come to be considered impossible. *Impossible*.

Impossible? Impossible?! Impossible is what they said about the rotary transport mechanism! Did John Wheel listen? No! John Wheel *gave* us the rotary transport mechanism! In what turned out to be a fabulous year for inventions, actually (it was my fourteenth and we'd been up at the lake since I could remember; in the space of a few months we got the "wheel", eggs and the Awkward Silence™, and when Jeremy Awkward had another hit that October with his Moment™, it seemed we were on a real roll).

It was the year my father undertook to plumb the lake for once and for all. I'll never forget waving them off from the shore. Mother went along with some sandwiches and to assist, as she often did. I was sent into town, to pick up some string for the tomatoes. There is no trace of doubt in my mind that my father—a saintly genius, incidentally—was entirely successful in securing a measurement of the utmost accuracy. It is therefore doubly unfortunate that they were never seen again.

That was it. All further bids to get to the bottom of the lake were outlawed by the Council. Nobody would have had the nerve to try anyway, except for me. It wasn't until many, many years later that my daily petitioning finally ground them down and they capitulated, permitting my own attempt.

Thus it was that I found myself out on the lake one morning with a spool, a pulley and—despite the undoubtedly historic nature of the occasion—not a single spectator.

For a weight I had Urine's jewelry case, willingly surrendered. The rings of iron that comprised its two handles had caught my eye—the string could be looped through them and tied around the box, keeping the drawers closed. This was important as I had not removed any of the jewelry; it would add valuable weight.

I had been prudent—although the lake's depth was a mystery, it was relatively small and I had prepared a full three hundred foot of string. I fed one end through the pulley which I had attached to the side of the boat and secured it to Urine's jewelry case. With nobody watching there didn't seem much point in marking this extraordinary event with ceremony of any kind so I braced myself and dropped the case into the water.

The spool spun. In the dark water it didn't take long for the jewelry case to vanish from my sight. I could see the line of string melt into blackness beneath the boat.

Fifty foot.

And still the spool spun—my pulley system was working perfectly. The depths must have been very clear as the case appeared to sink without hindrance. So quickly!

A hundred and fifty foot.

And still the spool kept spinning. The speed of it! Accelerating! The racket as the cantilever knocked and juddered! The creak of the truss! A great yowl from the stanchion!

Two hundred and fifty foot.

No sign of abatement, in the spinning. The spool accelerating still. This was a deep lake. Possibly deeper than three hundred foot, it now occurred to me. The spool almost bare.

A shuddering jolt!

The jewelry case with not the slightest intention of discontinuing its plummet. My little boat reared up at a near ninety degrees, spilling its contents in to the lake—my sandwiches, my coat, some angling odds and ends.

Three hundred and something foot.

Prow skyward, stern sinking, gunwale at water level—a boat is not a thing that should, under any circumstances, lose altitude. Incapable of swimming in any of the popular styles, I reached for my knife and cut the string before the water could take me.

The oars were gone. I paddled my way back to shore by hand. It took me a while—plenty of time to think. Nothing had been achieved and little learned; the lake was deeper than three hundred foot and that was all I knew.

I needed more string. And possibly a bigger boat. And a different kind of weight altogether. The jewelry case was unlikely to resurface, and would certainly offer no insight if it did. It was gone forever. A dead weight, as useless as its former owner. No, I needed something very different at the end of my string.

Something alive.

❋

Noranbole and Mark Fleming. Cow shed.

"The thing is I'm not certain I should say anything at all, Norrie. Not at all sure I want to be a runner in that race. Urine's cruelty knows no bounds—why, it's the very stuff of legend! Along with her peerless beauty and her incomparable shining grace. My adoration seeps from every pore in my skin. Surely you can smell it? But I'd fear for my own safety were I to actually tell her.

"She doesn't tend to take these things too well. For example that time Norman Spencer invited her for a shake at the ice cream parlor and she just about scratched his eyes out. She was wild. The boy needed stitches.

"Or the time she acquiesced to a rendezvous with young William Branston on the southern summit of Cleft Heights and not only did not show up but had in fact gone to quite a bit of trouble erecting an enormous wicker structure on the facing slope which spelled out the words "Fuck You William Branston" and which she set alight at the appointed time along with an effigy of the poor lad, who never really recovered.

"Or the time she garroted Timothy Spencer's pony because he had been sitting on it when he had glanced at the hem of her frock.

"Or the time she unscrewed the lids from Larry Tool's entire larder-full of winter pickles, slipped a note into each jar which outlined a trait of his which she found either unappealing or downright foul (there were over four hundred jars) and replaced the lids with glue which was unusually cruel even for her because everybody knows how poor Larry loves his winter pickles.

"Or the time she set Lance Holcroft's parents on fire because they had had the audacity to suggest she might share a pitcher of lemonade with their son at the upcoming county fair.

"Or the time she . . . and I'm quite aware of my peculiar sexual peccadilloes (as is everybody else, now) but it isn't as if any of the algae in my care suffer more than algae do anyway, in general, out there. My protists fare even better, living out their little lives in an aquarium until such time as I . . . need them. That is a state of the art aquarium; it is top notch. Anyway, Facebook was hardly the appropriate forum.

"Careful, Norrie!"

White mist over black lake water at daybreak. I was not alone this time—a motley little entourage set up folding chairs on the bank as I readied the much reinforced rig. Reinforced and considerably enhanced with all available technologies. Even the appalling Urine was there, no doubt to keep an eye on her property. Her presence was the closest she had come to recrimination for the loss of her jewelry case, about which she had never uttered a word. I had one foot in my boat and one out as I bent over and clapped my hands encouragingly.

"Come on, Spot!"

I tried to sound light—jovial even—but Urine's stupid mutt, willingly surrendered, was clearly going to be a spanner in the works. It hadn't even managed to get onto the boat yet, though to be fair it was having to deal with a number of impairments to its mobility.

I had learned a vital lesson from my first attempt. If anything were to go awry down there—an unanticipated depth or an obstacle of some kind, a rocky outcrop for example, or a tangle of vegetation—then I would want to know about it. It was vital then that in the event of failure Spot would be able to return to the surface with said information. To this end I had duct-taped a pair of flippers to the hind feet of the dog and this was understandably causing some changes to its gait—a circumstance it was struggling to cope with in good spirits.

In addition to the difficulties with walking, Spot could no longer see. I had secured a snorkel mask to the head, to house the underwater camera which I had carefully duct-taped to the snout. I had chosen the Clarocam 8600e for its timer which I would set to go off at around the three hundred foot mark. It was this final touch that made Spot a data collecting marvel, and that would perhaps earn him a place in the footnotes of the treatise on depth measurements that would no doubt be demanded of me.

I picked the whimpering mongrel up in the end and dropped it in the boat. There was no facility for oxygen supply—we would just have to be quick which, judging from previous experience, wouldn't be a problem. Now that we could make our way towards the center of the lake I concentrated on my new rig. I had five hundred foot of string—surely sufficient—this time, but that was the least of it. I felt I was at the very vanguard of scientific experiment with this new set up, which included not only string but also wire; a matching length of it ran alongside and was fastened to the string at regular intervals with loose loops. It was to the wire, and not the string, that my weight—a sizable rock that sat heavily in the boat—was attached. The dog would be attached to the string only and at full depth I would cut it, allowing Spot to swim to the surface, if he wanted to, which I assumed he would.

Although an audience had gathered, they were frustratingly out of earshot by the time we reached the middle of the lake; disappointing though it was not to mark the occasion with some appropriate words, I lifted the dog and dropped it in the water with the minimum of fuss. I heaved the boulder over the side as well and as rock and puppy plunged I monitored the rig. The abominable Urine was on her feet and looking anxious.

Fifty foot.

My wire and string assembly spun uneventfully till the three hundred foot mark, at which point the lake surface lit up like a lightning strike, the camera's flash amplified by the water's lens. A few of them fell back off their folding chairs in fright. I was momentarily blinded. Everything continued to spin.

Four hundred foot. The inexplicable acceleration. My well-oiled rig much quieter this time but no less worrying. Another great flash! The dog was doing its job—I salivated slightly at the thought of all that data. Four hundred and fifty foot. I took hold of my wire cutter. Another flash!

Five hundred foot. The boat rearing up again. As I looked below me at the depths a fourth flash in my eyes. Dazzled and panicked I put the cutter to the wire and snipped, congratulating myself on my preparedness. Goodness this lake was deep. With a bit of luck the photographs would be illuminating. As my sight cleared, however, my heart sank; I had cut through the string as well. It would remain tangled with the wire, and the weight. My data was sinking.

Another flash!

This was embarrassing. I looked to the bank and the tiny crowd. Most of them had their hands to their heads. That putrid girl was on her knees.

And another!

The upside was neither boat nor rig had been lost this time. I would live to measure again! I began rowing towards the shore. A good scientist gleans as much from failure as success. I tried to tune out the wailing from the lakeside so that I might review my process. The dog, it would seem, had not been a good idea.

A flash!

The 8600e is a thirty-six-exposure camera, so we could expect a few more of these. I pulled my boat up onto the bank; Urine's ugly, tear-filled eyes were on me. She didn't utter a word and just as well—I was short on patience. I felt her pup had let me down. The rest of them had their eyes closed against the repeated blindings as I pulled a tarp over the rig and set out for home so that I could think.

Another flash!

✻

Noranbole and Bernard in the Maypole loft. A shaft of dusty light through the one window at floor level. Old clothes and toys scattered and piled in the corner, chests and rolls of fabric, paintings and framed photographs, stacked. A compendium of nostalgias. The settled sediment of a home, from which memories rise like bubbles in beer.

"Careful with them teeth, sweetheart."

Bernard leaves his reminiscing aside for a moment so that he might address an important matter. He has been preparing for this.

"Been doin' some retrospectin' sweetheart. Got me in a brown study 'bout things an' I just cayn't rightly figger if it wouldn't be better all round to skip town and allot upon a real city job. Clerkin' or biscuit shootin' or some such."

Noranbole's head stops bobbing.

"N'est-ce pas? Workin' up to a declaration for ma whole years and fully expectin' to git the mitten. Cayn't see no good comin' frum all this heart-lovin' I been brewin' up. Strikes me I might consider it altogether more happifyin' to just git up and git: hit the trail and see me some elephant."

Bobbing resumes.

"Lingerin' here with a beat-up blood pump an' I'm more 'n likely to find maself among the willows. Bendin' too many elbows with any Tom, Dick or Sally that wanders through. Wearin' a californy collar 'fore you know it. Teeth in the ground and cold as a wagon tire. Buzzard food."

He sighs.

"It's a bad box, Boley."

Noranbole lifts her head and looks him in the eye.

"What is, Bernard?"

"What is? Why just the whole caboodle is all! The entire scene-aria, stetson to spur! Sure as shit the game is up. Don't wanna tell the girl but I just gotta. Ain't no room in that purdicament for the barb of a peacock's feather!"

"Pardon? No wait, never mind. Why don't you just tell her and get it over with?"

"Why don't I . . . well whaddya think I been talkin' about this whole time, chucklehead?"

"I could ask her to wait for you behind our lean-to this evening. She listens to me."

"Whut? Tell who . . . what in God's great bounty are you talking about Noranbole?"

Deep breath.

"Look, you like my sister. I can talk to her. Y'know, vis-á-vis . . ."

"Your *sister*? You reckon I got my heart fixed on that witch? I swear I do not know of any less appealin' young filly in this whole county! All that airish attitudinizin'. Plus the violence, of course. Tá mé eagla Fuail. You must think someone's stole my rudder. That I'm some typa gump! A sap-headed sonk!"

Noranbole pinching the bridge of her nose.

"Who are we talking about, Bernard?"

"Who . . . well jeez loueese girl you got some kinda waxy deposit in those holes each side'a yer cabbage? Ya great heffer! You gotta be off yer chump, ya soft-headed spooney! What a yack! There is clearly a problem north of your ears. Zut alors! You got no more smarts than a salmon got feathers! Idiot! Moron! If brains were beauty you'd be uglier than a burnt boot! Nastier lookin' than a dime's worth o' dog meat! I been talkin' about *you*, mush-head!"

A silence. A lengthy silence. A lengthy, uncomfortable silence. Long and uncomfortable and silent. Very long. Noranbole sitting back on her heels. Brow furrowed, lips all aquiver, eyes down. Bernard staring at the drooped lids of his one true.

He has said it.

He is ready for death!

He isn't breathing particularly well.

Her eyes rise in a cold stare that makes him feel sick.

"Bernard."

"Ja, mein Schatz?"

"You got any money?"

※

We'd meet up at the Fleming house every hour or so—the midpoint. I had brought some string and it had been secured there and pulled out to the Maypole corral and the Wakeling compound as well as up slope through the woods to the old sycamore: a tridental web that could be kept to in the failing light. The central prong that stretched from the Flemings' door to our porch was as long as the longest trek anyone dared undertake in these temperatures—my winter string.

There were a good few of us—it isn't every day that someone goes missing round here and to have two of our young people disappear at the same time had brought the neighborhood out. Blackening trees made needle shapes against the only just brighter evening sky, and heaved with wet snow. The wolves were hanging back, unnerved by our numbers, but we knew they observed us, just beyond the circumference of our sight.

I was, naturally, distraught and so grateful for the snowfall and the darkness. Ms Emma could not see my tears. Lines of lantern and torch shuffled up and down the wooded slopes—bobbing and little in the distance: our neighbors, searching.

Noranbole!

Our chances were slim. Nobody had the nerve to venture far from the stringed zone, away from the houses, the voices and people. The snow at this time of year was deep and progress was slow—over time repetitive expeditions in confined space had flattened out channels through the cold powder, so folks would follow these up and down and up and the whole effort became more hopeless as it went along.

Every time I turned around that idiot girl was following close behind. I had a mind to bolt into the blackness. Maybe the wolves would take her, maybe me. It hardly mattered now.

Noranbole!

I sat on the Fleming porch and waited for word. Urine skulked nearby. I could see Ms Emma's bonnet approaching from her place and a torch from the opposite direction. As it got closer it lit the brooding face of Pa (he didn't take kindly to being addressed as Patrice) Maypole.

"Any news, Pa?"

"Near fixin' ta throw up the sponge is where we're at I reckon. Folks is all dragged out."

He put himself down next to me and dusted some snow from his boots with his hat. Then he sat staring straight ahead.

"I'll be a cat's paw. Why this whole bee is a hornswoggle."

"Yes. Yes, I see . . . and the kids? Any sign of the kids, Pa?"

He retrieved a scrap of torn cloth from his overcoat and handed it to me. Gingham, yellow and white: certainly Noranbole's. I turned it over in trembling hands. It had been ripped, maybe by thorns and then again maybe by claws, or teeth. Along one edge the unmistakable stain of fresh blood. Ms Emma covered her mouth with her hands.

"She can't be . . . she has chores!"

"Now don't go gittin' all honey-fuggled," Pa spat. "We found Bernard's hair case too, up by the ol' tree, wet with blood. I'm tellin' ya it ain't nuthin' but a taradiddle. The Simon Pure of this is fornent to these here proofs or I ain't no Maypole. Atwixt my boy's splashin' and that girl's yen for stringin' whizzers this whole shoot is barkin' at a knot. We're gettin' it in the neck here and that's for damn sure!"

"What's he saying?" Ms Emma had moved in close.

"Shh . . . I don't . . . go on, Pa."

But Pa had gone quiet and turned his eyes towards the shadows that flickered where the torchlight failed. They were abysmal. His face was thinky. Finally he spoke again.

"Absquatulation."

He brought his forefinger up and ran it along his bottom lip. I looked at Ms Wakeling. She looked at me. I looked at Pa.

"I see," I said. "Sorry?"

Ms Emma screamed a little breathless, nasal scream. Pa turned and looked at me hard.

"It eventuates thus."

"Right." I nodded. "What?"

"It eventuates thus," he said. "Oughta seen it. Soft down on that girl since he wuz a button but lately worsewise; a barber's cat, dead-alive and clearly difficulted. Strangely biddable and so of course up to something. 'Smornin' he had his mud pipes on and we got some airtights missin'. Sundry prog and so on.

"They ain't gone goslin', no sir, but they sure as shit is gone. The girl got cow sense e'en if my boy is slower than cold tar on a slope. They'll be hidin' out or off to see the elephant but one way or the other they're above snakes."

He had rolled himself a cigarette, sparked a match off the side of his boot, lit himself up and blown a smoke ring.

"Of that I have no doubt."

Ms Emma appeared to be . . . *vibrating*. Her eyeballs looked swollen.

"Snakes?" she took a step back, then forward. "Elephant?"

I stood and placed a comforting hand on her shoulder.

"I think they're dead. Even if they're not they'll never make it out there. Let's go home."

❈

The melts are not long off.

  . . .

  Yes?

Yes.

The days grow lengthier and more detailed.

I'm not, eh . . .

You have been here for nine weeks.

Yes.

You may recall the conversation we had in November, Mr Seiler, which resulted in your entering my employ.

A bit formal.

Just answer.

I do remember, yes.

Your brief which I outlined at the time was to be of assistance to me during the winter in the monitoring of my two girls, both of whom were of marriageable age and one of whom was attractive—a siren to the lads of the county.

Yes.

I haven't asked much else of you.

No.

Apart from the sharpening of some tools. Indeed your . . . remunerations have exceeded what we originally agreed in both nature and degree. Despite your squirreling yourself away in that shed, increasingly. I am only trying to help, you know.

Yes.

A man's fluids require frequent liberation or they will stew.

Some of the tools are really *very* blunt.

I have asked for this little chat Mr Seiler because I wish to express my disappointment.

Oh?

Oh? I surprise you? Really? You are surprised? For reals? You didn't anticipate disappointment here, today?

Well . . .

You need reminding perhaps of yesterday's unfortunate events? The toe-snappingly cold trek through wolf-infested forest? The yelling and the wailing? The gnashing? The wet clouds of breath in the grief-stricken air, the frozen-teared faces of the bereaved? A quick recap?

No, I do remember.

Excellent. You would acknowledge then that as we approach the end of your tenure here one of my girls appears to be—and I recognize that there is some evidential uncertainty here—dead?

That would appear to be the case, yes, notwithstanding the as you say murky specifics.

I am to be grateful I suppose, to be *appreciative* of the fact that at least it isn't my Urine who has been lost.

Eh . . .

You give no indication, Mr Seiler, that you recognize the seriousness of the . . . the precariousness of your . . . hm?

Oh, no . . . no, no I can . . . what?

Be under no illusions, Seiler. One more dead daughter and you're fired.

That does seem fair.

Now lie still. Stop squirming!

✳

Naturally Urine looked even worse than usual that early morning up at the lake. Covering her in the goose fat had been just about unbearable. I don't know why she couldn't have done it herself. Still, there wasn't much of her and I would have plenty left to see me through the rest of the winter, for tatties and for Ms Wakeling to apply to my nether parts.

I had fashioned a suit from beaver skins which Urine would wear for added insulation. Of course I was very keen that she not mess this up as seven whole beavers had died for that suit and I told her so.

"I won't!"

I hauled my string and spool aboard the boat and not without difficulty— it was the longest I had ever made up till then and quite possibly the longest there had ever been. Certainly in this and surrounding counties or I would have heard something.

In fact it wasn't entirely string. Over the course of my two historic attempts I had plundered my stocks and when I could source no more I had used every sheet in the house, numerous horsetails and Urine's own hair, willingly surrendered. She was bald now and more hideous than you can even imagine.

Go on. Try to imagine something more hideous.

You see? You *can't*.

These then would be the last few lengths that I hoped would get her all the way down to the lake bed. The measurement, if I had gotten it right this time, would be a thousand foot of string, one hundred and eleven strips of sheet (queen size), four horsetails and Urine's head of hair.

A small entourage of local lads wept on the bank as we embarked. I pulled us towards the center along the string; in a master stroke I had recruited Lepidopter and it was from him that the string would extend, first across the lake surface from where he stood at the edge to the spool on the boat, and thence downwards. Nothing could move that mule when he didn't want to move. Not me. Not anything. Such a simple but commanding maneuver. I was almost smug.

The injection of Urine into the set-up had facilitated a certain back-to-basics approach. Gone was the wire and string combination (too experimental) and in its place was something much simpler. The repulsive and unpleasant girl would cling onto another rock as it sank, with the string fastened to her waist. In the event of mishap she could let go and resurface, though I admonished her that this course of action was to be considered in only the direst of eventualities, or once she had in fact reached bottom and secured a measurement.

In the middle the girl stood and cleared her throat, giving every indication that she wanted to say something. Appalled, I handed her the rock and insisted she leap from the boat without delay, which she did. As expected, the boulder dropped swiftly and without fuss for the first five hundred foot, after which it dropped swiftly and without fuss for the next five hundred. I was beginning to get a little annoyed with this lake.

She was a few lengths of sheet and her own hair away from having to abort and resurface. I waited for the now familiar jolt as the string reached full length, but it didn't come. Instead, Lepidopter was swept from his feet and pulled into the water. He proceeded to skim the surface, progressing towards the boat at an alarming rate. Then, for the briefest of moments, he was in it with me, apparently calm but for an almost imperceptible widening of the eyes. And then, he was back in the water.

Lepidopter! The stupid girl was drowning my mule! Momentarily, I clung to a hoof but I didn't have the strength in me to hold on. All I could do was hang over the side and watch as he sank from sight, wide eyed and braying silently up at me. Then, nothing: the lake was quiet and calm.

I was grief stricken. Oh, what a price to pay for my vainglorious obsession! I'd have leaped in myself, if I'd had a spare boulder.

Lepidopter!

There was wailing from the shore and some ostentatious (if you ask me) display of emotion, but my tears ran down my cheeks in silence as I contemplated the trouble I was in. A puppy was one thing but this would take some explaining. I stared down over the gunwale for any sign of improvement. There was none.

How typical of the girl! Never in all the time I'd spent carefully planning this had I supposed it could end in such tragedy, notwithstanding the jewelry box and the thing with the dog.

Lepidopter! My beautiful mule! Dragged to a cold end by an ugly idiot. I wouldn't be seeing the inside of that tool shed again either.

A hush descended on those at the lakeside, then a commotion.

I paid no attention at first.

Then voices were raised.

Were those *giggles?*

I wiped my eyes and peered towards the boys. Young Mark Fleming had removed his smock. The poor lad must have lost his mind. He was wading naked into the water and was decidedly perky below stairs. Strange, determined look to him. Once his member was submerged he bowed his head and raised his arms. In a few moments the water round his groin began to glow. And now, from the green glow, a green line grew and disappeared into the depths.

It really was an unexpected development.

A dreadful grin spread across his face and one of the others pointed excitedly at the water. From far below the surface a green light pulsated; the dome of a jellyfish-like concavity ascended as we watched. Against the light the unmistakable silhouette of a living thing! No, two silhouettes!! Before we could take it in it surfaced in a great upheaval of water that drenched my boat. Something landed with a thud, then something else.

Lepidopter! A little worse for wear but breathing and braying!

Oh Lepidopter!

I had my mule back! Whatever came of this, I could make more string! I might not have measured the thing I wanted to measure and I was certainly homeless but by God I would measure something! And I still had a mule!

But wait, the other figure. It was covered in weeds but I could see that it too was breathing. I wiped them away.

Spot! Alive and well! No sign of the snorkel, sadly.

I picked the dog up and waved it gleefully at the boys. We were nearing them now having been set adrift by the tumult. The sight of the dog didn't seem to impress anyone. Mark Fleming's jaw dropped and he sank to his knees.

"I'm sorry! I'm so sorry," he sobbed.

I leaped over the gunwale, took him by the shoulders and shook him.

"What . . . are . . . you . . . talking about? That was fabulous! I really thought I'd lost him there. And the dog is a bonus."

He looked up at me through tears. "But, Urine . . ."

"Ah, yes. Well . . ."

But I was cut short. Something was approaching through the bushes— a snapping of twigs and a great heaving in the undergrowth. They were pulled apart and Ms Wakeling's familiar figure stepped through, red-faced and glowering, vapor trumpeting from flared nostrils.

"Seiler!"

Part Two

Noranbole

Chapter One

OPENED ONE EYE. Noranbole, that is. Mouth very dry.

The alarm clock was the old-fashioned kind. She wanted to take it and batter it against the wall for a very long time, but she satisfied herself with a good slap and put a foot on the floor, waiting for the other eye. Bernard had saved up for the clock because it had pictures of puppies on it, knowing that she had never been allowed a dog. He was banging around in the kitchen.

It wasn't quite bright; traffic was still lazy and sporadic in the street. Even here in Notown, it was relatively quiet down there. A few footfalls, each set separated by the dim seconds. Blue collar breakfast time.

Another day in Big City.

Another good day.

She made straight for the fridge and some water. Bernard was heaving a sturgeon into the fish kettle.

"בוקר טוב"

"Morning, Bernie."

"לישון טוב?"

"Not really. Funny dreams. What's for breakfast?"

But she could see.

He always had to be at work by a quarter to seven sharp or Mr Dunkhorn would be on his case, so he went down to the wholesale fruit & veg market every single day at six to get her favorites. What he couldn't afford he grew himself in a thirty-square-meter greenhouse on the roof—made from plastic bottles—that he hadn't told the landlord about.

After a couple of harvests he'd really begun to hit his stride. This morning, he'd laid out her usual buffet of cereals and exotics—there was a giant granadilla and a cluster of Burmese grapes, some hairless rambutans fanned on a platter with cape gooseberries, safous and a few bilimbis. The centerpiece was a carpaccio of horned melon, sprinkled with lablabs and canistel shavings, which he'd arranged in the form of a radiant sun, and tilted for display.

Below it an array of home-baked breads, piled and clustered to resemble a little hamlet of huts. He'd been particularly busy this morning; there were nans and tandoors, pretzels, pumpernickel, quick breads, farls, ka'aks and a whole stack of yufkas. Between the little huts, droplets of condensation bejeweled the creamy surfaces of softly scooped Asturian butter.

"01000011 01101111 01100110 01100110 01100101 01100101 00100000 01101111 01110010 00100000 01110100 01100101 01100001 00111111," asked Bernard.

"Eh, tea this morning, I think," said Noranbole.

At the foot of the hamlet, he had spread out some rolled oats, pecans, cashews and pistachios, dried apricots, figs and raisins and in front of all of that a swath of cane sugar. The granules glistened like sand on a little half-moon beach.

"Now the hula skirt makes sense," said Noranbole. "Very fetching."

Bernard placed a garland of Arabian Jasmine around her neck and an orchid in her hair. He pressed play and, to the strains of Joe Keawe's "My Little Grass Shack", danced for her.

※

Mr Jespersen was opening up his grocery store and delicatessen across the street as they closed their building's clanking iron door behind them and took the front steps leisurely. It was a little brighter. Noranbole didn't have to leave so early but she did like to walk with Bernard and sometimes he needed her help, with Mr Dunkhorn or a neighbor.

"Morning, Norrie!"

"Morning, Mr Jespersen!"

The shop owner looked at Bernard and went back inside.

They ambled, in no particular hurry. Later this would be a busy street. It was lined with businesses but most of them were shut at this time of day. Lights had come on in the Two Star Laundromat and Dry Cleaners but all was dark behind the shutters of the Pole Pole African market.

Bernard had his hand in hers and a foolish look on his face.

"Onusowna," he grinned, "doin' it tabletops. Sooo partickler!"

He took her other hand and gave her a swirl.

"É nosso triunfo. Der Erfolg!"

She laughed.

"Yes it is, honey, and yes, we are."

Past the Greenville Organic Fruit outlet and the Sports Bar where Bernard would take her for a beer whenever he had the money. Mrs Alfandari and her elderly neighbor, Mr Van Cauwenberghe, were out on his steps, enjoying an early morning mélange of poisonous gossip and complaint. Not much happened on Myrtle Street that Alfandari, in particular, didn't either instigate or find out about.

Mr Van Cauwenberghe was updating her on the latest algorithm of lights-on-and-off across the street in the little apartment over the florist, where Anezka Le Breux lived—a topic of great interest to Mrs Alfandari—when she nudged his knee and shushed him.

"Good morning, Noranbole. Off to work are we?"

"Yes, Mrs Alfandari. Mr Van Cauwenberghe."

The widow looked Bernard up and down, glowering.

"Mr Maypole."

"Daddywank," said Bernard.

Her back straightened.

"What?"

"Sorry about that, Mrs Alfandari," said Noranbole, "He's Welsh, you know."

"Нет я не," said Bernard.

"Let me take care of this, honey."

"Welsh?" asked Mrs Alfandari, "I thought he was Flemish."

Her face was perplexity.

"Didn't you tell me he was Flemish?"

She was looking at a point in space, slightly to the left of the tip of her nose.

"Or was it Walloon?"

Noranbole had Bernard by the arm and they'd already walked on.

"He's been around, Mrs Alfandari," she called back as they took the corner onto Weaver Street.

Alfandari and Van Cauwenberghe exchanged disapproving scowls.

"Poor girl," said the old man.

"I'm sure she told me he was Flemish," said the widow.

The restaurant where Bernard worked was at the end of the street, on the corner of Stitch. It was daylight now so Mr Dunkhorn, who was on some kind of eco kick, had turned off the third floor neon sign. It was an illegible mess in the morning light but Noranbole knew it from memory:

Phineas Dunkhorn's 24 hour Schezuan Noodle & Burger Emporium.
Specialising in Kosher Chicken and Münchner Weißwurst since 2009.

And beneath that, the tag-line Dunkhorn's marketing people had come up with:

For heaven's sake eat something.
You look awful.

They stopped in next door at Farmer's to get Bernard a bagel for his lunch, since freebies were frowned upon in the restaurant. Outside she stood him in front of her and checked him over for facial breakfast and other stains.

He was well-dressed, and had been ever since discovering that the renowned Monsieur le Mesurier—Big City's foremost clothier—was a huge fan of tropical fruit. His shirt was a Joey Haemorrhage button down with French cuffs and a very fine, floral motif, his tie a rather demure, speckled Fuerziore.

The suit itself was a marvel: a subtle pinstripe, it sat softly but smartly on Bernard's frame, the pleated pants and three-button blazer blended from the wool of the Vicuña camel and a little quiviuk, which Monsieur le Mesurier's own team of trappers harvested each early Spring from semi-wild Arctic muskoxen on their proprietary Greenland reserve.

"So you think you might get to cook some noodles today?"

Bernard hopped from one foot to the other excitedly.

"Ooh! Stappit! Perchonce! Fooonlyitmoot! Yatink? Ah jaysus—"

"Well, you never know. Do your best, my love. Good things will come."

He gave her a long kiss and hurried off to Dunkhorn's six forty-five motivational talk.

Noranbole walked on wearily, slightly dreading her own day of drudgery, admonishing herself for doing so and envying Bernard's ability to enjoy the simple things, his relentless optimism, his inventiveness and his hope.

❀

In truth, Noranbole had been finding her working days a bit lonely. She spent them in Alltown, a much swankier part of the city, amid bankers and brokers and other people with whom she felt she had little in common. Businessmen and other high falutin' folk. Barristers, that kind of thing. It was isolating.

Bookkeepers. One or two botanists. Educated, humorless types.

A biochemist.

She longed for the company of her own kind.

A baker perhaps, or a biscuit designer. Those people knew how to shoot a breeze.

Beekeepers, though not good conversationalists, were invariably devoid of pretension.

The company of butchers had its obvious drawbacks, but there were discounts.

Real people.

She was on Wide Street now and things were different. The pavements were filled with the scuttle of commuters. They writhed and squirmed with it. People everywhere, tiny in the great steel and glass gorge. Wide Street was lined with the major players: palaces built to intimidate and glorify—Tamsac Inc, Palpon, the Campoz group, Xin, Rubrol, Dimfit.

Noranbole side-stepped the people stream and stood on the steps of her own building. It was the most magnificent of them all, hundreds of crystal stories high. At the entrance, a brooding portico. Unnecessarily massive Doric columns and ludicrously elaborate architraves comprised a colonnade, precursing the inner peristyle.

She looked up at the revolving plaque, itself the size of Phineas Dunkhorn's 24 hour Shezuan Noodle and Burger Emporium:

The Terra Forma Corporation
Totally Awesome Since I-Don't-Even-Know-When
Peace.

A lot of people, she supposed, would be thrilled to work for the world's most powerful organization, but the monolith just made her feel small. The self-consciousness began at the x-ray machines in the lobby as her plastic lunch box trundled along the belt, flanked by bespoke leather briefcases and Muy Caro™ handbags. At the elevators, a friendly face.

"Hey Norrie."

"Hey Mr Benedetto."

"Nuther day nuther fifty cents, huh?"

"Yup. How's Mrs Benedetto?"

"Oh great! It didn't turn out to be anything at all."

"That *is* great!"

"Yeah. It was a worry, I don't mind telling you. Makes you wonder what would happen if something really did happen, y'know?"

"Yeah."

"Eightieth floor?"

"Yeah."

And at the eightieth floor:

"It's time for you to change, Norrie."

"Yeah."

The eightieth floor was Noranbole's last chance to catch the elevator she needed, the one that went all the way to three hundred and three. At the top she stepped out onto a carpet so soft and deep she couldn't see her shoes.

The deep pile made it quieter here and thick mahogany doors ensured she couldn't hear a single voice as she made her way to the end of a low-lit corridor. There were fresh flowers in pedestaled pots at regular intervals and little refrigerators with complimentary refreshments, which she was entitled to take as much as anyone else around here. She could never remember the code, though.

She stepped through a double door into a large, long, empty room. It was at a corner of the building and a conference table ran down the middle of it. The wood paneling was lined with portraits and a stately, antique desk took up a wall at the far end.

Putting her lunch box on the table, she went over to stand at the floor-to-ceiling window for a second, looking out over Big City Avenue that would soon teem with taxis and delivery trucks, tour guides and tourists. It was still too early for all that, but a long summer had yet to release its grip and she could tell it was warming up outside. Shirtsleeves were short and the sun high enough to slice horizontally through gaps in the skyline, gilting the upper stories of a building here and there.

Where the gold light hit a facade head on, it lit up like a torch. Where it skimmed a surface, it threw unexpected details into relief—the otherwise invisible arcs and sweeps of concrete, the lunar chaos of pebble dash and stone—and seemed to unite all this artifice with the world around it, to subsume the invention, inviting it back in to the universe it railed against. It was the only effect in her visual field that could possibly have reminded her of home, where the same sun would burn the stubbled wheat fields today.

Nothing else came close. She was as far removed here as it was possible to be from the primordial contours of Spoon Ridge, of the bend in the river where the Bennetts lived, of the boathouse and its joyless liaisons, of her past—the blistering, callused monotony of a childhood spent in unthanked servitude. The years passed in affection's waiting room.

There was no trace, here, of the windowless scullery, no echo of the mother monster's nasal, task-announcing whine. She looked at the Tamsac building, at the illuminated hoardings of Main Square. Did it all sparkle for other people the way it did for her? Did it *smell* good? She took a deep, deep breath, despite the glass that separated her from the city and its oxygen. Its life. Out there in the purity of alien space.

She wanted this. Home—she wanted to apply that word to *this*. The old house was becoming a distant memory and the distance, though not yet great enough to snap the cord, was welcome. She wanted *this* to be her home. And she thought it *could* be hers. She just had to earn it. For Bernard too. To keep him safe and happy. Somehow.

Time had slipped away. Behind her the door opened and a nervous looking secretary slipped in.

"Ms Wakeling?"

"Good morning, Lucy."

"Sorry to descend on you so quickly, Ms Wakeling, but we have the Mayor on the line."

"Sure. Put him through."

"And also the President?"

"Ah," said Noranbole.

She gave Lucy a crisp but friendly smile and went to her desk.

"Then the Mayor will have to wait."

Chapter Two

IT had been quite a morning.

Noranbole had taken a number of calls from regional chiefs, and various Terra Forma strategy manifestos as well as the more recent annual reports were open on her desktop. She was still settling into the routines of her new position, having risen to it from the post room in a mere eighteen months and a series of fortuitous events so highly improbable as to defy description here.

Some of the chiefs had been argumentative—there was a degree of resistance to the changes that she was proposing and she was up to her neck in a hearts and minds charm offensive, under considerable pressure to make a mark within her first year at the helm.

The organization had become mired in a post-crisis corporate strategy dilemma. There was no consensus on whether the approach, going forward, should be fundamentally Classical in nature (as defined by Whittington) or Romantic, as advocated by the emerging Byronics—a think tank of academics from the University of Big City, who had been putting forward the argument (with some success) that the old paradigms had given way to a whole new strategic archetype and that rational approaches such as situation analysis, SWOT, forecasting and so on would actually *stymie* future growth and development, despite their proven effectiveness in antecedent market contexts. Instead, they were suggesting, organizations should be viewed as nebulous, unpredictable person clusters driven predominantly by lust. Optimal strategic decisions, they argued, could be expressed only in the language of unadulterated avarice or disgust, without recourse to the jargonized encryption of defunct methodologies.

Noranbole had no background in management, having spent her working life to date scrubbing things and peeling other things, but had instinctively felt uncomfortable with the debate from word go; she had little time in general for fallacious dualities of the kind, intuitively recognizing them for the anxiety-driven avoidance behaviors they were and so had refused to take sides or to forge any potentially limiting board alliances.

She had instead elected to enter the fray from a totally unexpected standpoint and the surprising nature of her opening gambit had gained her an early advantage. She was, in fact, making a little headway; the directors had been caught off guard and some of them were demonstrating an uncharacteristic willingness to entertain unproven ideas in the absence of any standard credential.

Her early successes in trade bloc liaison—maneuvering NORISUR into a customs union agreement that cleared the way for Terra Forma to grab a further 10% of market share in Region 5 over the next four years, with KOFTA following suit soon afterwards in Region 1, opening up a modest but significant increase in market share there of 2% over the next three years—had given everyone some pause for thought and solid grounds for listening to what she had to say.

Noranbole's aspiration for Terra Forma was to break away entirely from the binary restraints of Classical versus Romantic and to trailblaze a wholly new approach.

Something that no one would have seen before.

Due to its unfamiliarity, other organizations would be put on the back foot, she anticipated, allowing Terra Forma time to rewrite some of the market rules while its competitors reeled. The concept she was working so hard to sell to the directors was nothing less than a complete overhaul of the company from the ground up, starting with business practices on the front lines and culminating with deep reform at board level.

The goal was to create the world's first Gothic conglomerate.

She'd dubbed her plan Operation Pitchfork. An exorcist on the board, a healthy respect for white witchcraft at all levels, an annual séance: the three central prongs of her vision.

She was under deadline to get her proposal papers ready for the extraordinary board meeting she'd called, and sitting across from her was Vacuity Blanc, head of Corporate Branding. Vacuity had been an eager ally from the outset and was Noranbole's de facto right hand on the project. Despite an unfortunate tendency to deploy words like "creation" and "idea" as verbs, she had been entrusted with the construction of a three dimensional model of the proposed strategy for presentation to the directors. She'd made it look like a creepy castle and was going over the whole thing for Noranbole.

"Look at its little face," she said, gently fingering a gargoyle.

"Cute," said Noranbole, both feet on the desk.

"It's nearly lunch time," said Vacuity.

Noranbole was resting her chin on a hand and had turned to look out of the window. She could never quite shake the thought that her chores would be piling up back at the Wakeling compound.

"I'm going to do a fart."

The phone rang and she picked it up.

"I've got a Mr Phineas Dunkhorn on the line, Ms Wakeling," said Lucy, "again."

"Thanks Lucy. Put him through. Hello, Mr Dunkhorn."

"Really sorry to disturb you at work, Ms Wakeling. I know how busy you must be and on that, can I just say what a great job you guys up there are doing on behalf of all of us and also how much I absolutely adored the new Cogdat™ commercial? Genius, and an absolute godsend for families who might have been struggling with, you know, choices."

He waited for her to respond. She didn't.

"I wonder whether you intended to diversify? Birds and lizards would seem to be an obvious area for development. Blizzards? Horses and rabbits? Both lagomorphs, you know, so it should be straightforward enough on the engineering side. Habits? I have some ideas I would love to talk to you about sometime—"

"It's good to hear from you, Mr Dunkhorn, but I'm in the middle—"

"Yes of course. I'm afraid we're having some trouble with Mr Maypole again. He seems rather . . . upset. Needless to say we don't really know—"

"Put him on."

"محبوب؟"

"Hey honey. You seem to have them worried down there again. What's up?"

"我会告诉你，我这都失去耐心！他们已经做了一遍！ Θα κάνω τους λυπόμαστε γι 'αυτό. Θα θρηνώ την ημέρα! Я заліць мёдам у валасах! Падпаліце сваіх дзяцей!"

"Whoa, slow down there a little, baby. Tell me what's happened."

"나는 국수에 있어야합니다. 아무도 국수를 요리하지 않습니다. मैं आपको बता, वे मुझे आखिरी बार अनदेखी की है!"

"Ah. OK, put Mr Dunkhorn back on would you? Try to be nice, honey. And calm. I love you."

"Eh bien oui, je t'aime aussi, bien sûr."

"Ms Wakeling?"

"Yes, he's a bit put out, Mr Dunkhorn. I understand one of your noodles men is absent again, and you know how keen Bernard is to prove himself. He feels overlooked."

"This again," said Mr Dunkhorn. "Ms Wakeling, could you get down here? I think we all need to sit down and thrash this thing out. I wouldn't ask but . . . it isn't very easy . . ."

"You want me to drop everything and come down there right now?"

"Yes."

Noranbole looked across the desk at Vacuity, who was reattaching a demon to the Channeling Cauldron with some double-sided sticky tape.

"OK."

❋

When Noranbole got down to the Emporium it was all go, a great melée of sound and food in a maze of stainless steel and tablecloth. She was shown through the kitchen to Mr Dunkhorn's office in the back. Bernard was already there; he gave her an eager smile and gestured for her to sit next to him. His demeanor was upbeat but Noranbole knew when he was unhappy. When he felt small. She wanted to hug him.

Mr Dunkhorn was talking on the phone.

"Ms Furbush, a question. Why, when I passed the cold store this morning, was Mr Crackbone in there, stacking yams?"

He had hung his Jeeves & Hook jacket over the back of his chair and was working in Rayner Sturgess shirtsleeves, in a muted plaid, which he had rolled up to his elbows.

"No, I understand that the yams need stacking, Ms Furbush. It was I who highlighted the issue. If you remember, the delivery people were . . . It was? But I thought I . . . well either way, Ms Furbush, we both seem to be on board with the yam stacking. No, my issue is the Crackbone part. What is he doing in cold store when he's been assigned to the seafood tanks? I assigned him myself, didn't I? I did? I thought so. It should be Mr Pidge with the yams; it's crucial that we play our people to their strengths, Ms Furbush, absolutely key. I spoke about this at the quarterly, do you remember? Well . . . no, obviously I didn't mean . . . I know that, Ms Furbush, you're a very . . . absolutely, I never meant . . . OK, I grant you that . . . Look, let's concentrate on the problem at hand shall we? Where is Mr Pidge right now and what is he doing?"

Noranbole slipped her hand into Bernard's and squeezed. He gave her a wink.

"You have got to be fucking kidding me. I can't be hearing this."

Dunkhorn rolled his eyes at Noranbole. She held on to Bernard's hand.

"Who could possibly have thought it a good idea to put Mr Pidge in the cloakroom? A known claustrophobe. Of course you know what I'm going to ask next . . . well I have to ask, Ms Furbush . . . well it might very well be a never ending . . . but I need to keep on top of . . . if you'll pardon me, Ms Furbush, I do happen to be the mana . . . no of course not . . . no, I wasn't saying . . . I did not say that, Ms Furbush! Well I'm afraid I'm going to go right ahead and ask the question and you'll just have to live with . . . Ms Furbush? Ms Furbush! Oh, you're there. I thought you'd . . . Where is Miss Leaking? There, I . . . oh. Why not? Uhuh . . . uhuh . . . uhuh . . . I suppose that's . . . will she be in tomorrow? I see. I'll leave that in your very capable hands, Ms Furbush, if it's all the . . . you'll wish her our best of . . ."

The door to the office opened quietly and Mr Flucker came in as if by prior arrangement. He clicked it shut behind him and made for a chair at the side of Dunkhorn's desk, facing Bernard and Noranbole.

Rather daringly, he was tieless and wore a mandarin collar—in direct contravention of dress code—over a silk Jessie Taki with a floral pattern. Nobody else at the Emporium would have got away with it, but then Mr Flucker was a man who knew exactly how far he could push things. At the end of the day, nobody could touch his noodle department. Not in Big City or anywhere else for that matter, and if Dunkhorn didn't like it there was always Oodles, a mere two streets from here.

He sat down and crossed his legs, leaving the right half of a pair of Baker Brown ostrich-hide cap toe brogues prominently on display, and when he flashed a smile at Bernard the brightness in the room increased by a few lumens.

"Well yes . . . no . . . yes . . . no . . . yes . . . yes, we *are* going to need to get on top of this, though, Ms Furbush. Role allocation, I mean. I want it optimized. We *need* it optimized! Why on earth would we have gone through all those functional analysis questionnaires if we weren't going to . . . there's no way we can go into the next quarter in this kind of disarray. Pidge in the cloakroom, Crackbone in the fridge. It's ridiculous. I'll revisit the whole thing at our next quarterly. Will you remind me? Yes . . . absolutely. Perhaps you could prepare someth . . . yes . . . and you'll remind me? Oh, of course, absolutely, but you will remind me, won't you? Good. No, I think that's it for now, thank you, Ms Furbush. Oh, please tell Ms Titterton I like her projections. Yes. Yes, thank you."

Dunkhorn put the phone down and grinned at Noranbole.

"*So* good of you to make it down here at short notice, Ms Wakeling. It must be frantic up there in Terra Forma head office at the moment, what with this gargantuan crisis we're facing. Not to mention the other crisis, equally enormous. We really are beholden to people such as yourselves who work so tirelessly to steer us through all these crises, and can I just say, since we have you here—"

"Thank you Mr Dunkhorn. If we could just—"

"Yes, of course. Mr Maypole, I've asked Mr Flucker to sit in on this. Let's see if we can't hammer something out here today between the two of you.

You may not be aware, Ms Wakeling, of Mr Flucker's reputation within the noodle community. We were very proud here at the Emporium to secure his services just a couple of years ago. It was key for us at the time and without a doubt landed us squarely on the noodle map. It's entirely to Mr Maypole's credit, and a testament to his shrewd judgment moreover, that he has his eyes on the department. Mr Flucker is a giant among Big City's noodle people, at both artisanal and corporate levels. A leviathan, a colossus—"

"Fickety wook," said Bernard.

Noranbole held Dunkhorn's gaze and smiled.

"Indeed. Naturally, given his credentials, Mr Flucker is very, very protective of his department. Some would say insanely so. A vicious man, who may even have killed, somewhere along the line, on his ascent to the top of his profession. You don't need to respond to that, Mr Flucker. What I'm saying is this—Mr Maypole finds himself in a queue. He's a candidate, moving in the right direction certainly, but not perhaps all that quickly. It's a process. What we might look at achieving here today is delineating for Mr Maypole the parameters of that process and sketching out for him, with a view to clarification, a road map if you will—"

"Yes, I suppose I might interject here, Mr Dunkhorn," said Noranbole, unable for the moment to look away from Flucker's teeth, "to the effect that I can personally vouch for Bernard's cooking. Boiling in particular. He has spent many hours at home perfecting his technique. The man can cook noodles. He would in my opinion make a fine addition to the—"

"But of course! Absolutely! We're assured of it, Ms Wakeling, make no mistake about that. Mr Maypole is on his way to the noodle department. That is beyond question and I believe Mr Flucker and I are on the same page here. We're all agreed. I'm looking at Mr Maypole and I'm seeing a noodle department operative in waiting. That's exactly what I see when I look at Mr Maypole. What do you see when you look at Mr Maypole, Mr Flucker?"

"Noodles," said Mr Flucker.

"You see? What we're here to discuss today isn't so much whether as when. Timing is paramount. We have a hell of a lot on our plates at the moment, if you'll pardon the pun, and the elephant in the room, of course, is that Mr Maypole is already a crucial cog in our machine. A vital piece in a well-oiled jigsaw puzzle."

"Pfft," said Bernard.

"I think what Mr Maypole is trying to say," continued Noranbole "is that he feels he's earned his stripes vis-à-vis his current role and that perhaps the time has—"

Dunkhorn slammed his fists down on his desk.

"Dammit, Mr Maypole! You are not ready for noodles!"

The force of his ejaculation took everyone by surprise and, for an uncomfortable minute, nobody had any idea what to say.

Eventually, Dunkhorn stood and let out a slow breath through pursed lips, head bowed.

"Ms Wakeling. Mr Maypole. I apologize."

He went over to a flip chart that stood beside a metal filing cabinet.

"You can step out, Mr Flucker, thank you. I'll take it from here."

Without seeming to get up out of the chair, or move in any way, Mr Flucker quietly left. Dunkhorn flicked the front page over the back of the chart, revealing a mess of angry graphics in red and blue. And green. And yellow, and black, teal, mauve, aubergine, copper, terra cotta, chestnut, lavender and white.

"Take a look at this, Bernard. Can I call you Bernard?

"না," said Bernard.

"Great. Look, Bernard, we're trying to get this ice cream thing off the ground just now. You've probably seen people come and go and wondered what it was all about."

He picked up a pointer from the ledge at the base of the chart and tapped the graph.

"Each one of these lines represents a potential supplier. OK? Look at these guys here. The pinky ones. They're the go to guys for Madagascan vanilla. They do strawberry cheesecake as well. And salmon, actually, but we're not sure about the salmon. Anyway, the point is this—they don't do chocolate. They don't do *chocolate*, Bernie. I mean, for the love of God.

"So we go to these guys, the eh . . . what is that, would you say? Would you call that jade? Never mind. They'll do the Madagascan vanilla, at a slightly higher price mind you, and they do chocolate, so things are looking up, right? Wrong. They won't supply Tutti Frutti."

He threw his arms up.

"We can't seriously contemplate a foray into the ice cream sector without Tutti Frutti. We'd be sitting ducks!"

One hand scrunched his hair. The other tossed the marker back at the chart, where it bounced and fell to the floor.

"The rest of the mess you see here is just a bunch of variations on the same theme. And these are the complications that arise with the *basic* flavors. We have our eyes on a whole lot more—Peanut Butter, Black Raspberry, Tiger Tail, Lemon Donkey, Showered & Shaved: the works, Bernie. Can you imagine what the chart would look like?"

He was pacing now.

"Can you even *conceive* of such quandaries? Hm? The weight of managerial responsibility . . . oh, don't be in such a hurry to move on Mr Maypole. There's a lot to be said for a nice simple role, you know. A clear head at the end of the day. A clear conscience."

He had approached Bernard's chair and put a hand on his shoulder.

"You remind me of me, you know, Mr Maypole. I started off in your department. That's right. You didn't know that did you?"

He removed his hand, folded his arms and addressed the ceiling.

"Well, I did, and look at me now. I must seem a very distant, rather marvelous figure to you. But you could *be* this, Bernie. You have to keep the faith. Sometimes it isn't as quick as we'd like. I tell you there isn't a day passes by that a small part of me doesn't wish I was back where I started, nothing but ambition and potential. Not a care in the world if you don't count food, or shelter."

He circled around behind them and stood quietly for a moment at the window with his back turned. He appeared to be trying to stabilize his breathing. After a minute he leaned his forehead against the cooling glass.

"Every morning of my life, Bernie, I pass by not one but two ice cream parlors on the way to work. I look in the windows. You want to know what I see?"

He removed his head from the window pane.

"Hm? I see tutti frutti, Bernie. I see vanilla. I see chocolate."

There was a thud as he readdressed the glass with his head.

"*Chocolate*, Bernie."

His hands, which had been on his hips, became fists at his side.

"I see all three, is what I'm saying to you, in both parlors."

He looked up at the grey sky. It was going to rain.

"How are they doing it, Bernie? Hm? *How?* It's eating away at me. Every waking second. I'm losing sleep. I'm under a hell of a lot of pressure to get this thing up and running, because we have the pizza launch to think about in November."

He turned around.

"Do you realize I'd been thinking about you in relation to that? Hm? Something in delivery."

He parked himself on the corner of the desk and leaned forward, looking Bernard in the eye.

"Maybe even a delivery *vehicle*, Mr Maypole."

Taking the younger man by the shoulders, Dunkhorn spoke vehemently.

"*How* could I take you off dishes, Bernie? Now, at this critical juncture in the company's growth and development? And with the crisis, and the other crisis, and what have you, and the ice cream, and the pizza? You're a victim of your own success out there! You're *too good*, Mr Maypole!"

He shook Bernard violently, and screamed at the top of his voice.

"You're just too goddamn good! You're just too goddamn *good*, Bernie!"

Bernard managed to make eye contact with Noranbole. She shrugged. Then, thinking she should intervene, she opened her mouth to speak. There was no need—Dunkhorn had exhausted himself.

He slumped, gripping the desk's edge for a few seconds and taking shallow breaths. Then he dragged himself back to his chair and threw himself into it, spent. For a minute he just sat there holding his head.

"Think about the company, can't you?" he pleaded, finally. "About the *team*."

Making a visible effort to sit up straight and adjust his tie, he brightened.

"Look, Mr Paddock in burgers has made an excellent suggestion. I can see you're downhearted and I want to do something for you. Sproat has to pop out for an hour or so tomorrow afternoon. Take his kid to the dentist. How would you feel about filling in? I know it's not what you've been working towards, and it is only an hour, but it could be a real eye opener. Some of the burger people have gone on to table service and even, in one case, noodles, and as I mentioned, with the November pizza launch fast approaching, adaptability is a really key performance indicator for us right now. This could be great for you!"

"Really . . ." his clenched fists trembled and his face was cholesterol puce ". . . key!"

When Bernard walked Noranbole out through the kitchen door, they lingered by the bins to say goodbye, but he wouldn't look at her, so she held his face in her hands and gave him the stare till she got a smile out of him.

"Listen to me, Bernard. You are doing great. Look at me, my love. Just keep doing your best. Good things are coming. You are wonderful and I am very proud."

He looked close to tears, but he gave her a wink.

"That's better. I have to get back to the office now or those people at NATO will be getting all uppity again."

She patted his cheek and kissed his mouth.

"I'll see you tonight, OK?"

When Noranbole got in that evening, wonderful aromas traced twists in the air, curling scimitar sweeps from her olfactory receptor neurons back down the hallway and into the kitchen. She could hear a bath running.

"Hey baby."

Bernard didn't reply. There was an envelope with her name on it propped up by the telephone. She opened it and read the little card.

"Mwen pa kapab kwit li. Ou dwe jwenn li."

She smiled. A treasure hunt. Not the week's first.

"But there's nothing you can't cook!" she yelled at the kitchen door.

"How'm I supposed to find something that doesn't exist?" she asked herself, kicking off her shoes and leaving her lunchbox on the little telephone table. Bernard had poured a glass of whatever sparkling wine he'd been able to pay for and left it by the card for her. She took a sip and winced. Below the clue, an instruction:

"Sihirli olur nerede. Başlayın."

She chuckled.

"Where the magic happens?" she called out. "The kitchen?"

A disgruntlement of pan clatter. The cutlery drawer slammed.

"Uhuh, bedroom then," said Noranbole, wandering in there.

He had changed the bedding and prepared the room for some industrial strength romance. The lights were low and red. Petals on the bed. A bottle of wine in an ice bucket.

Barry White.

"Utterly devoid of originality," she said loudly. "But I don't hate it."

Bernard began to whistle. There was another note on the pillow.

"Enkel. Det er bak deg."

Noranbole turned round to face the little en suite. It was cathedral level candlelit in there and there was hot water running, pushing little steam puffs out into the bedroom. She went in and blinked while her eyes adjusted.

Bernard had arranged a very considerable number of candles around the bathtub. The water was hidden beneath bubble hills, and she caught the scent of some fruit or other as she leaned over to turn off the tap. On one corner of the tub a third card sat on top of a little black lacquer box.

She picked up the box first and opened it. The interior was lined with velvet, but empty. There was something on the lid but she couldn't make it out, so she brought both box and card back out into the brighter bedroom. There was an inlay beneath the veneer and in an elegant, cursive script—ivory white—the following words:

"It's A Good Box, Boley."

She smiled.

"Don't see what it has to do with whatever it is," she muttered, holding the box right up to a lamp and examining the lid more closely. She could see now that the inlaid script was in fact a weave of some kind. It reminded her of knot work and was exquisitely fine. With an intake of breath she realized what Bernard had used. Angel hair.

Noodles.

She opened the card.

"Gracias por cuidar de mí hoy. Un día, yo te mostraré cómo puedo cuidar de ti."

When she turned to go to the kitchen he was already there, eyes big and wet. She found herself in his arms

"I know you will, Bernie. I've always known that."

He undressed her and lifted her into the bath, refilled her glass and went back to his cooking. Noranbole set herself adrift in the candlelight. The scented water was a heavenly Hades, hot under suddy hills. The sweet aroma eluded her. It could have been muscadine, but might have been monkey apple.

※

It was obvious as soon as she stepped into the kitchen that Bernard had made an effort with dinner. She could see immediately that the table had been laid out to represent the open sea. It was covered in a thick and undulating carpet of blue petunia blossoms and in the center there was a ship built of dark chocolate that ran the full length—with sails of frosted candy that seemed to billow—and that may have been a cutter but then again, judging from its slender outline, might have been a sloop.

The nautical theme was in honor of the meal's main dish—slow poached sturgeon which Bernard had carefully laid out from stern to prow, placing it there when still just warm enough to melt the deck a little and make its own chocolate sauce.

But that was for later.

"અને હવે પ્રથમ કોર્સ માટે."

"Multiple courses," said Noranbole. "La-di-look at you."

She sat down and Bernard pushed her chair up to the table. He had, in fact, prepared six.

For the first, he served a cartouche of plum and roquefort-stuffed Iberico pork tenderloin wrapped in Bellota ham and served in a Sweet Tooth mushroom sauce, sprinkled with candied juniper berries and laced with manzanilla wine. To accompany it, the manzanilla, and when they had finished both, by way of amuse bouche, the rump of a quartered stag which had spent the night in salt.

For the second, a salad of dandelion greens, persimmon and pomegranate seeds tossed in red apple vinegar and argan oil, and served on a Murcian omelette. With it a large jug of a very lightly chilled Sangue di Giuda to bring out the fruit and, in a not dissimilar jug, a civet of wild hare.

As they ate and drank, Bernard regaled her with scintillating tales of his thrilling past. The time he got his leg quite badly bitten by a gypsy up behind the Fletcher cottage. The time they let Gideon Tupp's unbroken yearlings out of the corral and he, Paul Bennett and Michael Hilliard had to hit the ground in unison to avoid the wildly fired rounds Tupp was letting off in his panic. Fits of adrenalin giggles, not knowing for a few seconds there if they would live or die.

The time they broke into the Branston homestead and Michael Hilliard got mauled by the family cat. The stuttering stabs at explanation as sleepy Branstons emerged from their bedrooms. The blood everywhere.

The time the banks of the lake up at Swan Hill froze over and they walked out across the creaking ice, and how they swore they saw light beneath it, and how Paul Bennett swore he heard voices.

For the third course an enormous pie. Bernard cut a slice for her, releasing an ascension of rich steam and revealing the innards: a bit of a pig, a kid goat, two goslings, an indeterminate number of chickens and pigeons, three young rabbits, a heron and two leverets in a gloopy German sauce. Noranbole was beginning to feel giddy as Bernard filled her glass from a bottle of bacony Garrafeira port.

"Even by your standards, Bernie," she said, using the back of her hand to wipe a sliver of greasy capon from her chin, "you've done well here."

For the fourth a platter of dariole wafers infused with Guinea grains and a clear blue, perfectly pyramidal jelly flecked with pulled pork, along with a bottle of brandy.

For the fifth a stew of damsuns and gooseberries in orange blossom water, fennelled, filled out with custard dumplings and brought to life with a carafe of Grand Constance from the Cape.

Finally, the sturgeon in its vessel, complimented with a board of Alpine cheeses—an aged Beaufort with crunchy calcified bits, a creamy young Comté, a Grataron d'Arêches, a Reblochon—and repeated helpings of a Steinbeisser Williams Pear schnapps to aid digestion.

"Chocolate, cheese and fish," said Noranbole.

"Класическа комбинация," said Bernard.

"Absoyumminglutely," she replied. "Can't be beaten."

A certain expression oozed its way across Bernard's chocolate-stained face—a look that Noranbole recognized immediately. He stood and took her by the hand, leading her into the bedroom and there, wiping the sturgeon from her lips, he kissed her hard and threw her on the bed. Then he stood over her and undressed.

Although they did this on a daily basis, and sometimes twice, she never failed to be impressed with his length. What really did it for her though, she reflected as he removed her clothing, was the girth.

Observing a well-established routine, Bernard initiated the lovemaking of the crow, taking care to include not only the inner and outer pincers, but also some biting at the sides and touching. He had long ago mastered the art of foreplay with young Molly Stodder in Old Man Stodder's hay barn, and Noranbole was certainly getting the benefit now.

"Excellent," she said when an hour had passed. "Nicely done."

His preparations complete, he uncorked the bottle of wine, poured her a glass and penetrated her, taking great care to vary his ruts and breaking from their norms here and there to surprise her with some churning, some pestling, a bit of rubbing, a touch of buffeting and a good dose of hammering.

For Noranbole, it was the perfect end to what had been a rather difficult day. She was enjoying herself immensely. As light began to show through the blinds she surrendered to sensation, the corners of her mouth slid earward in a slow smile and, as Bernard worked away with a deliberate, pumping action, she lost consciousness at the summit of one of their pleasure peaks.

Interlude

"Some of the *beaches* I've been on," said Mitch. His eyes flicked from the monitor to the two girls lounging on beanbags in the foyer's chill out area.

"You should have *seen* those beaches."

He'd been biding his time for a shot at these two but they'd turned out to be the busy types. Days all planned out. Cultural shit and that. Boundless energy. He'd had a good long look at the various parts of both of their bodies and decided that everything was just tickety boo. As long a look, anyway, as could be had as they came and went.

"I've *been* on those beaches, man."

Today though they were lounging on the beanbags, having helped themselves to a beer each from the honor system bar, and were making use of the wifi. Mitch imagined they had all sorts of liking and sharing to catch up on— girls like that tended to have very large social networks. Neither of them had been openly hostile towards him yet and he found that encouraging.

"You guys like mountains?"

Before either could answer, his view of them was blocked by an agitated looking Olly.

"It's happening again, Mitch."

As well as agitation, Olly was exhibiting a certain amount of shame.

"Aw jeez," said Mitch.

Passwording the reception laptop, he headed up to the sixteen bed mixed dorm. Sure enough, she was in there and so were four of the male residents. They were sitting on the edges of their bunks with their trousers down or zippers undone. She was wearing a rubber glove.

"Miss?" Mitch found himself knocking politely on the door frame. "Could I please have a word with you in the hallway out here for a minute please, Miss?"

"Certainly, Mr Mitch."

She swept past him in a rustle of skirt, removing her glove and dropping it in the wastepaper basket by the door as she left the room. Mitch looked at the residents.

"Jeez. You guys look kinda sad."

"Yeah," said Aaron who was in Big City as part of a round-the-world which was to take up much of his gap year. He pulled his zipper up. "I *do* feel a bit sad."

"Me too," said Roddy, who came every year for the street theater festival and was clutching his Devil Stick for comfort. Teardrops sprinkled the jeans that were gathered round his ankles.

Mitch went out into the hallway where she stood waiting for him, upright and imperious. She had replaced rubber with the pair of elbow length lace gloves she usually wore whenever she left the building.

"Jeez, lady."

He'd worked in a number of hostels. They were his primary mode of income, in fact. He knew his way round the booking software and all the basic routines, the same the world over—breakfast and stripping the vacated beds, key collection and stocking the bar. It was easy work.

This was new though. Even in the city, he'd never had to deal with anything like this before, or anyone like her. If Mr Mørch found out about this he'd lose the gig. He *definitely* had to deal with it. Now.

For sure.

"Good heavens, Mr Mitch! What is the matter with you? Have you been taking opium?"

He was aware of being sweaty, and probably pale.

"Perhaps we could upgrade you to a private room?" he said.

"Whatever for?"

She looked puzzled.

"Who would milk the boys?"

At this point, a kind of calm came over Mitch. He shrugged and held his hands out, palms up.

"Look I'll be honest with you, Miss—I'm out of my depth here. They say you don't take any money. And your bed is paid for, y'know? It's all good. *But.*"

He tried to drill his meaning into her with his eyes.

Nothing.

"Y'know?"

She didn't.

"OK, lady. I've got enough on my plate, OK? I like a quiet life. Last thing I need on my watch is some skank tricking the dorms. This is a backpacker's hostel. OK? It's all very wholesome. We deal with a lot of arrested development, of course, but nothing like this. You'll have to—"

Something in the way she was looking at him made him stop.

"I shall assume from your tone, Mr Mitch, that skank is a pejorative term. I do not require a definition; I would merely point out that I have been nothing but civil towards you since my arrival here."

"Yes. Yes, I know that, Miss. I don't mean to. Yes. You've been very. Always been. I don't."

He'd run out of language.

"You seem tense."

He *felt* tense. She shook her head in exasperation.

"Well? What *is it*, Mr Mitch?"

His heart sank. Confrontation wasn't his thing.

"I don't know. I don't know, Miss. Is it Miss? Or Ms? I don't know. I guess I'm just tired or something. To tell you the truth, it hasn't been very—"

But he didn't have her attention. She had removed a lace glove and retrieved another rubber one from her bag.

"No! No, there's no need for that, Miss."

Her head jerked mutely back, as straight as a chicken's.

"I *work* here, Miss. I can't allow it."

"Oh come now, Mr Mitch," she said, snapping the glove, "you make a ridiculous figure of yourself, spouting this nonsense. I suppose that isn't an erection?"

Mitch looked down. He was wearing sweats today so pretense was futile.

"Aw, that's not fair."

He put his hand on himself, then thought better of it and took it away and just stood there, staring at the shape of his penis through heavy cotton.

"How did you *do* that?"

She shook her head but her face softened a little.

"I can hardly be blamed for your turgidity, Mr Mitch. It's your curse."

She was stretching the glove over her fingers like a surgeon.

"Is there somewhere quiet?"

Chapter Three

Yes, Jacintha—to disparage him is a pleasant diversion, because he is worthless.

Excruciating.

And to think he has latched himself on to the CEO.

Our CEO.

Our *leader*.

A towering figure!

A hulking presence.

Looming. In the mist and such.

A benevolent . . . a benevolence.

Wonderful woman.

Great gal!

Poor thing.

She'll never last.

Not with that sack of shit she's dragging round.

Holding her back.

Draining her.

Feeding off her *elan vital* like a yeast infection.

A tapeworm of a man. A hookworm.

A whip worm.

A roundworm and a fluke!

A scabied pinworm!

A plasmodic strep of a man!

Man is too elevated a term for he whom we discuss. He'd come across as out-of-his-depth in a petri dish.

Off in a corner of the dish somewhere, experiencing feelings of inadequacy, if he had any sense, which he doesn't.

Although petri dishes are round, generally speaking, Bethany.

A crawling moron!

A cystitic mass!

A long-fisted sloth!

A chested succubus!

It makes me smile to think about things that might hurt him.

Does it?

The sap-headed sonk!

Or humiliate. Makes my toes tingle. Warm tingly toes.

Apparently he can cook.

Silence!

He is so disgusting it makes you wonder about his poo. You know?

Not at all like Brett Blake, who has a salary in the six figure bracket, a gorgeous portfolio of pension, insurance and investment products and who is, in several other ways, admirable.

He certainly makes his numbers. Last year he had the highest quarterlies I'd ever heard of. Scarcely believable. Magnificent quarterlies, leading to enviable bonuses.

Which we, dutifully, envied.

Nobody had ever heard of quarterlies that high.

It must be *extra* disgusting, is what I'm saying.

Although some of us had heard of quarterlies that were almost as high.

But not quite.

No.

And not just Brett, to be fair, though I swoon at the merest glimpse of his shoes.

No. *All* of those who toil—

Even the ones who don't always make their numbers, bless them.

Toil at the coal face—

So to speak.

Sculpting our very future—the world itself!—from the spoiled clay of proletarian inertia.

Those indolent, resentful masses. Artists, beekeepers and so on.

Parasites!

And he their king. The king of the parasites!

The Parasite King!

He soiled himself, and shamed the rest of us, at the company picnic. Do you remember?

He literally soiled himself?

I have no way of knowing that. I wasn't there.

I was. He underdressed.

Mother of Christ, yes. I remember.

She seemed unperturbed.

She's a saint, is why. I mean, nobody expects you to turn up to a company picnic in a suit or pantyhose, but that doesn't mean you should come looking like you just rolled out of bed. Steer clear of sloppy sweats, holey or worn tees, denim cutoffs or anything inappropriate, such as a busty halter top or short-shorts. For men, jeans and a polo (or a plain tee and cargo shorts) are fine, while women can opt for a tasteful sundress or knee-length day shorts and a cotton tee.

It's not fucking rocket science, is it?

But he had to be all "check out my muscles" and "get a load of these upper arms" and what not.

And his table manners. Everyone else, including the children, had the good sense to avoid the spinach.

Bad dining manners are a huge no-no. Avoid overloading your plate and only go back for seconds once everyone has had a chance to serve themselves. Don't double dip when helping yourself to salsa or guacamole, and don't chew with your mouth open or try to carry on a conversation with a mouthful of food.

It was just *excruciating*.

You could have etched glass with those nipples.

Silence!

Well there's no way I'm inviting him to my upcoming Foreign Accent Syndrome fundraiser. Not after all the work I've put in, and not after the spectacle he made of himself at last month's Scurvy bash. I couldn't understand a single word the wretch said.

Apparently he's Belarusian.

Good God.

But you'll have to, Penelope. That's the bind; you can't not invite the CEO.

Poor girl.

Will Brett be there? I shouldn't even ask, of course.

What a man! Have you had the chance to take a look at his numbers?

Magnificent.

And that swing!

He'd be a great pairing for Noranbole, if he wasn't already married to Tilly Bumpus, a very dear friend of mine.

Plays off scratch, you know.

Hang on. A parasite, by definition, is—

Silence!

※

Noranbole sat on her desk looking out of the window while Vacuity did a circuit of the conference table, straightening dossiers and making sure the mineral water was evenly spaced.

"We had sturgeon last night," she said through a yawn, bending down to take off a shoe and give her foot a rub.

"I like pizza," said Vacuity.

There were patches of sunlight on the avenue below, but the sky was crowded with dark clouds, closing in. Through the toughened panes of glass the city was a stormy scene in a silent movie.

"That should do it."

Vacuity had her hands on her hips at the head of the table. Noranbole went back around her desk—she liked to be behind it when the board members came in. Remind them who the boss was. Remind herself.

The intercom beeped.

"Here they come," said Vacuity, and took her seat against the back wall, notepad in hand.

The double doors at the end of the room swung open and the board members and select executives brought their business and bustle in. Mr Elderkin, the Chief Finance Officer, was first to his seat, opening his dossier as Deer Spirit and Rood, the legal people, huddled with Mr Perigo, the Visionary and Mr Freeze, the Process guy, on the other side of the table. All four were whispering frantically at the same time. Rising, the accountant, sat alone.

"Where's Human Resources?" asked Noranbole as she sat down.

"Sick," said Vacuity.

"What's *she* doing here?" asked Mr Star Blanket, Head of Creative.

"Ms Blanc will be taking up a new role as Chief Brand Officer as of the first of next month," said Noranbole. "She'll be sitting in on our little get-togethers from now on and will be taking minutes at today's extraordinary meeting."

"Oops, going to have to correction that, Nor . . . Ms Wakeling," said Vacuity. "We already have an extraordinary meeting scheduled for early next week—your own, to go over the new proposals. Excitement! To avoidance any confusion, I'll go ahead and allocate *super* extraordinary status to the meeting currently underway."

The hum of chat around the room lulled. A number of the board members took a long second look at Vacuity.

"Fine," said Noranbole, "take your seats please, gentlemen."

Drinkwater and Poor from Engineering came in and closed the doors behind them. When everyone was sitting and quiet, Noranbole cleared her throat.

"Right," she said, resting her elbows on the table and weaving her fingers, "somebody tell me what I'm doing here."

"It's a disaster," said Mr Elderkin.

"A catastrophe," said Mr Amerideath, Chief Commercial Officer, as he came in. "Sorry I'm late."

"This could be the end of the corporation," said Mr Star Blanket.

"Yes, I think that's slightly over-egging it, Mr Star Blanket," said Mr Perigo, "but it certainly is a very grave situation indeed."

"Very grave," said Mr Freeze.

"Oh dear! Doesn't sound good," said Noranbole. "A detail or two?"

"It's the pipeline," said Mr Elderkin. "It seems we won't be building one."

"Total fiasco," said Mr Deer Spirit.

"Oh dear! If I recall correctly, it was quite important that we build the pipeline," said Noranbole, "vis-à-vis the future of Terra Forma and all that."

"Yes we were rather counting on it," said Mr Elderkin, "but it seems we won't be. They've gone and gotten themselves embroiled in a war."

"Oh dear! With whom?"

"With us," said Mr Poor. "The premier, Mr Stitz, doesn't seem all that keen on going ahead with the contract, now."

"We need to talk about a radical rethink, Ms Wakeling," said Mr Perigo. "A sidestep, or perhaps a ninety degree. I don't think we should exclude the possibility of a complete about-to, frankly."

"This could deepen the crisis exponentially," said Mr Amerideath "sending us spiraling downwards towards some sort of upheaval."

"Or worse," said Mr Drinkwater. "Upwards."

"What about any implications for the other crisis?" asked Mr Freeze.

"Well," said Mr Deer Spirit, leaning forward so everyone could see him, "on the bright side, it might actually resolve that one."

"Ooh," said Vacuity, "that would be good, wouldn't it?"

"Depending on how things go, of course," said Mr Elderkin.

"Of course," said Mr Deer Spirit.

"And we definitely can't salvage this?" asked Noranbole.

"How?" asked Mr Star Blanket. "I've been imagineering all morning. Nothing. And I'm the Head of Creative."

Noranbole sat back in her chair and thought for a moment.

"Well, for example, does he like money?"

She put her elbows on the table again.

"A lot of people do, you know, and we've got enormous sums of it. That's right isn't it, Mr Rising?"

Rising, who could give the impression of being behind a person even as he faced them across a table, kept his eyes on the documents in front of him and nodded.

"Sooo . . ." continued Noranbole swinging round and stepping towards the picture window. She could feel her business savvy kicking in. Her mind was all a-fizz.

Turning again suddenly, she faced the room square and gripped the back of her seat.

"Why don't we give him some?"

Her eyes were on the ceiling, darting here and there.

"You know. If he lets us put the pipeline there."

Silence.

Mr Drinkwater looked at Mr Star Blanket.

Everybody else looked at anybody.

Mr Amerideath looked at Mr Elderkin who, having cleared his throat, was the first to speak.

"Ms Wakeling, are you suggesting that we *bribe* Mr Stitz? A democratically elected head of state?"

All eyes were on Noranbole. The board of directors of the most powerful corporation in the world—they might as well have been kittens, her next words hanging over them like a soon-to-be-bloody cleaver.

"Not at all, gentlemen," said Noranbole.

Palpable relief around the room. The legal people were breathing again.

"Thank goodness for that," said Mr Poor, mopping his brow with a handkerchief, "because for a minute there I thought you—"

"What I'm proposing," Noranbole continued, "is that, on the understanding that it will secure a change of policy on Mr Stitz's part, we give him lots of this money Mr Rising assures me we have."

Another silence.

Prolooooooooooooooooooooooooooooooooooooooooooooooonged.

Mr Freeze was stiff in his chair. And pale. He looked at Mr Rising on his right, then at Mr Perigo, on his left. Then he looked across the table, at Mr Amerideath, who looked back at him.

"Eh . . . yes, yes I see," said Mr Elderkin. "Yes. Yes, I think I see."

A smirky smile smeared itself across Mr Deer Spirit's face.

"How clever of you, Ms Wakeling," he slimed.

"Clever?" asked Mr Rising. His face was reddening as he got up from his seat. Mad stary eyes on him. He slammed his fists down on the table.

"It's *inspired.*"

He sat again.

"We'll need to get a proposal typed up asap," said Mr Elderkin. "This would need to be in front of him before he attends the Peace Summit on Tuesday."

"Pardon me for piping in here, but I could to do that," said Vacuity.

Mr Elderkin scrutinized her.

"Excuse me, Ms Blanc?"

"I could to do that for you. Would you like me to to do it?"

Everyone but the Chief Financial Officer looked away.

"Eh . . ." His eyes shot around the room in search of assistance but all potentially available eye contact was withheld, " . . . yes, I believe I would, Ms Blanc. Thank you."

Vacuity tilted her head and beamed at him.

The phone rang. Noranbole picked it up.

"Sure, Lucy, put him through."

"Ms Wakeling? Dunkhorn here. So, so very, very sorry to disturb you at your work, Ms Wakeling. And what vital work it is! Why, if it wasn't for your steady hand at the rudder, Ms Wakeling, I don't know what—"

"You're very kind, Mr Dunkhorn, but I am rather in the middle of—"

"Quite so, Ms Wakeling, quite so. I'll come straight to the point. You've got to get down here."

"You're suggesting I take my leave of a *super* extraordinary board meeting of the world's most powerful organization, at this critical juncture in its multiple crises, to come down there to your noodle and burger emporium, right now?"

"Yes."

Noranbole glanced across at Vacuity, who was giving Mr Amerideath a palm reading.

"OK."

※

When Noranbole got to the Emporium there was a small crowd outside, peeking in through the slatted blinds, but she couldn't make out the cause of their fuss. When she pushed the door open she was taken aback by the flash of a camera. The photographer was aiming his lens at the rear of the dining space; she could see Bernard through the kitchen hatch, at the hotplate in a hair net and apron, spatula in hand. He was flipping burgers, surrounded by a huddle of his colleagues. Some of them wept openly, vocalizing their adulation. One or two were on their knees.

He looked a little harried, like someone who didn't quite know what was going on. He looked like he always looked. Their eyes met but Mr Dunkhorn had her by the elbow so she just blew him a kiss.

"Ms Wakeling, thank you so much for coming down here and so quickly. When I think of what I might have pulled you away from. Weighty matters of great import, without a doubt. I probably wouldn't even understa—"

"I'm still rather in the dark, Mr Dunkhorn. Could we—"

"Yes of course. I'm just going to go ahead and give it to you straight, Ms Wakeling. We've never seen anything like this. Never. I don't have the words. It's unlike anything. Ever. I tell you, I knew we'd made a good hire with Mr Maypole, but I did not see this coming. It's a game changer. It changes everything. Everything."

He ushered her into a booth where they joined a circular little man who wore tinted glasses despite the low lighting and who had a head shaped like a rugby ball on its side. A chunky gold chain hung from his neck, on the outside of his shirt, and each finger bore at least one heavy ring. Somebody had put a macchiato in front him but he showed no interest in it as he tapped the ash from a squat cigar directly onto the white tablecloth. He glared at Mr Dunkhorn as the restaurateur continued.

"Everything, Ms Wakeling, changes today. Now. This is the moment. The *key* moment. Nothing is the same, from here on in. Nothing. It's all going to be different. I took the liberty of making a couple of calls before picking up the phone to you earlier. We have some press here, as you can see, and this is Mr Feuchtwanger, somebody you definitely need to talk to."

The little, round, bejeweled man spoke for the first time.

"Ms Wakeling, my name is Mr—"

"Feuchtwanger," said Noranbole. "Yes."

He nodded.

"I see my reputation precedes me. You'll no doubt have come across me in my capacity as a promoter of any number of spectacularly astonishing and entertaining events around the globe."

Noranbole and Mr Dunkhorn exchanged a glance.

"The International Concourse of The Dark Arts comes to mind, or Festivale perhaps," he said as he finally picked up his coffee, holding it a centimeter from the surface of the table, "but never mind that now. Ms Wakeling, you are aware of the imminent Palpon™ World Meat Patty Flip Finals?"

Noranbole thanked the waitress, who at that moment had brought her a hot chocolate. She placed her handbag on the seat beside her and reached for the sugar bowl, emptying its contents into her cup.

"Please don't patronize me, Mr Feuchtwanger. I could hardly get across town today with all the security cordons they've put up. I sometimes wonder whether meat patty flipping is worth all this fuss, though I confess I'm as enthusiastic as the next girl."

She giggled.

"Oh indeed—," said Mr Dunkhorn.

"Shut up, Dunkhorn," said Mr Feuchtwanger. "You no doubt allude to the reason for all that security, Ms Wakeling. 'Flip' Mc Side, reigning world champion, was due to arrive in Big City today."

He took his glasses off and pinched the bridge of his nose.

"I sometimes wonder whether *he's* worth all the fuss."

"Well he certainly is dreamy," said Noranbole, her eyes glazing a little. "You need only ask a lady."

Mr Feuchtwanger put his coffee down.

"Dreamy or not, Ms Wakeling, he's been nursing a very severe case of burger elbow for some years now. All kept hush hush, of course. We've been getting him through with cortisone injections but that isn't going to cut it this time. I hate to sully him for you but the truth is his confidence is shot."

"It's absolutely—" said Mr Dunkhorn.

"One more word, Dunkhorn," said Mr Feuchtwanger, "and you're a dead man."

"I'm afraid, Ms Wakeling, that Flip won't be competing this time round. Or ever again. He appears to have had some kind of breakdown. He'd already become quite reclusive this last year and when I visited his ranch earlier in the week I found only a gibbering, incontinent mess."

"How heartbreaking!"

"Absolutely, and none of the narcotics we've been pumping into him in the intervening few days would seem to have done the trick. We're up against it, Ms Wakeling. You can appreciate the billions that are tied up in an event of this scale. How many people depend on its success."

"Yes, I can see how that would be a problem for you, but—"

"*Problem?*" interjected Dunkhorn, "It's a—"

Mr Feuchtwanger had quietly placed a hand on his associate's forearm, and with the other picked up an item of cutlery from the table.

"You see this fork, Dunkhorn?"

"I'm still at a loss as to how I could be of any help," said Noranbole, "I take it this has something to do with Bernard? He's done well today?"

Mr Feuchtwanger didn't immediately reply. He looked from Noranbole to Dunkhorn as if to work out whether she was serious. Having satisfied himself that she was, his shoulders began to shake. Replacing the dark glasses, he sat back on the leather seat and smacked his knees. A single laugh, like the bark of a dog. Then another. And then a stream of laughter, head thrown back and howling at the light fixture overhead. *Roaring* at it.

Dunkhorn kept his eyes down.

Noranbole took a sip of her chocolate and, as Feuchtwanger's outburst went on, another.

At last, the attack seemed to subside. The saddest, and happiest, and deepest of sighs came out of the little man; from beneath a tinted lens, a crystal clear rivulet of salt water emerged to probe the wrinkled gullies on the skin of his face.

"Ah, Ms Wakeling." One last shudder. "*Yes*, Ms Wakeling. Bernard has done very well."

He waved his hand in the air towards Dunkhorn, who leaned forward.

"Ms Wakeling, he's phenomenal. A phenomenon. That we haven't seen his like here before goes without saying."

His head shook in disbelief as he spoke, eyes misty with worship.

"When you see someone that good at something. At *anything*. You know? When the privilege is ours to bear witness . . . it just brings us so much closer to . . . to things we know nothing about."

His body convulsed and the tears came.

"You know?"

Feuchtwanger glared at him.

"Jesus," said the little promoter, and weaved his fingers.

"Ms Wakeling, I want Bernard in that tournament. Not only will he save the whole enterprise by replacing Mc Side—I think he could win it."

"The finals are two days from now, Mr Feuchtwanger," said Noranbole.

"Yes. Could you have a word with him, do you think? I don't speak . . . eh . . ."

"Well, yes, I could run it by him," said Noranbole, "although he did rather have his sights set on the noodles thing."

Interlude

"**B**EYWARD PHENN,**"** (a man of papery complexion who had been with the section a good twenty-three years, or rather the department, which he had entered—at the lowest pay point of the lowest grade—straight from school, eschewing the riskier options available to him at the time such as overseas meanderings of some kind or a stint in sales with Uncle Milus [who drank heavily and kept bad books and was not to be trusted with the medicine cabinet let alone his own business—kitchens] and who through hard work and application [not to mention gnawing self-doubt, brooding aspiration, vindictive scheming and pure spite] had raised himself up through two more grades, those being Executive Assistant and then Executive Officer and who at the end of that time—an unpleasant period, once the situation with Miss Wilted [having reached such levels of both aggravation and complexity for all concerned that *human resources* had gotten involved] became public knowledge within the department, leading to a miserable few years of particularly tortuous office politics for Mr Phenn—thereafter known in water cooler circles as Wayward Heyward—had secured himself a position in the office in which he now sat, an office from which he felt he could credibly sneer back at the Wilted mafia [a coven!] and within which he had since attained not one but two further promotions, those being Executive Officer to Higher Executive Officer and Higher Executive Officer to Senior Executive officer—a position that placed him within sniffing distance of a Grade Seven appointment and which he had now held for eight years—and who had been almost entirely personally responsible, he felt, for the name change of said office [at the rear of the building and not normally accessible to the public] from Research Section to the altogether more satisfying Investigative Services Section), "has dropped his pen."

You'd have had to have been right next to him to have heard him mutter—ass in the air and one eyeball to the mean, musty carpet, he could feel an imprint develop on his cheekbone, made by the coarse material as he tried to get a line of sight beneath the drawer unit.

"Heyward Phenn has dropped his pen."

No sign of it. Odd because the hidey holes were few—Mr Phenn kept a clean, uncluttered office and in the dim space beneath his desk, under the drawer unit had been his best bet.

There was another, just like it, in the pen tidy above him, but that was not Heyward Phenn's way. He could not abide waste. Reported it frequently.

Had, in fact, accepted—on a voluntary basis—responsibility for coordinating the section's material resources and waste management scheme (the MWRM program).

And what would I do when I had finished with *that* one, he thought to himself. Down to office supplies again, I suppose, to swipe another handful from the hemorrhage that is the stationery cupboard (which is not to say there's anything amiss with Mrs Tank, who as far as I can see runs a very tight ship down there and has a summery air about her and who simply doesn't have the brief to question stationery requests signed at Higher Executive Officer level or above). Down to office supplies, again, to grab more swag. To take, take, take and all the time, *all the time* a perfectly good, recently acquired, as-new pen languishing in some shadowy nook of my own workstation—taunting me, the MWRM officer, with its discarded utility: a dreadful, pen-shaped breach in the security matrix through which all the good things are being inexorably sucked, all the time. All the good things that work properly getting sucked out. All the time.

Taken away.

This wasn't good. He knew what he was like, when he got like this. Unlikely to calm down sufficiently, now, to carry out an effective and systematic search, the mandatory sessions had at least provided him with the wherewithal to recognize the signs and step back: better to tackle this problem afresh, later.

"Heyward Phenn has lost his pen."

He raised his face from the floor and gave it a little rub, going through two cycles of his centering mantra and arching his back. Then he got a) back into his seat, and b) the fright of his life.

Sitting across from him was a woman of severe appearance, hands hidden in elbow-length gloves, one of which was extended towards him.

"Yours, I presume?"

His eyes went to the contents of her outstretched hand. An Advantage Velocity™ Gel-ink Roller. That was it all right. He took it and placed it in the pen tidy, next to the other one.

"You're not breathing."

It was true. He took a breath.

"My name is Emma Wakeling," said the woman, removing the gloves and what he could only describe as a bonnet and revealing a head of tightly pulled back hair that culminated in a shiny bun. If a twenty-three year career in the administrative arm of a public sector archival body had furnished Heyward Phenn with anything, it was a keenly honed sense of 1) madness, and 2) danger. Both were in the room with him now. He was sure of it.

"I'm told that you are the gentleman to help me with my problem, Mr Phenn. It's a perfectly straightforward matter that I'm hopeful falls within your remit—a question of tracing a relative of mine, whose documents I carry with me. I'm sure I needn't take up too much of your time," said her mouth, while her eyes said "I'm a crazy lady, and I'm not going anywhere."

"I see."

"You will be recompensed, of course."

"This is a government department, Ms Wakeling. We don't charge, although there is a nominal administrative fee of—"

"No money will be changing hands, Mr Phenn. I'm from out of town, you know."

"But—"

"It doesn't mean I cannot pay you."

She was pulling on a rubber glove.

"I most certainly can."

Mr Phenn's eyes went to the door, which he usually left open. It was closed. He wondered what things might be like on the other side of it right now. The staff kitchenette. The innumerable functionaries. The delightful Mrs Tank.

"My daughter, Noranbole," the woman was saying, "a girl who I am afraid is rather hopelessly bereft of any semblance of gorm, is lost in the city with her ape. My aim is to bring her home. Those chores aren't going to do themselves."

"I see."

"I propose the following—payment in installments, each payable whenever you can provide me with information which progresses the search for my girl. I am more than happy to make a down payment this instant, as you can see."

"Yes, I'm afraid I don't quite see what you're getting at, Ms Wakeling."

"What I'm getting at, Mr Phenn, is that I am perfectly happy to milk you, in return for any attention you can give the matter," said the woman with a note of fatigued impatience.

"I offer the arrangement, which I consider a fair one, in the hope that, given my candor, we can skip any feigned reluctance on your part and get straight to it. Why you lads insist on such ridiculous posturing is quite beyond me," she continued, rolling her eyes. "I consider it an essential service. You people simply don't function properly, all juiced up."

Heyward's mouth was hanging open. He closed it. Then he opened it again, to speak.

"Well, I've never heard of anything like . . . I'm sorry, did you say *Noranbole* Wakeling?"

"I did."

His eyes dropped to his desk, to the newspaper that was open on it, to the business section feature he had been reading on Terra Forma's new, dynamic young CEO and to the half-page color photo of her. Glancing up from it to the woman's rubber-gloved hand, he stood.

"Ms Wakeling," he began, avoiding her eyes, "what you suggest is not as straightforward as you might think."

Making a show of tidying the top of his meticulously ordered desk, he closed the newspaper and dropped it into the recycling basket.

"One, you can imagine how many Noranbole Wakelings there are in Big City. Two—"

"Be that as it may, Mr Phenn. I am determined to find the girl and prepared to pay a handsome price."

He went to the filthy window and looked out over the staff car park. It was an overcast September afternoon and as he turned to his visitor, he wasn't at all sure how to feel about his decision to bin the newspaper.

"All right then, Ms Wakeling." He shrugged.

"Let's make a start."

Chapter Four

"**A**ND AS THAT MAGNIFICENT and colorful opening ceremony draws to a close, it falls to me to welcome you, an estimated two point three billion viewers around the world to this, the seventy-seventh annual Palpon™ World Meat Patty Flip Finals. A fascinating night of sporting excellence ahead of us folks, and I know you're all just as excited as I am. On a personal note, this is my eighteenth tournament, and what an honor it is to be here once again among what really are the elite athletes of our time. What wonders await? Which magical moment will you be taking away with you this time round? That's not important right now—just sit back, grab a Palpon Meatstick™ and a can of cold Palpale™ and enjoy. Palpale™ is the delicious and refreshing meat snack you can drink. Brian."

"Thanks Phil. I didn't even know flamingos could do that."

"I know."

"Seriously. I'm stunned. Speechless."

"It really was magnificent, as I said."

"And an apt launch for the Palpingo™, the new flamingo patty your kids will love, served in a crraaazy pink bun with a beak. Price point to be announced. And I'd just like to say, Phil, before we get into this year's stats, that it really has been an honor for me to be here at your side for five of those tournaments, learning from the master. Here's to many more."

"Thanks, Brian. An honor."

"A real honor, Phil."

"Thanks, Brian. Let's roll those stats."

"OK, but first let's take a look at the elephant in the room. The big news of course is the absence of 'Flip' Mc Side after an apparent breakdown. Rumors coming out of Mc Side's ranch are not at all encouraging, Phil, with unsubstantiated reports of uncontrolled blubbing and indiscriminate urination."

"The big baby."

"Right. 'Loser' Mc Side. Am I right, Phil?"

"You nailed it, Brian. 'Flip' Mc Loser. So that's going to mean some radical changes in the patty landscape?"

"Oh, you can forget everything you thought you knew about burger flipping, Phil. Word from what we're now calling the Maypole camp is we can expect something pretty special from there this year. Major new player."

"Course nobody's ever won on their first outing, Brian, and that's got to count against Maypole."

"Right. A largely unknown quantity, Maypole remains a rank outsider according to the bookmakers. Plenty of buzz around him but we've yet to see him flip a single patty. Gotta say though, there's a quiet confidence to Feuchtwanger that I haven't seen since he signed Mc Side."

"All of this would make local boy Chris Blancminster a favorite this year, wouldn't it?"

"One to keep an eye on, for sure, although I can't help observing that Blancminster isn't getting any younger. For my money, Phil, Mc Side's humiliating descent into mental illness, embarrassing for all of us, has blown this baby right open, as we'll see when we take a look at the stats."

"Right. And just before we do that, Brian, have we had any details from Feuchtwanger on what exactly it is that Maypole will be bringing to this year's table?"

"Matter of fact we have, Phil. At a press conference earlier today, Feuchtwanger, who normally plays his cards very close to his chest, as you know, shocked members of the media by announcing Maypole's intention to incorporate the infamous double helix overhand patty flex and dismount into his routine. It's a number of years since the double helix overhand patty flex and dismount has even been brought up and if Maypole could pull it off then it's difficult to see anyone beating him. Gotta say though, as you'll see from the stats—"

"Sorry to interrupt, Brian. Did you say the double helix *overhand* patty flex and dismount?"

"Yes, Phil, I did. As you'll know folks, we've seen the double helix patty flex and dismount performed on a number of occasions in recent years, but always underhand. Overhand we haven't seen. The maneuver was originally made famous by the legendary Art Merrill back in '49, when—"

"It was '47, if you'll pardon me for correcting you there, Brian."

"That's right—of course it was. '47, excuse me folks."

"And he died."

"He did indeed, Phil. He did indeed. A famous night."

"As a matter of fact, nobody's ever survived the double helix overhand patty flex and dismount, have they?"

"I don't believe so, no, Phil, so this evening promises to be a real doozer, one way or the other, and statistically—"

"You might almost conclude that the double helix overhand patty flex and dismount was impossible, Brian."

"Ha ha! OK, folks—sit back and strap in. In just over ninety minutes we'll have a new champion. Sounds so simple, doesn't it? Just the small matter of a tournament lies between us and that delicious upswelling of adulation in our breasts that we so dementedly crave. But who will rise from the victor's pit? Who will ascend to the top of the hydraulic winner's podium and look down on us with disdain as we weep? Nobody knows. Yet. But who will it be?"

"Roll the stats, Brian."

"Sure thing, Phil. Gotta say, I'm psyched about this one! There's a certain frisson this evening, don't you think? I'm reminded—"

"Stats, Brian."

❈

Extreme wide shot. Final round, latter stages.

The crowd, a heaving basin, sparkles here and there with the flash of a camera. In the middle, lit from above by a huge rig, the pit like a plug hole, sucking in the swirling energy. Blancminster and Maypole in there. Bernard taking a real pounding.

Pitside. Tracking shot.

A graceful twin slice and pickle-flick, even now, from the exhausted Blancminster. General sense in the arena that this is his moment. The form of his life!

Bernard drops his burger—another humiliation for the newcomer who nevertheless impresses with staying power, and spirit.

Close-up. Handheld.

He doesn't look good. There have been a number of mishaps with the spatula. Both eyes are badly bruised and closing up. He can barely see!

Back to mid wide.

Blancminster rouses the crowd with a textbook syncopated triple toss, side on.

Bernard smacks himself in the face again. Staggers. Noranbole, at his corner, covers her eyes.

Still he battles on! A respectable if uninspired patty-spin and pirouette.

The bell.

Handheld. Maypole corner.

Bernard with Feuchtwanger and Pressborg, the trainer. Noranbole behind them, tearful. They confer, voices picked up by the mike.

"Non possum videre quicquam," says Bernard. "Succidit me."

Pressborg hesitates. Wants to throw the towel in. Noranbole translating.

"Do it," says Feuchwanger. "Cut him."

Streams of blood. Vision a little improved in his left eye, he stands and waits for the bell.

It rings. He turns to Feuchtwanger.

"Si vos subsisto is," his voice is cool and lucid, "Ego mos iuguolo vos."

Final round.

"What?" says Feuchtwanger. Noranbole translating.

"Oh."

Bird's eye from the rig.

Blancminster doesn't look like he has another figure-of-eight half-spiral relish flop left in him, but you'd have to fancy him at this stage to see the young upstart off with a couple of back hand table-top bounce-and-buns, or perhaps a three-sixty overhead roll and serve.

Bernard smacks himself in the face. He's all over the place!

Pitside. Dolly shot.

Doesn't seem aware of Blancminster anymore. Looks around the periphery of the pit frantically, searching for something. Someone.

He may be delirious!

Surely we all just want his opponent to finish him off quickly now? Put an end to this!

Noranbole's hands to her face.

Now Blancminster falters!

Loses his patty!

A trivial failing so close to the final bell, surely? As he doubles over, fingering the floor for the disc of slippy meat, however, young Maypole sees his chance.

Straightens.

Takes a breath. A slow, deep breath.

And launches himself!

Pitside, far end. Static.

A beautifully executed helicoidal lunge!

A second twist to complete the double, his patty pert, flexed and poised as he executes a perfect half rotation.

Absolute silence in the arena as he achieves full extension, and . . . the fabled overhand release!

But wait.

Will he stumble on the dismount?

No!

Another half-second of hush.

Cut away. Crowd shot from Pit level.

The roar. Thunderous and sustained as they realize what has happened. In front of their very eyes!

Blancminster sullen. Great reversal-of-fortune feeling about the whole thing. Somewhere in the tumult the bell rings.

Mid wide.

Pit invasion. Big band music—real or imagined, it doesn't really matter. Reporters descend on both competitors. Bernard surrounded.

"Boley!"

Close-up, hand held.

Microphones to his mouth.

"You did it, Bernard! You pulled it off!"

"Boley!!"

"Mr Maypole, how does it feel to—"

But Bernard is looking past them, desperately scanning the edge of the pit.

"Boley!!!"

Noranbole can't get to him. Blocked by the throng as the decision is announced, lost in the noise, blinded by flashbulbs.

Extreme wide.

The assembled masses commence fawning, their champion now illuminated in the PalCone™ of Sanctifying Victory Light.

Many swoon while others moan, and sway.

Crowdcam. Miked.

"Look at those knees!" cries Nicola Basset of Farley Wallop, Berkshire, from one of the expensive seats as Bernard is hoiked by attendants to the top of the platform.

"Boley!!!!"

"If I could just loiter behind him in the bathroom as he shaved and glorify myself in the reflection of those Byzantine features," cries Imelda Chinchón of Calle Tucumán 222, Viedma, Argentina, "I wouldn't be any trouble."

"Yes!" cries Fiona Batemen of The Hollows, Carmel 93923, "Oh, how that would elevate you!"

Placed on the upper dais, the champion is crowned with a garland of glittering pork and swathed in the Palpon Cape of Glory™. At last he spots Noranbole, below.

"Boley!!!!!"

"That is not the leg hair," shrieks Betty Wendell of Hamilton Hill (just off the 14), Perth, Australia, "of an ordinary man! See how it undulates!"

She falls to her knees and wraps her arms around herself lest the love in her bosom burst her own ribs.

"I could surf those silken waves of bliss! I could fall in and sleep the deepest, saving sleep."

In the pit, handheld.

Noranbole at the base of the platform. She clambers up towards Bernard, eyes filling, hand stretched up and out, Bernard leaning out and down to grasp it.

"Boley!!!!!!"

Crowdcam.

"The nerve of him, to sport a codpiece of that particular kind!" yelps Anita Hodgeson of 5575 Fonseca Drive, Brampton, Ontario.

"I may be a bubba," cries Maureen O'Halloran of 34, The Meadows, Clonakilty, "and blind in one eye, but the thought of spieling with its contents is making my back schvitz."

Finally he holds her in his arms.

"Boley!!!!!!!"

Champcam. The couple framed in the PalCone™. Camera flashes in the darkness around it.

A microphone is lowered and Bernard takes it, facing the amorphous mob and opening his heart to them on the only subject he has ever cared for.

"Tenei wahine ko tetahi anahera!"

Bit of a lull.

Noranbole takes the microphone.

"He says I'm an angel!"

She blushes.

A cheer! Bernard leans in again.

"Таа е само една Сакам!"

Nothing.

"He says I'm the only one for him!"

A hurrah!

"Би түүний төлөө үүнийг хийсний!"

Zip.

"He says it's all been for me!"

A standing ovation!

Throughout, her eyes never leave his as they cling to each other in the shaft of light.

Crowdcam.

"Monotony!" screams Phillipa Duncan of Stone House, Fort Augustus, Scotland. "There's a certain escalation in tone each time but the message is essentially the same!"

"What a *bitch!*" cries Jacintha Lexington (long-standing member of the Terra Forma Ladies' Association and a pivotal figure on the Water Retention Committee) from the twisted mouth of her sodden face.

※

Bernard on the cover of Totally Everything magazine, Noranbole at his side. Embarrassingly sycophantic editorials in the Daily Existence. Voted World's Hottest Couple in Celebrity Despair Weekly. Front page of Global Planet, Noranbole at his side. Keys to the cities of London, Rome and Berlin. Quite the weekend.

Tuesday—the day of the extraordinary meeting—dawned.

The board assembled high above a sun-speckled Big City. Vacuity had the castle hidden under a sheet at the head of the table, ready for the big reveal. The mood was anxious and somewhat distracted. Something in the air. Noranbole was late and Vacuity beamed at anyone who looked her way, head tilted.

"An item to add to the agenda, Ms Blanc," said Mr Elderkin, "before we get to Ms Wakeling's proposals. Of the utmost importance. Total disaster."

"Utterly catastrophic," said Mr Star Blanket.

"Yes, thank you, Mr Star Blanket. I think it's probably quite important to maintain some sense of equilibrium," said Mr Perigo, "or we'll never get through this."

"For surely, Mr Elderkin," said Vacuity, opening her pad, "If you might just facilitate my ascertaining as to of what said item might be comprised?"

"Pardo—"

"Ah!" Vacuity closed the pad again and took her seat. "Here she is."

Noranbole's tiara was giving her a little trouble in the doorway so she backed up and came in sideways, keeping her head very still as she walked the length of the conference table and lowered herself into her seat as smoothly as she could, to minimize the tinkling.

"I'm sorry I'm late, gentlemen," she said. "I've just flown in from Paris, where I had to attend a glamorous and spectacular gala event for Mr Maypole, who was decorated with the Médaille de Tout—France's highest civilian honor, as you know."

She wasn't getting any eye contact. Trying not to move her head, she looked at Vacuity.

"Too much? Bernard got it for me."

"Oh no!" beamed Vacuity. "It's lovely."

"I better kick things off, Ms Wakeling," said Mr Elderkin. "We're in a hell of a pickle."

"Oh dear!" said Noranbole. "What sort of pickle?"

"We don't know," said Mr Deer Spirit.

"We're looking into it," said Mr Drinkwater.

"OK. But I should be worried?"

"Probably, yes," said Mr Amerideath. "As Mr Drinkwater rightly says, it's very early days but it could be . . ."

He removed his glasses to give them a wipe.

"That is to say, there's an outside chance . . ."

Mr Elderkin leaned forward.

"Ms Wakeling, I'm afraid it looks like there might be a possibility that we could be seeing the beginnings of a—"

With a shaking hand, he took a drink of water and put the glass down again.

"—crisis."

The word dropped from his mouth like a pebble, sending a ripple of astonishment around the room.

"Another crisis?" asked Noranbole.

"A *third* crisis?" asked Mr Poor.

"Fucking hell," said Mr Freeze.

"Not necessarily."

It was the first they had heard from Mr Rising, who seemed remarkably composed.

"If one of the current crises were to be resolved then we'd still be look-ing at a total of two. We might even contemplate the eventuality that both current crises are sorted out before this third one really gets going, in which case it'll be a considerable improvement."

"Right, but that's not the likely scenario, is it?" asked Mr Elderkin.

"No."

Mr Poor was fidgeting

"So it's definitely a crisis?"

"As I said, we're not sure at this point. You know Geoff?"

"Can't immediately—"

"In Analytics."

"Oh, Geoff. Yes."

"Well we asked him and he doesn't know either."

"Hm."

"I suppose it might be a little self-serving of me to mention, gentlemen," said Noranbole, "that we'd have seen this coming if we'd implemented my proposed divination ritual."

Mutterings.

Mr Elderkin turned to her.

"If I might be allowed to pace, Ms Wakeling?"

"Certainly."

He got up and began to pace.

"There's no point kidding ourselves," he said, looking out over the city. "We're sailing uncharted waters here; there simply isn't a protocol in place for a third crisis. We were having quite a difficult time of it with just the two, if I'm being honest."

Murmurs of agreement.

"Completely unprepared," he continued. "However, this isn't exactly amateur hour here. This is Terra Forma. We're awesome, and have been for a very long time. I propose we immediately set about recalibrating our quarterly . . . what is *that?*"

He was looking out of the window. Vacuity went to see.

At the other end of Big City Avenue, a disturbance of some kind—police lights and traffic parting. It was difficult to make out exactly what was happening from here but as the others joined them at the window the thing began moving slowly down the avenue towards the Terra Forma building.

The police vehicles were in escort formation and the thing was between them, veering dangerously in either direction as it approached. It didn't look like a truck or a car—the motions were more complex and discrete. Pistons maybe, or legs, like a giant spider crawling through the city. It was getting closer, becoming more resolved.

"Legs," said Mr Deer Spirit.

They were pulling something along at a wild rate. Wheels could be seen now, behind. Whatever it was, it included a person, straddling the wheeled part and reining in the legs with a rope clenched in both gloved hands.

White gloves.

"Are those horses?" asked Mr Perigo.

Yes. The police were keeping a cautious distance as four savage-looking steeds bolted through the panicking traffic, the cart behind them bouncing and tilting as they glistened with angry sweat, steam trumpeting from flared nostrils, teeth bared, eyes maniacal, rolling back in their sockets.

The board members had their foreheads to the glass now, peering down their noses as the scene came to a halt at the portico, far below them. The figure leaped from the cart and raced up the steps into the building.

"Was that a bonnet?" asked Mr Freeze.

"What do you thi—" asked Mr Elderkin, turning to Noranbole, but she had gone to her desk and was speaking into the intercom.

"Lucy, could you get Mr Maypole on the line please? And ask him to meet me here? Thanks so much."

She looked up at the board members.

"You're going to want to call an extraordinary meeting, gentlemen. I have to be off now."

She picked up her lunchbox and her Book of Proposals and went to the door.

"*Another* extraordinary meeting?" asked Mr Amerideath.

"I thought we were at one of those," said Mr Poor to Mr Rising.

Mr Elderkin was incredulous.

"You're leaving, Ms Wakeling? But your proposals! The crises!"

Noranbole turned in the doorway. The tiara had slipped a little. It teetered.

"Yes, I'm afraid so," she said, her hand on the handle. "I have chores."

Behind her, the ping of the lift as it reached the top floor, and before the door had slid fully open a voice emerging from it that made them all tremble.

"Noranbole!"

Part Three

Emma Wakeling

Emma Jope

Y EIGHTH HUSBAND was a rickety man by the name of Sampson Jope. At this stage my father had given up any pretense of vetting my suitors—in fact he rarely emerged from behind the closed door of his study to speak to me and never came to the table anymore. The decision therefore was entirely mine. I had been masturbating Mr Jope in the little room at the back of his ice cream parlor on Sycamore Street for many months and besides, he was good enough to waive any expectations he might have had in the way of a dowry; it was enough for him to take up residence in my father's house and spend his afternoons gloating over the collection of sickles I kept out back, running his bony fingers up and down the curved blades lasciviously, spittle running from the corners of his paper-cut lips.

We honeymooned out by Salt Bog in the little shack that Mr Tuttle had used for gutting deer when I was a young girl and my father would send me to help with the entrails. Though Tuttle was long dead, his hut had become a den for lovers' assignations and it was with some considerable satisfaction that we took it over for the week, knowing full well we were putting paid to the nefarious contrivances of any number of local casanovas.

The genital reek that hung over everything—the bench and broken sideboard, the chipped water basin, the dirty lantern and the damp bed—was hardly inappropriate and not at all unpleasant. In fact it seemed to excite Mr Jope, insofar as such a word can be applied to so old a man. He would rock back and forth as I washed his little fellow and grin at me through that hard stare of his. I couldn't very well begrudge him his pleasure; it isn't every girl who has sea lions at her wedding and I had two. Mr Thripp, master of ceremonies, kindly had them perform some very clever tricks for us before he broiled them.

It was a lavish affair—a wedding reception provided the perfect opportunity for Mr Jope to express his contempt for his neighbors by intimidating them with expense. As well as the sea lion there was horse meat and we were served boiled eggs to start which—much to the children's delight—contained delicious, crunchy little half-formed chicks. Dessert was an iced fruit and mutton cake which, even if slightly over-cheesed, was widely enjoyed.

The whole party in fact—the grand marquee, the fine pewter, the parlor games and botanical lectures, the bowls of candy, the ornate tableau that

Ms Standlack had fashioned from moss and stuffed crows, the unspeakable revelations concerning Mark Fleming, the dwarf stripper—was to be the talk of the county for many months.

Neither Mr Jope nor I paid much mind. On concluding the frivolity that had been our wedding we quietly retired to my father's house in order that we might embark upon the very serious matter of a marriage.

We were content, at first. He would address himself to his sundry concerns and I would apply myself to mine, the days passing peaceably. We would meet in the evenings to dine on something simple—an unseasoned chop or perhaps an austere stew of beans and water. I would have Noranbole serve Urine her meal in a separate room, as afterwards I would invariably administer a masturbation while Mr Jope, wobbly-voiced, read from the book of Leviticus. Our cohabitation facilitated a daily attempt and perhaps it was that—along with his creeping antiquity—that finally did for Mr Jope. Just a few months in he began to exhibit the symptoms of a strange and debilitating palsy.

One early morning in March neither I nor Noranbole could straighten him, even with our knees in the small of his back and a good strong rope around his shoulders. For fear of snapping the man we desisted and over the next few days the contortion increased. He would shuffle around bent over, requiring one of us to support him—at first by taking his hand and later, as expedience dictated, by the scruff of his shirt collar.

By Easter the process was complete—my husband was bed-ridden, having curled up into the shape of a perfect 'o', turned a jaundiced yellow and begun secreting something waxy from his skin that smelled of paraffin. A stoic, he never once complained and nor did I; an abandoned tractor tire in the outhouse became a mobility aid—we would roll him out to the tool shed to see the sickles each morning, rolling him back to the kitchen for some almond milk and a wipe down in the afternoon. On the day we first noticed he was dead we couldn't be sure how long we'd been rolling him around in that condition, since he'd neither spoken nor taken refreshment in some time.

Mr Smalledge, the parson—credit to him—rolled his sleeves up and helped us bury Mr Jope, who we were unable to retrieve from the tire, in a perfectly round grave in the front garden. Though poorly attended, the interment was jovial enough—I had Noranbole take round a platter of quails and Molly Stodder gave us a tune on her Arab lute.

My husband's executor, a Mr Pond, came that evening to go over the necessary business. Red-faced and unaccountably jocular, he could barely get himself through the particulars, having to break off on numerous occasions to suppress another fit of the giggles. I gave him sherry, to no avail.

He finally managed to communicate that I had inherited Mr Jope's old house and of course the ice cream parlor. The house I instructed him to sell; I would use the money to augment my collection of bagging hooks and, if there was enough left over, purchase a new pig scalder.

As to the parlor I admit to being at a loss. I am a lady, and have no experience of running a business but I am considering, and I have not the slightest doubt that Mr Jope would spin in that grave of his if he could hear me say so, a stab at frozen yogurt.

The M39

THE NORTH-BOUND FLOW, where a slip road drops the driver down onto the M39 turnpike from an aortic cluster of junctions, is four lanes wide—the fast lane, the middle, the slow and an outer lane for horse and carriage, along which Emma would have thundered with her errant cargo, almost a year ago now, passing the airport almost immediately on the left, passenger and freight aircraft sloping in on a perpendicular, very loud and low overhead.

The tram terminus.

The Palpon™ stadium.

After that, the business developments: Brobdingnag Semiconductors, Illustrated Graphics, Mallard-Hewson and so on.

Then another drop onto a great plain peppered with ugly installations: the chimneys of United Alchemies, the Assembly Construction Building like a shard of broken glass driven into the ground, the sprawling mess of Forge & Foundry Manufacturing Industries and the tinted-window, low-lying mystery of the Blitz Defense and Apologetics Corporation.

As the Wakeling carriage descended the trio would have been able to see Middleton on the horizon, though it would have been hours before they reached the sleepy satellite town and left it behind—no rest for the horses, no let up for the mournful lovers as Emma rode through the nothing that followed, out across the plain as light faded.

The rush of distance measured here in exit signs offering access to places that are for most people what they would have been for Emma and the sorrowful pair—notches on a mile count.

Holbourn, Raymonde, Freemount and Riverbed, Edding, Kingtown, Timbroke and Hooksy and then pretty much nothing for a hundred miles till the M39 merges with the Ampleton Ring and the old towers of the university can be glimpsed from the road on their mossy, manicured campus.

At the far side of the orbital they would have passed the exit for the continuing M39 and ridden on for five more miles before taking the Ampleton West slip road, joining the traffic that moves through an outlying industrial zone and eventually the M27, westbound.

Through the night, the monotonous tree-lined miles, foliage a murky brown in the orange glow from the median strip, dropping from tall t's and covering everything below them in a veil of piss light. Belmount, Accord, Ironia and Quieton slip by in their sleep, the whisper of their passing a lullaby to tired hands taking turns at the reins.

Big Lake on the right, Little Lake on the left as the road bends into the Northern Basin and the broken tooth outline of the snowy Sierra corrupt the horizon. The mountains rise while the road meanders lightly, linking up a twisting line of little outposts known for game and fishing—Pig Island, The Harbor, Cunningham's Bight—then straightening out for the gentle ascent onto the lower plateau.

Another day to reach the Sierra, The Gap and the steep climb to the top along the R2203. The end of the road for the motorist, the tarmac terminates here at the source of Rangan's River and the track that makes the long and gentle descent through Rangan's Gorge is unpaved, starting out near river level and, as the white waters drop off and the gorge deepens, seeming almost to rise as it imperceptibly dips. Before long the rider is a good half-mile above the river, carriage wheels pinging pebbles from the edge of the path.

At the bottom, some wooden buildings and then a wide main street. A saloon, a barber's shop and a little bank.

Fishing tackle and hunting gear in the store. An old mule tied up outside with a heavy load of string on its bowed back. Girls in gingham and boys in pants they're all too tall for. An internet café, an eating house and a chapel and at the end of it all, as there was at the beginning, a little wooden, hand-carved sign for the benefit of the rare visitor who makes it this far.

Welcome to Small Town.

※

Up to Fearing Copse and the magistrate's house, and out past the Shit Heap to Mallows Gulch where the bridle path splits and Tiny Village is signposted on the trunk of an old sycamore. The way there is a shaded track through bramble at first, then opens out onto fields on one side, overhung by oaks and horse-chestnuts on the other. Here and there the brown outhouses of farmsteads are visible, pines on the higher slopes behind them.

Everything except for the occasional stretch of fencing is old and encrusted; most of it has been around long enough to earn itself a name. Even the fields here have names—Pike's Field and Topley's Corner, Keene's Patch and Doughty's Garden, Doggett's Bank, Puffer's Meadow and Chickering's Plot. Even the older trees have names.

All of it named and pinned down, given root, gathering moss. Everything heaves with its own history, the land and the people like an old couple who no longer need speak to each other because all has been said; to give voice to it would only add a tinny echo. The road forms itself into divots that cup wagon wheels silently. Old walls and ditches part to make shortcuts for children. Cowbells give cadence to the odd tiny church. Breezes blow to justify the swaying of the trees. Rivers keep the fish wet.

Out onto the marshy flats where the flies swarm, sprinkled with a hundred ponds. Emma would have struggled here to keep the horses calm and the wheels on the wooden causeway for the long haul—no question of setting down for a rest in the flurry of biting insects.

Through the small hours, scarves pulled over faces, the sodden black silence as unsettling as the flies, broken by the cries of invisible creatures in the waters of Salt Bog. The day breaking. The horses jittering. Shoulders cold under damp shawls. Towards Spoon Ridge, up out of the mire and then back down into it as the sun found its strength, across the gentler landscape of Sugar Bog—reed grasses and islets, water birds and willows, sweetgums, sycamores and swamp oaks.

When finally the land lifts itself out of the morass, there are signs of human settlement: paltry hamlets that the inhabitants refer to by the name of whoever happened to build there first—Healde and Twelves, Adams, Blunt and Silvester and at last, where a low range of hills rolls in from the south, Tiny Village and in the distance to the west, the low peak of Swan Hill rising over the lake. To the east, pine trees crowd around a snaking river. In one of its bends, the Bennett house in a clearing and further along, the Maypole place. Further still, the forest path forks—one prong for the Flemings and the other twisting away from the river and up where Bernard would have tethered the horses they are tethered now, at a post outside the low iron gate.

The tool shed and the lean-to and the old wooden house, none of them visible through the dense woods except for the pointed tower that seems to peep over the tops of the trees with its one eye—the little round window that gives into Emma's attic.

Emma Naranja

MY SEVENTH HUSBAND was Paco Naranja, internationally celebrated butcher and marmalade artist from Sitiomalo—the seediest, grimiest, most cockroach-infested slum in Seville. A proud man, he had started out selling roadkill from a wheelbarrow he would push from bar to bar, just a scrawny lad amid the uproarious, work-shy drinkers, deafened by their mockery and even dodging fists in the rowdier salons.

It was the only time he would ever bump into his father. An amiable enough man, Álvaro Naranja refused point blank to acknowledge the fact that he had reproduced. Nobody could ever tell, as he'd look at his runt of a son through glazed and baffled eyes, whether or not it was a put on.

"I'm pretty sure I'd remember something like that," he would say, and then he would return to his gin.

When little barefoot Paco got home in the evenings—and once he'd swept the roaches and fly carcasses aside so that he might cower in the corner awhile and perhaps, if circumstances permitted, close his tired eyes for a minute or two—his mother, a less than amiable woman, would beat him to a pulp with a stale stick of bread she kept for the purpose.

The hard-working boy quickly picked up a favorable reputation in the barrios, always making good on the promise he'd scrawled on the side of his barrow—nothing sold more than a week after discovery—but his already solid little enterprise really took off when he cottoned on to marinating the less appealing meats, which he did with rind from the oranges that grew in the streets.

From a small premises in Triana which he secured on turning twenty-one, he grew his business, phasing 'found' meat out entirely over a couple of years, after which time he could afford to procure the choicest cuts of beef, fox and barbary meat from Gibraltar. With such fine wares to trade in he had no further use for his orange marinade but, reluctant to squander his hard won skills, he turned them to marmalade and an application of it that was to make him the most famous man in all of Spain.

A millionaire by the time he turned thirty, he had already cut a dashing figure on the covers of Tonteria!, Vague and Parochiale.

"Dalí never tasted this good!" proclaimed Madrid's El Periodico on the occasion of Naranja's debut exhibition. "A mesmerising, burnished gold, tangy and somewhat sticky tour-de-force!"

"Picasso's all very well," sneered London's Daily Evening, "but he isn't much use on a slice of toast."

"I will never abandon butchery!" said Naranja himself when interviewed publicly for the first time, and his declaration of blue collar humility endeared him to millions.

But fame was to turn to infamy. In conservative Spain, Naranja overstepped the mark when, the following year, he smeared a group of girls and boys in marmalade and flung them at a blank canvas for the gathered media in the Plaza Mayor. The sexual inappropriateness of the act would probably have been enough to sour his reputation but the injuries sustained by the children turned the public mood downright ugly and before he knew it, Naranja was on a plane and headed for the anonymity of a butcher's life in Big City.

It wasn't granted him. Paparazzi and mobs of fawning groupies made a mockery of his attempts to sell so much as a pork chop from his—admittedly ill-advised—glittering Big City Avenue premises and soon enough he had removed himself to a mountain retreat, a reclusive (and exclusive) vendor of charcuterie and fresh victuals to the stars and starlets of the day. They would arrive by arrangement in helicopters, touching down inside the protective walls of the heavily guarded complex where he lived alone, save for his mother, and unloved, save for no one.

I was astonished to bump into him that day in the general store on one of my rare visits to Small Town, recognizing him immediately from the likenesses I had seen so regularly in the gossip columns. He further surprised me by instantly falling to his knees and paying homage in the most colorful language to my "eternal and devastating beauty". I invited him to tea and, evidently pleased with the masturbatory welcome I offered, he proposed to me soon afterwards. Father was thrilled.

"You're marrying up," he crowed contentedly, "for once."

The wedding dispensed with, Mr Naranja was pleased to abandon his lonely villa in the mountains and move into my father's house, hanging his gold-plated wheelbarrow over the mantle and installing his mother in the spare room, whereupon he promptly forgot all about her. Every few days, I would take her a bowl of mustard soup and I found her a most compatible woman, often loosening the restraints a little as we sat together and spoke of our disappointments.

"Won't you befriend her?" I would press my increasingly withdrawn father. "You never talk to anyone these days."

But the pastor persisted in his silence and kept to himself. Raising the possibility of our parents providing companionship for one another with Paco was no better—he would stare at me as though I were daft.

My new husband continued to vend to the great and the good who completely destroyed my rhododendrons with their helicopters. He'd have their meat waiting for them in the drawer of the telephone table in the hallway, wrapped in newspaper, but of course it was a pretense—they'd always come in and stop awhile and I must say it was the gayest time. We had Flex Rigby sing for us in the parlor. Mimi Tourette wouldn't have dreamed of going anywhere else for her monkey offal.

Sporting icons like Guy Alabaster and Malcolm Bunt, the actor Morley Crawley who took rather a shine to Urine. Of course she was far too young to appreciate the pedigree of the knees that dandled her but Noranbole's head was turned a little and I had a time of it keeping her to the larder so that she could be prompt in bringing us all our sandwiches. Where we found the time to eat I'll never know, with the constant hum of chat so resonant it made the crockery tinkle in its cabinet. I remember a discussion with Sven Litting himself on the chaise longue outside the dining room, but I never had quite grasped the subtleties of post-structural hermeneutics and I couldn't wait to get away from the weasely little man.

Responding to the doorbell one afternoon I was presented with the following sight: a slender young woman with jet black eyes and hair to match, tied back tightly into a bun every bit as shiny as my own, a single lock of it allowed to fall over the flawless skin of her forehead in an artful little curl. Her dress was tight and ankle-length—a bright red sheath that revealed her femininities, it was covered with white polka dots and frilled at the sleeves and neck. She had both arms raised high above her head, palms out, the fingers of her left in serpentine motion, those of her right clutching an ornate fan of fine lace.

"Hola!"

She lowered one hand to hold the fan below her eyes and with the other still raised she spun clockwise till she was looking at me once again. Then anticlockwise. Then clockwise again, her feet in a constant rhythmic shuffle till she startled me with an almighty stomp on the decking, both hands up.

"I am Lola!"

There was a little red bag hung on her shoulder and she opened it now, retrieving a cigarette and a book of matches and replacing them once she'd lit up and blown a trumpet of smoke a little too close to my face for my liking.

"Enough of this. Where is Paco?"

By the time I could summon the presence of mind to tell her, she had brushed past me. I closed the door hastily and followed her into the parlor, where Mr Naranja had raised himself from his favorite armchair and was buttoning his fly.

"Lola!"

"Paco, this person wishes to—"

"You remember me," said the intruder, tapping her cigarette over my aspidistra. "At least that."

"Remember you, guapita? Not for a single moment did—"

"And the night of Tio Pepe's wake?" she said. "We slipped outside. The moon itself bowed down before our love. The very cicadas sang of it."

She had stepped towards him but turned away coquettishly, cigarette hanging from her parted lips. Paco spoke quietly into the nape of her neck.

"You wore jasmine in your hair."

"We danced the fandango."

"Am I to boil the kettle?" I asked.

"I wonder my dear," said Paco, addressing himself to the interloper, "if I might have the briefest of words with you on the veranda?"

I never saw him again. He sent instructions a few weeks later to forward the wheelbarrow to his mountaintop abode. I was only too happy to comply and sent his mother in it, though she hadn't been mentioned in the note.

The Attic

OBODY HERE. Nobody ever comes up here these days. There is only a dance of dust in the single shaft of light, bright and bobbling, that reaches the middle of the floor on a low diagonal. It catches the corner of a pile of old papers before touching down on the boards in an ellipse that reaches towards an old bicycle, propped against the back wall. Black and bulky, no more give in the slender wheels, no comfort in the hard saddle, but then it never had been comfortable; it would creak and complain under the weight of Charles Wakeling each Sunday—a long, thin stick of a man—as he peddled over unlikely cycling terrain to Tiny Village for scripture meetings.

It would creak and complain under his weight as he cycled on, protesting each protruding stone and muddy dip, quietening down awhile when left leaning beneath the window of Sarah Twelves' pantry where the pastor would pass each Sunday afternoon praying for her redemption. He was not well known in the county, being a private individual and having arrived from other parts in his midlife, but as a churchman he was shown respect. The house up above the Fleming place had barely emptied itself of the previous pastor's wake attendees when he took it and installed a housekeeper by the name of Phinoola Quigg. Nobody knew her either.

For a single man he was getting on a bit, and busy besides with the rehabilitation of the county's wayward women; apart from his Sunday afternoons in the Twelves house he was diligently at it Friday evenings and mornings Monday through Wednesday. Nevertheless, the scattered community was uncomfortable with the notion of an unmarried preacher and began to line their daughters up. The resulting courtships were variable in character. Some of the women only just qualified as daughters—tireless nursing responsible for the continued, if negligible, presence of a parent— and Emily Jenks was to scandalize them all by continually exposing him to the flash of her petticoat at the annual courgette race.

Still, a match was inevitable and come the month of May in the year after his arrival, the pastor found himself spending more and more time (Thursdays) with young Rose Flimsy. It was a potential union that the locals looked upon with great favor, particularly as Miss Flimsy—a retiring slip of a girl who could barely bring herself to whisper a breathless Good Morning to her own parents—had such poor prospects for finding a husband. Charles was heard to mutter approvingly of her following their sittings on the low bench outside the Flimsy cottage and in conference over bridal terms with her father described her as 'unobtrusive'.

A dowry agreed upon and the wedding costs accepted by Mr Flimsy, arrangements were made for a simple and somber ceremony in the little chapel up by Sergeant's Knoll and the pastor himself undertook to oversee the preparation of the flagellating implements. Come the day, however, Miss Flimsy was so overcome with nerves that she was completely unable to place herself within the sight of her groom, let alone the little wedding party that consisted of her parents and sisters, Agatha Pinch—her old school mistress—and Phinoola Quigg.

A hinged room divider was hastily retrieved from Ms Pinch's boudoir and the ceremony went ahead behind the protective panels of Chinese silk and their scenes of stork and peacock, spring blossom and love tryst that separated the bride from the onlookers, and a lowered veil—bolstered with a face cloth—that separated her from the pastor. On neither side of the room divider could the girl's voice be heard and, at the insistence of the visiting priest, her consent to the union was confirmed in a hand-written note that emerged in a trembling white hand from the folds of her dress.

Up in the Wakeling house young Rose got the life she'd always wanted, which is to say no one paid her a blind bit of attention outside the weekly flagellating which she found rather unpleasant but surprisingly easy to put up with. She was very rarely seen again in fact, quickly making an art form of her own disappearance into a new house and marriage. If the pastor and whatever company were in the parlor then she was in the kitchen, preparing. If he was in the kitchen then she was in the yard, fetching, and if he was in the yard then she was in the study, dusting. Preparing what, fetching what and dusting what, nobody could say, since it was well known that Phinoola Quigg did everything that needed doing around the place.

It would creak and complain even under little Emma's weight when years later her short legs would struggle with the pedals on her way to old Ms Twelves' house, now half-blind and dementing nicely, not so much a fallen woman as a broken one and given to screaming libelous obscenities concerning the pastor, which he as a man of the cloth was obliged to endure. He sent Emma there in his stead in those days; he might have given up on the aging woman's salvation but the dressings still needed changing weekly.

"Father," began the girl one day at supper (soup had been served and Phinoola Quigg had taken her seat so conversation, as long as it was brief and to the point, was permitted), "what's a Perry Knee-um?"

Rose, as usual, was nowhere to be seen.

The pastor placed his spoon on the rim of his bowl.

"I am absolutely certain that I have no idea whatsoever, Emma."

His eyes were on the ceiling.

"Why do you ask?"

"Oh!" said Emma, evidently surprised. "It's just that Ms Twelves told me that you had the most curious one in the county and I thought I might like to see it."

She returned to her soup, taking care to scoop away from herself and not to slurp.

"More lies!" screamed the pastor at Phinoola Quigg, who stood, brought her empty bowl back to the side cabinet and turned away, taking a knife to the boiled piglet she had placed there. His eyes bore into her back.

"Will I never be rid of the woman?" he pleaded with it. "Or Martha Dewey, for that matter, and *her* inexplicable delusions?"

"Isn't it the price of God's work?" said Phinoola Quigg, ripping a cheek from the bone for the pastor. Having put it in front of him, and a couple of trotters for the girl to gnaw on, she left.

"A heavy price," said the pastor, "but I am a servant of the Lord. I'm only sorry that you have to listen to these diabolical fantasies, Emma."

He took up his spoon again to stir his coldening soup.

"Particularly the details."

Little Emma knew well enough not to respond while she was sucking on a trotter. She let her eyes wander over the flock wallpaper and its Egyptian motif, the cracked old photograph in the silver frame of her father's grandfather—of whom he would not speak—in military uniform, the young, smooth-shaven face streaked with tears. Below it on the sideboard, a green glass oil lamp that she hadn't noticed before and that now sits on the floor beside the bicycle's back wheel, up in the attic.

It has spent most of its days here, just inside the door and pale grey with dust—all of them in fact since the time of the previous pastor, except for those few weeks that it passed in the dining room where Rose had put it and where Phinoola Quigg would glare at it every mealtime till her patience gave out and she stowed it away again. In Rose's single act of defiance, it would reappear downstairs for a spell, years later, only to be once again disposed of by the housekeeper.

The copper ring between the lower bulb of green glass and the obsidian base is loosened and greening but the collar that cups the upper chimney— also green and tulip curled—holds tight. The inner circle of the brass burner, ornate and in the Queen Beatrix style, is protected by the glass and still sparkles around its blackened old wick.

It had first come to Rose's attention via that lower bubble of glass, blown in the shape of a pineapple and studded to replicate the skin sections—at the center of each a little five-pointed star, some of which were quite sharp and had caused her scalp to bleed a little as it rubbed against them.

Charles had come in from the outhouse and passed brusquely by her in the parlor, bidding her follow, his voice thick and his back bent as she climbed the stairs behind him. He was walking strangely, this barely a month since the wedding. She thought she might have made the bed improperly or left wet soap in the dish but her husband surprised her by going on up to a little attic in the tower that rose from a gable at the back of the house.

He stood by the dirty window and asked her to close the door behind her and to remain quiet. She did as she was told and remained by the door while the pastor closed his eyes and joined his hands in prayer. Rose couldn't hear what he was praying for but she could see his lips move. When he opened his eyes again he went to the pocket of his smock and retrieved a little plastic lemon with a tiny lid on top.

"Do you know what this is?"

She was desperate to get away and hide and cursed herself for sitting in the parlor at that time of day, where she should have expected to be seen. On the other hand she was relieved to recognize the object and thus to have an answer to Charles' gravely asked question.

"Lemon juice?"

"No."

He took a few steps forward, ducking his head beneath the crossbeams, and stood over her, at no time lowering the lemon. It took all of Rose's resolve not to flee. Her breathing was quick and shallow. Her husband's eyes drilled into her from above.

"I have filled it with holy water. Take it."

He put it in her trembling hand, closed his eyes and stepped back.

"You must wash me."

She hadn't seen him unbuttoning his fly but his trousers were all of a sudden gathered in a heap round his ankles. Against her will her eyes climbed the line of his hairless legs till they were affronted by the most horrible sight of her young life.

It seemed to look at her.

Charles was quick to pick up on her lack of enthusiasm and rolled his eyes.

"For heaven's sake, woman, I'm not asking you to touch it. Just aim the lemon and squeeze."

But Rose was already in a swoon. The plastic lemon fell to the floor and so did she, knocking her head against the green glass lamp.

"Blast it! I'll do it myself!" said the pastor, sinking to his knees and grabbing the lemon. Squeezing it, he aimed the fine jets of holy water at his member.

"It must be sanctified, Rose. You have been very acceptable, in a sinful sort of way, since our wedding day. I trust this evening will be no different."

Eager to be a good wife, Rose raised herself up on an elbow to take the lemon and complete the pastor's ablutions, but she was too late and he too keen; he had grabbed one of her ankles and had it high in the air, and was fighting his way through her undergarments. In a not especially short amount of time he had defeated them and fumbled the wet thing against her repeatedly till it went inside.

It hurt her and so did the glass lamp against her head, but she was pleased to be a wife in every sense of the word as the churchman on her grunted and strained. That is why she took the lamp downstairs the following day and put it on the sideboard—as a trophy of her accomplishment and submission. And that is why, in the bravest act of her life thus far, she took it down there again for a second time, so that the little girl with the piglet's foot in her mouth, the tiny little person who frightened her so, could see the green glass that had made her mother's head bleed at the moment of her conception.

Emma Butters

BY THE TIME I married Devyn Butters, my sixth husband, he had grown into a big, burly and very, very bad man. I can't think why anyone would have been surprised; he'd been a very, very bad boy from the beginning. And I don't know why I proposed to him; I think he'd been waiting for me to do it forever, which was as long as we'd known each other.

When I was nine or so (it was the year of the long summer and the fires that took the Goffe and Bartoll farmsteads and that only Sugar Bog, in the end, could stop) Tim Whipple found his mutt whimpering in the porch. Its jaw was broken and pulled wide open and there was a slimy trail of blood and innards on the lawn it had crawled over, that had come from the slit in its abdomen. It died there looking up at its master and it broke the old man; he wouldn't last another year.

They found Devyn a mile and a half away where a wooden walkway leads across a little stream to the cornfields. He was sitting in the road with a bloodied trowel in his hands. Crying, his mother said, though I've never in all my years, outside of sexual congress, seen him cry. He was eleven at the time and where he got the strength to snap a dog's jaw I'll never know. Nobody could conceive that a boy so young would have done such a thing unless he'd been scared senseless and so people were happy enough to accept the child's account—that Lemonade had attacked him.

It didn't seem likely to me; I'd watched the daft creature chase bees in Mr Whipple's back garden all summer, but then people round here don't concern themselves much with what seems likely or not to a nine-year-old girl. Either way, a mile and a half was a long way for that dog to go in that state, desperate for his master's help or just to say goodbye. I'd be surprised if I was the only one thinking of the poor thing in the chapel at Mr Whipple's funeral that January when Devyn winked at me from the opposite pew. It was the first time a boy had flirted with me and the hairs on my neck stood on end in response.

It was when he killed again at the age of fourteen that he earned the reputation he would revel in for the rest of his life. Another dog, but there was to be no pretense this time; it was revenge.

Devyn had had an eye for Emeline Cheap that whole trimester and had told her as much, making the girl blush each and every day with his lewd suggestions, when classes had finished for the morning and the children would gather in the little yard behind the schoolhouse. He had an odd way about him when he liked a girl; it was as if he didn't like her at all, but instead had her in his sights. More of a threat than anything else. He made Emeline cry on many occasions by loudly bragging to his cronies—he always had a few—in the yard about the kiss he would have of her and when he finally got it by punching her to the ground one day and taking it, her big brother Patrick gave him a hiding.

Not being one to let things go, Devyn nailed the girl's Norfolk Terrier to the Cheap's front door that following Sunday when they were out at service. He nailed it there alive but it had died by the time they got back. He didn't appear to give a thought to the trouble he'd be in, bragging about it at school on Monday morning. His mother somehow convinced the Morals Committee not to send him to the Shit Heap, arguing that the previous attack by Lemonade had 'loosened' him somewhat and blaming old Tim Whipple for raising such a dangerous dog. The boy ended up painting the Cheap's fence—a torment for Emeline who would watch from a window as he leered at her. Nobody ever crossed him again.

By that time he was well able to raise his penis and I was the only one to whom he would entrust his masturbations, insisting that we perform them at a distance from town, down where the river bends and a cluster of tall rocks hide a series of pools from view. He would squeal and cry like a girl while I did it and presumably this was the reason for his concerns over privacy. Afterwards he would become angry and mean, spitting at me and not at all shy with his open hand, but he never blackened my eye and I came to regard the arrangement as an insurance policy; Lord knows there were plenty of girls around the county who didn't get off as lightly as I did.

He never courted me publicly and would spend his adolescent years causing several different kinds of trouble. Always getting caught, always getting away with it; his mother was something of a force of nature and ended up with a seat on the Morals Committee, which suited them both. In his own way he believed he ran our little corner of the world, I think. Certainly nobody troubled him, but then nobody troubled about him either. An ever diminishing matrix of opportunities for mischief (since everybody was on to him they quietly went about the business of proofing themselves against him—pets never left unattended and daughters neither) led him to a holed-up life out back of his mother's where he and a couple of sidekicks would drink beer and shoot at birds, tin cans and small woodland creatures. Everybody called it the Wasp's Nest because you'd be all right as long as you didn't disturb him there.

My riverside obligations towards him continued both between and during my marriages and despite a long series of local obsessions on his part. It had become something business-like and benign for the both of us, I believe, by the time I found myself between husbands and bored enough to toy with the notion of taking him on. His mother had him dressed up in a ridiculous powder blue suit for the occasion and spent the day fussing over him, smoothing his hair and straightening his top hat. By this time I'd become rather blasé about the whole process and had worn the same plain dress for the previous three ceremonies, over none of which had my father condescended to preside.

Since nobody had responded to the invitations, we went straight back to the house afterwards and he got into his dirty smock. Within ten minutes, two of his cronies had arrived, whereupon his mother rolled her eyes and left. The three of them went out back with a crate of beer and some guns and that was my wedding day. It was to be my marriage as well.

My father's house was the wasp's nest now and even I, as I went about the chores, was careful not to disturb it. On my way to and from the clothes lines at the bottom of the back garden, laden with smalls and linen, he would leer and snigger and, if he wasn't alone, mutter to his mates with his eyes on me while they doubled over laughing.

He still wept when I milked him but now it was in the privacy of the under stair cupboard, gagged so that neither father nor Noranbole would hear it, and he rarely made it to the bedroom at night, passing out instead on a hammock in the yard or on the kitchen floor.

His mother provided him with work of sorts, out in the wood mill on her land. Nobody needed any wood from him but I suppose she felt it more seemly that her son, now married, should go to work. He would turn out the odd desultory plank. She kept her own house but was in and out of ours on an almost daily basis, pouring her poisons into his ear, coiling him like a spring, ratcheting the mechanisms of his rancor a little more each day. Perhaps it was that, or perhaps it was the sense of entitlement that matrimony bestowed on him, that made him snap.

Maybe it was my fault. I answered back one day, down at the bottom of the garden with a basketful of his underpants and socks. I quipped that he might consider wielding a hammer or a hacksaw, and not merely his tongue, and getting something done about the place for a change. His face near boiled off his head as his idiot playmates guffawed, this time at him. I didn't realize what I'd done and went back up to the house with, I fancy, something of a haughty air about me. Nothing more was said about it that whole afternoon; I was particularly busy since Bridget had been dispatched to sit with Sarah Twelves for a week—the ancient woman's episodes had been more than usually severe—and I'd sent young Noranbole, who always seemed to be under my feet, along with her. Down on the kitchen floor with a brush and up to my elbows in suds, I didn't think anything of it when those other two stumbled up the path and off home for the night.

He was in the kitchen doorway instantly, wavering and slurred.

"Where'r my boots?"

"Out the back next to the bench. I cleaned the mud off them this morning."

I listened as he laced them up but thought better of asking him where he was headed at that time, and got on with my scrubbing. The brush was noisy on the boards so I was caught off guard by his toecap in my belly. There was not a shred of temperance to the kick; I had no time even for the feeling of pain as the force of it knocked me onto my side and I curled up instinctively, unable to breathe. He knelt heavily on my neck and hammered at me with a closed fist—my belly and my face, I don't know how many times. He was silent and I, winded, was too. The deed was done thus—methodically, without yelling from him or any screaming from me.

I cursed myself silently as my mouth filled with blood. At some point in the series of blows, Devyn Butters disappeared, leaving me alone with a fist I was wielding myself. I had questions—how did I get here? Why am I doing this? When will I stop? Where is my father? But they stuttered in my mind, the fist pipping the question marks to the post every time. The transition from beating to rape was barely noticeable to me, except for the crying. Then the boots on the wooden floor. Then the steps outside. Then nothing.

I hid under the veranda for three days straight—down where we kept the firewood—rolled up in a ball and making little runs to the pantry in the middle of the day when I knew he wouldn't be there, then darting back quickly to gulp down some dry bread dunked in a mug of milk to soften it so I could swallow. The water closet I couldn't risk lest I be stuck sitting on it and he should appear unexpected, so I wet myself where I ate and slept beneath the house. No sign of father. I was in a lot of pain and, I think, the frights; never in all that time could I fully subdue my trembling. I had no notion of what was to come next, of anything that might follow. I watched myself do this strange thing through somebody else's eyes. As well as the pain, deeper than it, there was such dispassion! I long for it even now.

By the afternoon of the third day—disgusted by my own smell—I chanced a run to the bedroom upstairs for a change of knickers and dress. Father was nowhere to be seen. As I reached the top of the stairs I heard footsteps on the front porch and my heart stopped; the door to my old nursery was ajar and I went in, pushing it back behind me but afraid to click it shut in case I was heard. I sat on my old cot. Every single floorboard in the room creaked and so it was impossible to move even an inch. I listened as he made clappers of the kitchen cupboards and got himself something to eat and then I stayed there for the evening as he hissed and whistled his way through the radio stations.

The radio was still on, caught in an unresolved space between two frequencies, when I heard irregular steps on the stairs, the bedroom door pushed roughly open and then, in no time at all, his snoring. I stayed where I was, unmoving and, in the morning, regulating my breath so as not to be heard as he used the bathroom noisily and went downstairs. It was Saturday, I supposed, because he did not leave the house. And so I passed another day and night, stock still and incontinent.

He spent most of the day downstairs or out back. I never heard his voice so he must have been alone. From time to time he would stumble upstairs for something and then down again. I cannot describe to you, despite the terror of his approaching steps whenever he'd pass by the nursery, how safe I felt as they receded. I believed these were the safest moments of my life—just my silence and his departures. I knew of nothing else, no yesterday or tomorrow and no other people on the Earth. I could have sat there, breathing steadily, till I died.

On Sunday morning he caught me. I suppose it was the stink that gave me away. As his footsteps passed by the nursery door and just as I was anticipating their sublime retreat, they paused. I knew instantly. When he pushed the door open he just stood there and looked at me. I couldn't really describe the expression on his face as he contemplated his shit-stained, wet-dressed wife, her blood-matted hair and battered face, but it wasn't kind. Having taken it in, I lowered my eyes and awaited the approach. When it came it was wordless.

He pulled me from the bed by my upper arm—practically the only bit of me that wasn't soiled by blood or waste—and dragged me to the bath, forcing me to my knees inside it. The blast of cold water from the shower head seemed to hurt as much as the beating had; I cowered beneath it, frozen and only slowly realizing, through the icy torrent, that he was laughing.

He told me to take off the dress and I did so, happy to get rid of the rancid thing and ready to get out, to be dry. In that moment I thought he would leave me alone—I don't know why. I was grateful, if you can believe it, for being clean. In my mind's eye I saw myself taking to my bed, to heal while he drank in the yard with his idiot friends. Sore but warm beneath the blankets, pulled up over my head, in the dark like when I was a girl. I even had a fancy that I might be brought a mug of milk and a biscuit; Bridget would be finishing up at Sarah Twelves', and surely father would be back soon from wherever he was.

The sun was blinding in the bathroom window as he knocked me to the floor and stood over me, unbuckling his belt. The wetting had given me a jolt and I had the wits about me to be mildly surprised he didn't whip me with it, but instead dropped it to the floor along with his breeches.

In all the time I had known him and how thoroughly bad he was, and about all the awful things he did, I had never been so incensed as I was at that moment—to see that he could have done what he did to me, found me in the state he had, and somehow be aroused by it, as perky as a hungry otter on a trout farm.

I punched it with all of my might, my own fist clenched now and quicker than my mind. My husband fell back against the bathtub and his feet gave way on the wet floor; he went in and banged his head against the other side. I was up like a shot and had a handful of his hair held tight before I knew what I was doing. None of this was becoming of a lady, I grant you, but then there wasn't a lady present; somewhere between all the blows that followed, I disappeared—there was only Devyn Butters, bashing his own head against the porcelain, once for every bad deed of his spluttering, waning life.

When it was done I dropped to the floor, exhausted and breathing hard, and heard the garden gate go. I knew it would be his mother, even before I looked down over the windowsill: nobody else ever came on a Sunday. The contents of her son's mashed head were dropping gloopily to the floor from the side of the bath.

"Devyn? Devyn, sweetie?"

She had let herself in and I could hear her tramping up and down the hall-way, so I changed into a new dress and straightened my hair—nevertheless I must have been quite a sight with the bruising to my face and a badly swollen eye—and went downstairs to deal with her, finding her in the kitchen. There was no mistaking her surprise upon seeing me and her wide-eyed expression remained largely unchanged as I put the bread knife through her neck.

The most unpleasant of my marriages, without a doubt. Bridget turned up later in the afternoon. Wordlessly, she put Noranbole down for a nap and helped me bury the bodies in the yard—far enough from the well not to contaminate it, at the back of the lean-to. She was such a good girl but she never would look me in the eye again, and she didn't linger long after that.

Explaining their sudden absence would not be an issue, since not a single soul ever asked after them, not even his so-called friends. Apart from my missing teeth I healed up quickly enough. Two nights after we buried them, my father finally showed himself. It was already dark; he had taken a candle from the front window and was outside the door of his study. He took a good, long look at me and I took a good, long look at him, and then he went inside and closed the door behind him.

But what is it about bad people that makes them so adhesive? Even from his grave in the back yard, with his mother's muddy, corpulent corpse draped face down on top of him, Devyn Butters managed one more leer. By the time a fortnight had passed I knew I was with child; I filled the house and the best part of a week with inconsolable sobbing, thoroughly disgruntling Bridget, who had never before seen me in such a state, or had to play nursemaid.

It was disgraceful of me, of course, but in the end I pulled myself together. I like to think that Emma showed herself again, that morning in front of the mirror in my bedroom; I wasn't crying anymore and I didn't look such a sight, leastways with my mouth closed. I tied my hair up in a tight bun and wore a dress to work in; I would scrub and prepare every square inch of this house for the baby. Noranbole, little as she was, was big enough to peel and scrub—she would be put to work as well. I had Bridget promise me she'd stay till I'd had my Grips and was free of the child. We would birth the thing into a spotless world, a disinfected world—wiped clean of the horror, washed of its soiled beginning.

And then I would despise it.

I would visit a life of torment upon it. Every moment. Every day. We would see if it was human, and if it was we would ruin it.

My term was uncomfortable, painful at times, as if Devyn was still kicking at me but from the inside. I spent it filled with revulsion and resolve. Every kick I would repay with a kick of my own, for every stretch mark I would leave a scar, for each and every cramp the child would do a spell tied to a post in the shed. When I finally got the Grips, I let Bridget know and took to my bed. I would have frightened any man or woman who saw my face as I climbed the stairs, so much was I looking forward to punishing the baby.

My labors were predictably arduous—not a single thing related to that man had managed to be anything other than grueling. I held, and probably hurt, my larder girl's hand through the night, the last time I would ever hold it; finally, just before dawn, the thing was out of me. She swaddled and offered it to me but I waved it away and she put it in the cot by the window. A girl. I fell asleep.

When I awoke Bridget was gone, for good, and the room was quiet. I assumed the child was sleeping and went over to the cot to check. There it was, and wide awake. There she was, calm and silent. Not at all wrinkly, as I had expected. Bright blue eyes.

I wanted to see Devyn in them—I had come over to mete out a first horror, if truth be known.

But he wasn't there.

They say a baby can't see more than a few inches from its face but I swear she looked right at me. I swear upon my life she looked right at me and forgave me then and there. I picked her up and held her to my chest. For the last time in my life, my eyes produced tears and I soaked her in them, on my knees on the floor, then held her back to look at her again. He was gone; there was nothing of him. This was her gift to me.

Still, there has to be a price. That is only proper. Since I could not expel the stench of my own water—it had lingered in my nostrils since the child first grew in my belly—I called her Urine.

But I could not hate her. I cannot. Just the opposite—I owe her everything. I hate myself instead. I always will. I will despise myself. I will despise any husbands I happen to pick up along the way, and all men. And women. I will despise the world I live in and the sun that revolves around it. I will despise the rain and the wind and the rivers.

And I will despise you.

The Nursery

THREE ROTTING STEPS drop down from the locked attic and point across the way to a door painted pale blue and stenciled with an alpine scene. It too is locked, the room unused. Just inside and to the right of the door, the shamrock-shaped brass attic key hangs on a hook, its teeth dangling Damocles-like over the head of Penelope Rabbit in a pretty bonnet, on her way to church.

Below that sits the mahogany sideboard where Phinoola Quigg had the towels and water when this was the birthing room, near nine months into Rose Wakeling's term and during the worst storm anyone could remember. The Flemings down the way were to lose their lean-to that night and cattle would be found dead in the morning, far from their field.

The elusive pastor's wife had been commanded to take up residence in the room now that her time was close and the Grips might come at any moment. She would pace the creaking floor, almost unable to bear her confinement; for Rose Wakeling, the worst thing imaginable was to be in a place where anyone might find her.

On that night though, sitting in a soft chair by the window where Phinoola Quigg had put her when the first Grip came, with the net curtains billowing a little in the draft from the old window and water bucketing against the panes, back lit sporadically by lightning bolts and rattled by thunder, Rose was calm and coping and in comparatively good spirits.

Remarkably good, in fact.

"Such a fuss!" she said to the bustling figure of Phinoola Quigg, which was back-and-forthing to the sideboard with no apparent purpose or result. The young woman's water had broken and she was looking out of the window when she wasn't watching the housekeeper in amazement, and smiling because she liked the thunder; she never had before but somehow that night she did.

"There's really no need. Won't the pastor's dinner be . . .?"

"Dinner is it?" said Phinoola Quigg. "Dinner? With me on my knees, wiping his wife's fluid off the Persian rug? He couldn't cut himself a sandwich for once in his life?"

She looked up from the towels she was laying out between Rose's legs and gazed at the lady of the house, perplexed.

"Well aren't you in fine form, for a woman on the verge of her torment?"

"Torment?" said Rose, tapping the astonished housekeeper's head with the little book she held in her hand. "Not at all, you silly!"

She sounded positively assertive.

"Are there any biscuits left, do you think?"

The window was shaking its way out of its frame with the thunder. Phinoola Quigg went to it and drew the curtains, then checked that the wick of the table lamp was well oiled before planting her hands on her hips.

"Biscuits, ma'am?"

"Yes," said Rose, opening her book and leafing through it to find the page she was on, "Lemon creams, if at all possible."

※

Charles Wakeling sat on a stool in the study, eschewing the comfort of the walnut office chair he usually sat in for reading and contemplation. He felt it behooved him at a time like this to maintain a straightness of spine without recourse to the pampering of a back support and the slight give of rattan. He might have been praying, with his hands clasped on his lap and his head bowed, except that he couldn't concentrate and was simply grinding his teeth and looking very intently at his knees.

It was past nine, near the end of October and they'd been up there since darkness had fallen in the mid-afternoon. Nothing. No sounds or signs. Nobody had told him anything. An old drop dial clock tocked on the wall and the lamp sputtered, spitting its last little bit of light into an irrelevant corner of the room. He decided he would go up to see for himself if anything was happening and, having given his legs a good squeeze to gird himself, stood and made his way in the gloom towards the stairs. At the study door, however, he stopped dead—Phinoola Quigg was at the bottom step, her first foot on it, and had turned when she heard him.

"And where, might I inquire, would you be going, Pastor?"

The churchman wiped some imaginary speck from his waistcoat, eyes on the ceiling, then on the floor.

"I thought . . ."

He unfastened his cuffs.

"Shouldn't I . . . ?"

Then fastened them.

"Isn't there something . . . ?"

"A *man*, Pastor?" asked the housekeeper. "A *man*? With the rivers of blood up there and a baby to pull out of your wife and my arms up to their elbows in her vagina water? Now is the time, is it, to introduce a *man* into the situation? Is that what you're suggesting, Pastor?"

She'd already turned her back and was near the top of the first flight. Charles stood impotent, mesmerized by the biscuit tin.

"Sure isn't there always a sinner somewhere," she said as she disappeared from view, "that you could be praying for?"

❊

"There you are, Phinoola Quigg, and with the biscuits, bless you!"

Rose lounged in her seat, thumbing through her little book, a compendium of gingham patterns, and helped herself with relish to a lemon cream which she pulled apart to lick the filling.

"Well aren't you a fine one ma'am, with your baby nearly here and not a sign of distress on you?"

Phinoola Quigg had a handful of towels again but nothing to do with them. She leaned over Rose like a half-coiled slinky.

"Oh, it'll be along I'm sure," said Rose. "When I know if it's a boy or a girl I can decide on the pattern for its little smock. I'm such a silly—I can't quite make my mind . . . up, between . . . oh . . ."

"What is it ma'am? Is it the Grips?"

The housekeeper had dropped to the floor and made stirrups of her hands and was searching Rose intently for any signs of progress.

"No . . . I don't . . . I don't . . . ah . . . ah . . . ah . . . ah choo!"

"Mary and Joseph, did you ever see such a thing?" said Phinoola Quigg.

"So silly!" Rose couldn't suppress a fit of the giggles. "It was just a silly sneeze, Phinoola Quigg!"

But the midwife had her head down and, having birthed at least a dozen babies in her time, was expertly cutting the cord, counting the fingers (ten) and the toes (ten) and wiping the wrinkly little face before wrapping the thing (a girl) up warmly and raising it into the sight of its laughing mother.

They say the screams could be heard from the Gribble ranch clear all the way to Salt Bog, and all around the county. Screams to freeze the blood in a vein, crack a tooth and pluck the hair from a head. The loudest sounds Rose Wakeling had ever made and that's for sure.

Charles Wakeling knelt on the study floor and prayed hard, assuming the Grips had begun and bracing himself for a night of it, so he was perplexed when roused by Phinoola Quigg just a moment later—on her way back to the kitchen with the biscuits—to tell him he could go upstairs if he wished.

The screaming hadn't stopped.

Beginning the very next day, the room was made into a nursery. A Parisian swing cot japanned in white and gold was installed, and beside it a cast-iron rocking chair with red velvet cushions where Phinoola Quigg would sit and keep watch over the baby, stock still and refusing to rock the rockers.

Opposite the window there is an ornate little hearth with a surround of ceramic depictions—rural scenes in green, white, yellow and red—and above its mantel Charles hung a map of the county: from Small Town at the very center to the gorge above it and Tiny Village at bottom right.

Rose had disappeared back into the house and nobody would see her again for months. Her interest in the baby was evidenced in the daily jar of breast milk she would leave for Phinoola Quigg to find outside the kitchen or at the nursery door, always tied round the lid with a gingham ribbon, but she could not bring herself to enter the room or to be in the terrifying little creature's physical presence.

A week after the birth a note from her was found on the side table in Charles' study, requesting that the child be given her own mother's name, Emma, "if at all possible" and a week after that the name itself, in fine needle-work, was found framed on the landing, along with a tiny smock in yellow gingham; Phinoola Quigg put the frame on a shelf within sight of the cot and the smock on the baby—they were the only things, apart from her milk, that Rose Wakeling ever bequeathed to her daughter. The needlework still sits there, between a base metal crucifix and a mechanical calendar that would change the day and date on its display if anybody re-membered to wind it, and that doubles as an ashtray. The shelves above and below hold the few toys that waited for Emma's growing fingers—a woolen pig and an unfurnished doll's house, a rubber ball and one bat. On a single shelf opposite, a bible and several volumes of stories from scripture as well as hand-written copies of Charles Wakeling's sermons.

And everywhere, Penelope: off to church where the attic key hangs, pic-nicking with a brace of ducks below the window sill, remonstrating with Gabriella, the supercilious goose, beside the wardrobe and tying her little bonnet up beneath her chin over the cot. She too watched over Emma, from every possible angle but nowhere more so than from the wall separating the room from the landing, where she sets off on her way to Sunday service.

If the Penelopes along that particular wall seemed especially watchful, it's because they were. Rose would never set foot in the room again but she felt compelled to look at the child and to this end had Phinoola Quigg drill an unobtrusive peephole—aligned with church-bound Penelope's eye—so that she could stand by the door outside and observe.

Phinoola Quigg would become aware, the moment she settled in the velvet chair and opened the book of nursery rhymes that she would read to Emma, of the rabbit's roving iris—a blue searchlight sweeping over the cot, the baby hands and baby feet, the gurgling mouth as soft and slight as a wet dimple.

Thus passed the early days of Emma. When she was old enough to sit up in her cot, Charles took it upon himself to begin her spiritual education. He would relieve Phinoola Quigg for an hour or two at a time and read to his daughter from the bible or from one of his own works, which concerned themselves exclusively, and to his housekeeper's consternation, with the pitfalls of womanhood.

Eve, Jezebel, Mary Magdalene, Sarah Twelves—Emma was to become familiar with them all, in as much as a babbling infant could. She would look at her father, transfixed, as he read and gesticulated. She might have been able to tell from his tone that something terrible was going on, something of which she should not approve. Something infernal.

The pastor too would feel the eyes of his wife bore into the baby as he read, and with considerable irritation. He did not appreciate any interruptions to the child's indoctrination but couldn't help himself—his eyes would go to the peephole at regular intervals and he would lose his place in whatever text he was subjecting the baby to and have to begin again, a renewed fervor in his voice on these restarts that would make Emma's eyes widen even further and fill with tears.

It didn't matter to Rose. Her fear of her husband, of being seen, of everything notwithstanding, she was compelled to look at the little girl. Nothing in the world could have stopped her. Not, that is, until the day the clever thing—rapt in some biblical tale of fornication her father was telling—followed the pastor's line of sight to the little emptiness that was Penelope's eye and, on seeing the glistening blue circle that moved within it, gave a little smile and waved her hand. A squeak was heard from outside the door and the blue eye disappeared in an instant. The pastor threw up his hands in exasperation as the child began to cry, staring at the now black void where the blue had been.

And so began the migration of Rose. She would plead (in a note left at the top of the stairs) with Phinoola Quigg to drill a new hole and the housekeeper did so, picking another Penelope's eyeball at waist level so that Rose had to peer in over the surface of the sideboard, on her knees. Across the wall from door to corner, Penelope appears in various states, and she never does make it to church. At this second peephole she leaps over a wooden gate at great speed, the tiny shadows of a farmer and his dogs in the distance.

It bought Rose another few months as the child learned to drink from a teeted cup and to say its first word (harlot) but it wouldn't last—inevitably, the day came when Emma spotted the flick of her mother's eye in the wall and cried again as it vanished and inevitably, Phinoola Quigg was asked to drill another hole, this time necessitating a stepladder for Rose on the landing, on which she would perch to watch her daughter's first toddles from the eye of a Penelope who hangs from the jaws of triumphant Fergal Fox, her back legs twitching and her snout still puffing out a bit of panicked breath as the housekeeper regaled Emma with the heroics of Hudden and Dudden, and the cow they managed to kill and Donald O'Neary who was a terrible nuisance.

As she told the child of the horned women and the disgraceful lack of hospitality shown them. Of their undoing by a daubed sieve like the one Munachar had used to carry water for the makings of a threshers' cake so they'd give him a bit of straw to bribe the cow for the milk the cat wanted, and for the cat the butter wanted for the dog's paw, and the deer to swim and the water to be swum in and to wet the flagstone to sharpen the axe, to cut down a rod for the gallows. Another hole drilled when again the squeak of discovery was heard and Penelope's eye emptied and the child wept.

This new hole at barely knee level and in the eye of the pretty rabbit again, miraculously free of Fergal's teeth, hind leg mangled and paws bloodied, digging desperately with the pack of hounds closing in behind her—the worst of all the peepholes for Rose who had to lie down in a very awkward position to use it and get a terrible crick in her neck, never mind that by this time the child was crawling and might come right up to this low Penelope at any time.

She didn't wait to be discovered. For the fear of it alone she left another note for Phinoola Quigg, begging for a peephole higher up. In her exasperation, the housekeeper—who was not above the occasional show of petulance—drilled one for her: in the corner at near ceiling height.

Rose had to unfold the stepladder and lean it against the wall on the landing, climbing to the top of it to watch her child from a precarious height, pressing her nose to the point where the two walls and ceiling met so she could get her eye to the hole. On the other side, in the nursery, Phinoola Quigg had once again used the eye of a Penelope, this last one hanging lifeless from the farmer's belt.

It was terrifying for the lady of the house, because having her face turned towards the corner made it impossible for her to keep one eye on the top of the stairs and being right at the top of the ladder made it very difficult for her to flee if she were to hear someone approaching. Still, she was driven to watch her daughter, convinced that by doing so the girl somehow fell under the protection of her mother.

She would peep from the hole in the corner for the remainder of the little girl's infancy. On the day that Emma, in a new pair of heeled shoes, found that she was able to reach the door knob and, turning it, open the door, she heard an almighty clatter and a heavy thud; when the curious child stepped out onto the landing for the first time, the ladder still shuddered where it had fallen, but there was no other sign of life.

Emma Dobrovolny

THE SPIDER IS DEAD,
Rots like blueing bread
On a hopeless tongue that dallies
O'er absent teeth in crescent—
A wreath of Aunt Sally's
In a gallery of gum
And spittle in spots
At the corners of the mouth
And in the middle.

And you, too, are dead.

All of you.

"Well?"

Klement, my fifth husband, swiveled in his chair a little as I stood over him, hands clasped at my waist. I may have been tapping a foot. He held the poem in both hands and had yet to look up at me, so for the time being I found myself addressing his bald patch.

"Well," he said, "it's, eh . . ."

On first impression I had found Mr Dobrovolny the airiest and most oblivious of men. It had attracted me to him. He was a writer of fictional stories and Tiny Village was his chosen retreat that year—a quiet place in which to seclude himself for the completion of a story collection.

None of the villagers had anything remotely interesting to say about fictions and he was therefore left to his own devices—enjoyed from a distance as an exotic addition to local life. Although he was foreign, I considered him quite the catch; he'd been accepted as a Fellow of the National Institute of Letters and cut a handsome figure in his heavy wool weave, three-piece suit. He kept the barber busy with the grooming of his unusually complicated beard and was the only man any of us had ever seen who made use of a monocle. Moreover, I thought it very obliging of him to tolerate the presence of Noranbole—a very noisy baby—whenever I was called upon to address one of his frequent and unpredictable arousals.

But it didn't take long for the grumbling to begin.

Despite the presence of a host of literati (George Brock, creator of the Mrs Besbeech Mysteries, was there with his wife Dorothy—an eminent essayist in her own right—and just about the entire Barnstable Group turned up, lounging around the place in their foppish and gender-bending outfits) the wedding reception which we held in the house was a subdued affair. This was largely due, I would argue, to the laudanum cake that Ester—my new husband's rather stern elder sister—had prepared. An inappropriate choice in my opinion. I was keen, though, to accommodate Klement's wishes since he was being so good about the baby. As a consequence of the cake, our dancing was clumsy and conversation impossible, but our incoherent reveries carried on well into the night.

"Yes. And you've begun with a spider, I see. And it's dead. That's . . ."

The trouble began as early as the following morning and would brew for a year. I wanted to know what Klement expected for breakfast and was surprised to find him in my father's study, arranging the desk with his own typewriter and various papers. When I pointed out to him that the room already had an occupant he looked at me uncomprehendingly. I don't know—perhaps they do things differently in Prague. Perhaps there is no requirement there to respect one's elders. We were not in Prague, however, and I insisted he organize a corner for himself in the parlor where I assured him he could work undisturbed. He acquiesced but there was something about the altercation that changed things between us. So soon after the wedding!

"You've certainly evoked the oral cavity so . . . well done there . . ."

It also seemed to sow a seed of resentment between husband and father. To the best of my knowledge, they were never to exchange a word. Klement secluded himself as best he could in the parlor and got on with his stories, but it quickly became apparent that the house made a poor workplace.

The baby was a dreadful burden to me and an impediment to this new chapter in my life. Bridget, a young woman now, had no time for childcare, busy as she was digging the new pit out back. It was to take her eight months to dig that pit. It therefore fell to me to tend to the ill-spirited child that cried its way through each and every afternoon.

It wasn't easy. In my desire to make myself useful to Klement, I had appointed myself his amanuensis. However, since he refused to discuss or even reveal the content of his stories to me, it proved impossible to fulfill the role. Instead, I would sit nearby, shuffling papers and sharpening pencils and feeling very redundant and foolish. The baby would cry in the pram in the hall and Klement would work through gritted teeth.

"And the punctuation, Klement? The *spelling*?"

I'll confess I've never really understood the need for fictional stories. Bob and Barbara Nettleton have four grown boys, the eldest of which lives now in Little City. Nobody knows his exact age but from the salt-and-pepper of his beard the last time he was back, it's unlikely to be less than twenty-four—the length of his parents' marriage. Never mind his green eyes. Ed Ingalls bought his ranch from the municipality for a hundred dollars, in a rising market. Surely there's enough in all that to keep us going? Why make things up?

"Oh!" He seemed to perk up a little. "Well the punctuation is . . . well of course, with poetry it's so . . . and the spelling is absolutely . . ."

He looked up, finally, and handed me the page.

"Emma, I cannot find fault with the spelling here. It's perfect, as far as I can see," he said and turned back to his work.

My failure to appreciate the art no doubt made me poor company in the parlor. After some months, Klement arrived at the conclusion that my time would be better spent pacifying the awful child and he advertised for an assistant who on arrival turned out to be a very pretty young woman from Czechoslovakia by the name of Žofie Láska. She and my husband got on like a house on fire as he pounded away at her proofs those next few months. It must have been a blessed release for him.

But not for me, lumbered with the infant. I had settled back down beside the pram in the hallway, my perfectly spelled poem sitting smugly on my lap. Noranbole was as usual making plenty of noise and I was trying to stare her down when Klement put his head around the corner and cleared his throat.

"Žofie and I will be attending a conference."

It was Žofie's day off and she had doubtless gone to Small Town for more shopping, courtesy of the generous and, as far as I could make out, indeterminate wage my husband paid her.

"What kind of conference?" I asked. I thought I might like to accompany them.

"A . . . fictional story conference," he replied. "No . . ." his eyes were on the pram, " . . . babies."

So I let them go and I don't suppose it will come as much of a surprise that they never came back. There are some, I have no doubt, who would take comfort in being immortalized—as I strongly suspect Noranbole and I have—in his now celebrated tale, "The Harpy's Changeling", but I would have preferred a marriage.

Still, these are the trials of a single mother with a young child.

The Bedroom

THERE'S NO ONE in the room at the end of the landing, a distance from the pastor's and next to the one that Phinoola Quigg took for herself. Emma was moved here once she'd outgrown the swaddling accoutrements of the nursery. The bedroom hangs beneath a gable of the house so the window is low to the floor; the bed, made new for the girl, appears big and tall on the opposite wall, on the other side of which Phinoola Quigg would sit and press her ear to a tumbler, listening.

The bed was built for Emma to grow into; at first, its roughly turned bobbins and balusters of light and dark wood dwarfed her—asleep, she might have been mistaken for a doll tucked up in a real child's bed, a miniature in a life-sized world. Awake, the discrepancy was every bit as marked—the little girl found herself in a grown woman's room, furnished with just one stocky wooden wardrobe, two stick chairs, a writing desk by the window, and the one concession to her youth—a gray rocking horse which took up the rest of the space and which she was soon enough forbidden to use, on account of the noise it made on the floorboards.

"How many sides on an enneadecagon?"

"Nineteen."

"A tetrakaidecagon?"

"Fourteen."

"What is the capital of Bolivia?"

"La Paz."

"And what could they possibly have in La Paz that would be of any interest to us?"

"Tin."

"And what would we be doing with tin?"

"It is malleable, ductile and has a highly crystalline structure. We coat things in it. We cover them up. It slows down the inevitable corrosion of everything. It staves off the rot."

"Do *we* rot?"

"We do."

"When we die?"

"Before we die. We are rotting now."

"Even you? A child?"

"Especially me."

"Can we not stop the rot?"

"No."

"Can we not slow it down?"

"Perhaps."

"With tin?"

"No."

"Then how?"

"One: submission. Two: work. Three: prayer. Four: unseasoned vegetables. Five: in the winter, dress for winter. In the summer, dress for winter. Six . . . six . . ."

"Ah, isn't it well for you that you only need to take five steps, and the rest of us laboring away over here with our seven?"

"Seven. For every confession, a denunciation. For every denunciation, a light snack or similar reward."

"Well isn't this a fine state of affairs? We can count to seven, can we, without passing six? It's a new way of counting, is it?"

"Six . . ."

There still hangs, above the bed, a framed painting that Phinoola Quigg put there to edify the child—a bar scene depicting the brawl that has broken out over a card game and all of the protagonists, despite their clothing and their recognizably human bearing, are canine. The card table is upturned and behind it a Cuban Dogge, for example, with a cigar hanging from its jaw, stands in the half shadow. Next to it, a Cordobese Fighter in a bowler hat with its paw on the haunch of a pipe-smoking Bullenbeisser. The three friends spectate gleefully as a big old Molossus pins a Blue Poll Terrier to the floor—the latter in a three piece suit—and slits its belly with a switch blade.

On the day she presented the painting to Emma, the little girl remarked that perhaps it wasn't the nicest of things—to kill a dog like that, over a game or, for that matter, to look on and laugh while the deed was done.

"Wasn't it foolish of him, in that case, to play poker with five aces," said Phinoola Quigg as she straightened the frame on the wall, "and no knife?"

Anything the housekeeper did or said around Emma had the barb of a lesson to it. She would spend many hours in one of the chairs, drilling the girl on her times tables, bible readings and such general knowledge as she thought appropriate for the daughter of a man of the cloth.

"Six: the prophylactic . . .?"

"Six: the prophylactic wisdoms of the progenitors—the teachings of Deuteronomy, the erections of Haggai, the disputes of Malachi. Matthew, Mark and Luke, but not John. Television's Gary Fulwell. Language that enshrouds. The admonitions that stand sentinel on the threshold of thought. The Holy Constrictions."

"Is that it?"

"Yes."

"And what must we have to take the Seven Steps?"

"A quieted mind."

"And what must we do to quiet the mind?"

"Close the eyes."

"Will you be having porridge or bread?"

"Porridge, please."

"Because bread would have been too easy, is that it? Because I need you to fill up my empty, idle hours with your food orders?"

Somebody up at the Butters' wood mill had truncated the wardrobe so that it would fit beneath the diagonal of the roof. It is tall enough that the girl could hang her clothes in it but short enough for her to keep her childish treasures on top. She might have arranged her dolls there if she'd had any, or framed photographs if she'd been interested, but what she put there was a wooden board of sixty-four inset squares, black and white, that she propped up against the wall so she could see it better.

Emma loved that board and kept two felt pouches—one with chess pieces and one with checker stones—in her school bag. She never got to use it in the house; Phinoola Quigg thought it improper that a housekeeper should compete with a child in her care and Charles Wakeling, who thought it very dubious indeed to be beaten so consistently at both games by his own daughter, had long since given up.

Once a week, the girl was permitted to tuck the board under her arm and take it to school where she would stay behind for an hour and play a game or two with the crumbling schoolmistress, Agatha Pinch.

※

The schoolhouse was a one-room shed of horizontally slatted timber, painted white with a bell tower and a porch at one end. Much of the time, the responsibility for ringing the bell fell to Emma, as Ms Pinch felt she displayed the requisite gravity of demeanor. Inside, it was even barer than was hinted at by the spartan exterior. One long blackboard and nine desks in perfect square formation. A map of the county on the wall opposite the board. An old upright piano in need of a tune. Nothing else.

In the early autumn, the late afternoon sun was still high in the sky, creating little rhombi of light on the floor beneath the windows along one side of the classroom. It also cast a near vertical shaft from the skylight which illuminated Emma's desk—the one in the middle—and warmed it a little in the gloomy room, so that is where she and the doddering nonagenarian would sit to play.

"Your mother is well?"

"I have no idea."

"Of course. Well, no news is good news where your mother is concerned. I suppose if something were awry they'd have found her . . . found something . . . and your father?"

"Father is very well and sends his regards."

"You must thank him for me, Emma. Perhaps I'll send a note with you. He hasn't come by in some time, or shown as much of an interest in . . . school affairs."

One of the old teacher's arthritic hands had found its way to a stray lock of gray hair.

"I could give you his email address?"

"I know where you live, Emma."

"No, I mean his electronic mail address. It's like mail, but electronic."

"Well then it isn't *very* much like mail, is it? Whatever it is. I'm afraid you've rather lost me, as you youngsters so often do. A fanciful notion. How on earth would one get an *electronic* mail into an envelope?"

"It works on the phone line. You read the messages on a screen."

"Like a television?"

"More like a telephone."

"A telephone? With *pictures*?"

"Yes. Pictures and text."

"*Moving* pictures?"

"Yes, there is video."

"Good heavens! And anybody can send messages with this thing? *Ordinary* people?"

"Yes. There is a cafe in Small Town with a machine."

"Oh how delicious! How *wonderfully* emancipating! Why, this'll be an end to tyranny! The technological embodiment of the democratic will of the people!"

"Do you think so?"

"I'll stock up on candles and tinned food. Are we playing English or Russian?"

"Misère?"

"Good. Mind you, we've never had much use for telephones around here. Everybody lives so nearby. The Bosworths are a little out of it, up on the ridge, but nobody likes the Bosworths."

To play, Emma sat at her desk and put a stool in front of it so that Ms Pinch could face her across the countless obscenities carved into its soft wooden surface. The slant of the lid was slight enough to make the game possible; chess, with its taller pieces, was more of a challenge.

The desk at Ms Pinch's back when they convened like this was the front middle and belonged at that time to Patrice Maypole, a brooding boy who bitterly resented Ms Pinch's attempts to correct his elocution and who nobody understood, either in the school yard—where he would arrange twigs on the dusty ground beneath the great oak tree, according to some scheme of his own impenetrable devising—or when asked to read or recite in the classroom. He steadfastly refused to answer even simple mathematical conundrums in recognizable English; if the answer was four he would say *Beat the devil round the stump!* or *Right as a trivet!* and when called upon to produce the square root of a hundred and forty-four he would more than likely recount some old folk tale in which the only terms anyone could make out were *a hog-killin time* and *cayote*.

Even though Ms Pinch disapproved, the boys (all seven other pupils were boys) would periodically fabricate reasons to swap seats and make such a fuss of it that she would eventually capitulate. Thus they orbited around the Wakeling girl like moons around a world, or to her mind like pieces on a board. The only two exceptions were Patrice, who held on to his place for dear life and showed willingness on more than one occasion to take the matter outside and Devyn—the Butters boy—who never budged from behind Emma where he could blow paper balls at her from the hollow shaft of a pen or just stare into the back of her head till she could feel it, and whose own analogy for the dance of the desks was flies round shit.

That September, the place to Maypole's right was vacant, reserved each year for the foreign boy who never came and who lived with his parents in a trailer on a strip of common land up by the lake. Nobody minded them—the father was some kind of engineer and volunteered his time with the council on all sorts of innovative building projects and repairs; Frau Seiler too gave her time to the community, forsaking her patch of geodesic tomatoes once a week to teach German at the Ladies' Association to a group of women who would never use it but who thought it a terribly novel diversion and mainly went because they were curious about the foreigner. The family were generally considered benign despite their having notions, such as the home-schooling of their boy and the wearing of organic shoes.

"Your move, Emma."

On the other side of Maypole sat little Henry Mason; a red-haired, gap-toothed boy in dungarees and relentlessly good spirits, Henry was the class darling. He never had a bad word to say about anyone, and very few words to say about anything, but always wore a wide grin and a constellation of freckles designed to endear.

"As nice as pie," was Agatha Pinch's daily verdict, despite the fact that she never did manage to instill in him a single fact or calculation.

"It's you again, Emma. Dear me, you're dreaming!"

Behind Emma and to Devyn's right sat Gideon Tupp—a ruddy boy from way up country where the huge Tupp ranch sprawled. He stayed at his aunt's nearby during the week so that he could attend lessons and got picked up by his brother direct from school each Friday to work the weekends. He was strapping and wiry and sturdy and strong and the only boy in the school who could or would stand up to Butters.

And because he could, Ms Pinch put him there and always moved him back eventually, and so Devyn would turn instead to the left and reserve his special attention for young Oldman Stodder, the class baby, who in all the power play and negotiation over seating arrangements would usually draw that short straw. His schooldays would be a misery of slap and spit, knee and fist, and his own daughter when he was grown would be kept home, and away from the classroom at all costs.

"Three of your men captured, Emma. Lucky."

That term, Emma found herself flanked. On one side, Shane Holcroft, a spineless giggler who found comparative peace in the Butters slipstream, born to crone and happy to take the regular abuse that Devyn dished out in return for a kind of protection—Holcroft had no neck and too much ear and he didn't like being reminded. Butters had no kindness in him but he was canny, and would mete out a fair dose of malice to anyone who brought either subject up, in return for the boy's deference.

"That's you in the dog hole, Emma. Clever girl."

On the other side, Darryl Horse. Another adjunct to Devyn, young Horse was as memorable as a ninth pint and seemed to exist only as a faint satellite in orbit around Butters, visible only in the refracted glare of the class bully. In terms of the trouble the trio were responsible for perpetrating, Darryl took charge of the psychological department. There was something distinctly admiring in the way he would look at Devyn that Devyn was not entirely comfortable with, in the sense that he didn't quite know how he felt about it.

"I suppose you'd better crown me, Emma. Unfortunate."

The game had contracted now to a nine-square field. It brought Emma's classmates to her mind and how they, in her imagination, were stones to be jumped one at a time and how the empty desk beckoned—a resting place on the king row at the end of a winning move.

"I have you pinned, Emma. You win again, devil take you."

When it occurred to Charles Wakeling that his daughter—a solitary girl—might benefit from some companionship other than that of Phinoola Quigg, he could have chosen any of the schoolboys or nominated a girl from a distant nook of the family, except that he never appeared to maintain any correspondence with family and had a very practical approach to selecting a suitable boy. He settled on Devyn, since the Tupp boy lived too far away and the Butters were people of property who owned one of the few businesses in the area.

Much to Emma's consternation then, her nemesis was presented one Saturday morning to a skeptical Phinoola Quigg on the Wakeling porch and shown into the parlor where the pastor was composing a sermon. Devyn had had his hair smoothed down to a shine by his mother, who had dressed him herself that morning in a navy blue sailor suit with short pants that Darryl Horse (who happened to be kicking stones around beneath a cherry tree as they'd passed by on their way to the Wakeling compound) would not soon forget.

"The Butter boy is here."

"Butters," said Devyn, face flushed with malevolence.

Charles propped his quill in the inkwell and turned to the boy, eyes on the ceiling.

"Yes. My daughter is waiting in her room. I trust you'll provide each other with some beneficial diversion, Mr Butter," he said, turning back to his work. "Including play, if necessary."

"Butters," said Devyn, red crescents dug into the palms of his hands.

For four hours, Emma sat in one of the chairs in her room and Devyn sat in the other. Not a word was spoken. There was very little difference between the encounter and others that had taken place in the classroom except that here, Devyn, who had brought along a pocketful of chewed paper and a pen, was able to spit balls at Emma's face instead of at the back of her head. For her part, the girl was patient, wiping each one away and returning her playmate's cold stare, augmented perhaps with a smirk for his outfit, until Phinoola Quigg came back (ear bruised from being pressed to the tumbler) to retrieve the boy.

"Have you enjoyed yourself, Emma?"

"No," said Emma.

"Well isn't that lovely? And you, Butter? Have you enjoyed yourself?"

"No," said Devyn. "And it's Butters."

"I don't suppose we'll be repeating the experience, so, will we?"

Her hand was already on his shoulder to shoo him out of the room but the boy's eyes were on the painting that hung on the wall over Emma's bed. He'd only just noticed it, not being the curious type, and as Phinoola Quigg pushed him towards the door he made the only remark he was ever to make in Emma's presence that could possibly have been interpreted as kind.

"I like your picture."

Emma Cleverly

F Noranbole's father, my fourth husband, I do not speak.

The Kitchen

A T THE BACK of the house, behind a door at the end of the hallway and to the left of the stairs. Nobody in it now. Another door opens onto a small porch at the rear right-hand corner of the building where boots, bicycles and wet coats are kept, and a third into a small pantry that leads to the dining room.

It has seen better and busier days—first when Phinoola Quigg ran it like an oiled engine and later when little Bridget grew into the management of it. Now though it has sagged and dust has collected in the crannies. The cracks between things are congealed with gummy residues, the corners webbed and discolored by damp. At night a strip light blinks from the ceiling. Two old gas lamps of gathered glass protrude, defunct, from the walls and the old crank telephone hangs there too, next to a mounted salt box.

The linoleum—scuffed and peeling—is one of only two things in the room, apart from utensils and such, that isn't white; it is merely near-white, streaked with veins of jade green for a marble effect, though long past looking elegant. The edge of it curls up the skirting board under a kitchen table laden with mason jars, spice tins, coffee pots and a sugar bin, and over which some copper pans, a griddle, a fly swat and two wine skins are hooked. A drum of flour on the floor keeps the lino at bay. Next to the table, an ancient Hoosier cabinet.

In the pantry behind, another old cabinet with an array of doors and drawers so scatty and irregular as to make the use of it intimidating and which hasn't been opened for years. At its side an old iron grille food safe has been made a vegetable rack and smells of potato must. On top of that the microwave.

It's dark back there in the pantry and there is no bulb, only the dregs of fluorescent light by night and the indirect illumination that comes by day from the one bright window back out in the kitchen, a big old Belfast basin beneath it. The only other item that isn't white is the largest thing in the room and is very far from white—the kind of black that isn't just black but a black event horizon, that doesn't just fail to reflect light but seems to suck it in.

The monstrous old Glenfield range was Phinoola Quigg's domain; it hogs most of the outer wall so its over-sized flue doesn't have far to go to spew its exhaust into the open air. If anyone can claim to have seen a wave of true pleasure roll across the housekeeper's face, and that is doubtful, she will have been looking at this machine at the time.

She was the pilot and this was her cockpit. For as long as she lived in this house, no other hand was to touch it. Every morning of that life she would stand before it, hands on hips before firing it up, and admire it: the heavy-hinged oven door with its two pull-handle latches behind which, usually, a baby animal of some kind roasted, the broiler above it and the boiler beside with a tiny tap for running off hot water. Of the black ceramic levers that regulated gas flow to the six burners, she was particularly fond, often finger-ing them needlessly. There was something validating, for her, in the other oven. A second oven: something of which she had never had the temerity to dream.

The bread warmer that scented the kitchen.

The plate rack.

The sauce shelf for her gravies.

By the side of the black giant she kept a tiny, three-legged stool and would sit there when not laboring elsewhere, to keep an eye on the machine as it boiled and fumed and to make sure the Flimsy woman got nowhere near it. She was capable of sitting there for a long, long time without needlework or scripture to occupy her mind. No pea splitting or potato peeling—just sitting and listening to the rumble that came from somewhere within the heavy plates of hot black iron, which once in a while she would pat like a mother on the leg of a dozing child, to keep it that way and to ward off the anxiety that its stillness gives rise to.

It was a skill that came in handy as Emma grew and began to spend time outside the confines of the home and the housekeeper's direct supervision, particularly as the girl embarked upon her puberty and began to produce scents for the attraction of boys. Her absences were a taunt for Phinoola Quigg who had a habit of imagining the worst; it was from that stool that she would endure them, upright and measuring time. No matter how qui-etly Emma, on her return from a school dance or a birthday party, would shut the front gate, Phinoola Quigg would hear its click and leave her post, intercepting the girl at the front door to get a good look at any escort there might be and to make sure there were no shenanigans on the veranda.

※

Patrice Maypole knew just how to jive. A strange, rangy boy and never any good with girls, in his later years he would somehow raise a son—much to the consternation of the Ladies' Association, who were pretty sure that none of *them* had facilitated. He did well, it has to be said, to carve out any kind of life for himself, since from cradle to grave, nobody but the boy would have any idea what he was talking about and, despite the fact that a good nature shone through in his behavior, he was generally shunned by the opposite sex—occupying himself instead with pigeon trapping and the whittling of twigs.

But the boy could dance; there was no two ways about it. Grown-ups would attend the annual ball—for which girls were shipped in from Nutherham, a girl-heavy village about half a day upriver—just to watch him throw their delighted daughters around the schoolhouse, desks pushed back against the walls and Agatha Pinch a surprisingly lively pianist. Patrice was an impeccable chicken walker. His throwaway was out of sight. Furthermore, none of the older boys could match his mooch.

And it wasn't just the jive; young Mr Maypole was equally adept in the Pasa Doble, the Tango and the Lindy Hop. Any number of styles, in fact—they all came effortlessly to him and so, although disdained elsewhere and never for a single second considered beau material, he was a popular dance date and would be Emma's first.

Neither her father nor Phinoola Quigg would have considered allowing her to attend at the tender age of twelve, but for all her antiquity Ms Pinch was still a force in the village and wouldn't play a note unless she felt she had sufficient numbers. It was therefore generally understood that her pupils would show up at these things or send a cast iron excuse—something in the way of a bereavement or debilitating head injury—and so Emma found herself breaking quite the sweat in her efforts to keep up with Patrice who, well aware of his linguistic limitations, danced right through every tune played and through the gaps between them too.

Danced Emma to her coat hook afterwards and danced her across the yard outside and up along the river. Danced her past the Bennetts' house and past the Flemings' letterbox and uphill in a swirl of quickstep and cha cha cha. Waltzed her through the garden gate, and danced her down the garden path where she could finally take a breath, a little too flushed and busy being dizzy to be intimidated by Phinoola Quigg's crossed-armed frown on the porch.

"Foxtrotting, is it?" said the housekeeper, not removing her eyes from Patrice for a moment as she detached him from Emma and pushed the girl into the hallway before any sentimentalities could arise between the two.

"And you call that a feather step?"

She needn't have worried. Emma had enjoyed herself, to a degree, but couldn't be said to have picked up anything like experience in the ways of courting; in fact she came away from that first date under the distinct impression that the company of young men was largely a matter of centripetal force. Practical-minded girl that she was, she simply ticked the encounter, and Patrice Maypole, off her list. A stone jumped, a piece taken, and merely the first in a series of moves—none of which would bring her any of the satisfaction she found on her black and white board, at a desk in the sunlight with Agatha Pinch.

That was the year that Devyn Butters' riverside masturbations began. By the time the next ball came round, Emma was a dab hand, having come to regard the activity as a disciplinary measure and herself as an accomplished boy tamer. No fewer than seven of the young men at the dance that evening were to feel the benefit of her newly acquired expertise, as a consequence of which her tumbler of red lemonade and vanilla ice cream floater was kept topped up throughout. The resulting ice cream mustache would drive young Oldman Stodder—Emma's actual date and one of the few there she didn't get round to draining—so wild with lust that the poor boy, who had never felt it before and didn't know what to do with it, made a spectacle of himself on the floor behind the piano.

Although she was to remain very busily occupied with the juicing of boys, getting to know one to any appreciable degree eluded her. The Stodder debacle very much set the tone for subsequent dates—a series of clownish disappointments—and males were to remain a lifelong riddle.

It was always going to be that way for Emma; the girl had nobody to turn to for advice. No one could have been less available than Rose Wakeling and her father was worse than useless, invariably referring her to scripture with his eyes firmly on the picture rail, or doling out some laborious household folly to 'cool her blood'. Phinoola Quigg refused point blank to discuss shenanigans and at the merest mention of them would retreat to the kitchen and to the old sink under the window there. The number of times, in any given day, that the housekeeper would wash her hands in that sink—whether to rinse them of flour or of some perceived affront to her decency—was extremely high. There is still a worn spot on the lino where she stood and a discernible thinning of the basin's enamel where she leaned. She can almost be seen there still, hands held under the spout of water and head straight, looking not out of the window but at the gingham curtains which covered it and which she never opened. They are faded now, sun-bleached of their pale blue check.

They were bright and clean the day Emma, just a few days after her sixteenth birthday, met her mother. It was the first time she'd been allowed in the kitchen.

The pastor, who liked to think of himself as an open-minded man had, as part of his ongoing efforts with the county's wayward women, turned to psychology. He had been leafing through a copy of Dr Hans Sittlichkeit's *Mother Abandonment: causes, symptoms and role in the development of the contemporary strumpet* and one or two of the eminent scholar's theories had struck a little close to home. As Phinoola Quigg was fussing about him one afternoon in his study, wiping pristine surfaces and rearranging decorative items, he put his quill down.

"I would like your advice, Phinoola Quigg."

"Would you indeed?" asked the housekeeper and stopped her dusting.

"Yes. I've been reading this book—"

"Have you indeed?"

"Yes. And it says here—"

"Does it indeed?"

"Does it . . . ? But I haven't . . . The book is about girls, Phinoola Quigg, and how we might, with the use of cutting edge scientifical interventions, go about the prevention of their loosening."

"Well, isn't that nice?"

"Yes, let me just . . . The point is, Phinoola Quigg, that I am of the opinion that some of the theories presented by Dr Sittlichkeit—"

"Are you now?"

" . . . may pertain, indeed may pertain very closely, to our own situation, and—"

"*Our* situation?" The housekeeper clasped her hands.

"The situation in this house, yes. The long and the short of it is that according to modern science, it would seem that young Emma would almost certainly be the better for it if she had rather more to do with her mother than is currently the case. Rigorous studies have shown as much."

"Have they indeed? It all sounds very clever, doesn't it?"

"At the very least, I think a formal introduction is called for, don't you? That is the matter upon which I would like to consult you. The fact is, I don't know how to go about it. I haven't seen the woman since last October, although there is not the slightest doubt in my mind," and here the pastor's voice became shrill as his eyes darted around the room, "that she is listening."

"Right, and I suppose that'll be my job, will it?"

"I am asking for your help, Phinoola Quigg. It is, as always, very much appreciated."

One of the housekeeper's hands went up to keep a strand of undisciplined hair in check.

"I suppose it might be helpful of me, then, to mention that the lady of the house does participate, from time to time, in the preparation of legumes?"

"Does she? Does she now? Well, there's our opportunity. Can we have legumes with lunch today?"

"It isn't Monday today? The day we have carrots?"

"I see. We'll have to do it tomorrow then. If you—"

"We're not to have soup and crackers, is that it? As we always do on a Tuesday? I'm to put them in the bin, am I?"

"Yes, perhaps you might just tell me when we're next having legumes, Phinoola Quigg."

She had her hands clasped again.

"It would shock and appall you to learn, would it, Pastor, that the regular Saturday morning broad bean delivery is expected on Saturday morning?"

Charles Wakeling slapped his knees and stood, bringing the exchange to as decisive a close as he could.

"Saturday it is!"

When Saturday came and Emma awoke, the housekeeper had been in her room and laid out an outfit on the back of a chair, having gotten it into her head that when meeting her mother for the first time, a girl should look as girlish as possible. There was a powder blue, puff-sleeved dress with a white pinafore, a matching headband and socks and, under the chair, a pair of plain black ankle strap shoes. The adolescent was dismayed but sufficiently intrigued to go along with it all.

Nothing was said at breakfast. Afterwards the pastor went for a walk. Emma sat on the chaise in the hallway and waited to see what might happen. Phinoola Quigg could be heard rolling dough in the kitchen and at half past ten the vegetable man turned up in his cart and left the delivery box at the back door—Emma could hear the housekeeper remonstrating with him there. At eleven, her father returned and went straight into the kitchen, quickly coming out again and planting himself in front of his daughter.

"Come with me, Emma."

She stood and followed the pastor to the kitchen door. When he pushed it open and beckoned to her to go in, she hesitated on the threshold, momentarily blinded by the brightness that came pouring into the gloomy hallway.

She timidly put one of her feet into the new space, and then the other. Her father closed the door behind them. Her eyes adjusted to the light.

She had imagined it many times, putting it together with bits of kitchens she had seen in other houses, wondering often about all the marvelous things in it that she would so much like to see. Here it was, even more beautiful to her eyes than it had been in her mind. A fresh, white world—quite the opposite of the house she knew—resplendent and smelling of bread. Flowers leaned out of a jar on the bottom shelf of the dresser and the crockery above them gleamed. Against the blue and white glare of the window was the silhouette of a woman. Her father placed himself beside it and looked at the ceiling. She could see up his nose.

"Emma, this is your mother."

Rose Wakeling turned around slowly and Emma got her first look. Her mother was an amiable looking woman with round, rosy cheeks and stray hair at either temple where it had come loose from her bun. Wiping a hand on her apron, she held it out towards the girl.

"Emma, how nice to see you," she said through a broad smile, eyes narrowed to slits. "How are you today?"

"I'm very well, mother," said Emma. She curtsied. "Thank you for asking. How are you?"

"Very busy with these broad beans," beamed the woman, "so if you'll excuse me," and she turned back to the basin. Phinoola Quigg, who was sitting by the range with the beans in a bowl on her lap, rolled her eyes.

Emma looked from her father to the housekeeper, to her mother's back, wondering what to say. There was a silence, broken by Phinoola Quigg who—noting the tremulous shoulders framed by the window and the white knuckles on the rim of the sink—stood, put the bowl of beans down on the table, took Emma by the shoulder to guide her back towards the door, and looked at the pastor.

"Enough?"

Emma Lapel

ARRYING SILKY LAPEL—my third husband—was, with the benefit of hindsight and the best will in the world, not a very good idea.

"Table manners!"

His first words to me. We were both guests at a luncheon at the Anthony's. The village had a new milliner, a Mr Bouchier who hailed from Ampleton and was sprucing up local heads with his urban chic creations; Thomas Anthony and his wife Barbara had wasted no time in arranging the get-together, which to all intents and purposes would be an interrogation. The Antennae, was the clandestine nomenclature, such was the fishmongering couple's sensitivity to environmental change of any kind. Mr Lapel, a solicitor by profession, had only moved to the county a week or so before the hatter and was also to be scrutinized.

I was at a loss as to what I had done to offend. Mr Lawter, owner of the general store, wouldn't lift his eyes from his plate. Neither would Mrs Sutton. Ms Tradshame was looking intently at me as if in an effort to determine exactly what it was she ought to disapprove of.

"No, no," said Mr Lapel. "Not at all, Mrs Harsykes. Not at all."

He took the bowl of buttered corn that Mescaline Stroop held out to him and helped himself to seventeen kernels, one at a time.

"No. I meant generally," he said, passing it on and accepting a sliver of boiled bacon from the lady of the house. "So important, don't you think?"

There were nods of accord, not only from myself but from the company in general.

"I have undertaken to make an authority of myself on the subject and will be pleased to share my findings here, for the overall improvement of village life."

Barbara Anthony's face was the same color as the beetroot Mr Lawter was shoveling onto his side plate.

"Oh, Mr Lapel, I do hope you don't find us coarse! You must take us to task *instantly* if you find any of our country ways at all denigrating," she said, trying very hard not to look at the shopkeeper who, having amassed a quantity of beetroot, was putting some bacon in his pocket.

"I wasn't alluding to any deficiency in the manners on display around *this* table, Mrs Anthony," said Mr Lapel, casting his eyes slowly and deliberately over each guest and their cutlery. "To do so would be impolite."

He was polishing his knife.

"However, it just so happens that I am currently putting together a pamphlet for the ignorant which I intend to distribute locally and the contents of which I would be delighted to outline here. As long," and here he bowed in acknowledgment of his hostess (Mr Anthony was busy fashioning a kind of sandwich from two slices of steamed turnip and a smear of parsley sauce), "as nobody objects."

Nobody did.

"Very well. There are a number of requirements pertaining to arrival and reception, of course, but my expertise is limited to that which takes place once guests are seated, so I shall begin there."

He put his knife back in its place and straightened it.

"Before a meal commences, a firm resolve to enjoy it should be unanimously expressed. Men's hats must never be worn at the table. Ladies' hats may be worn as long as it is daytime and the wearer is visiting. The occupant of the hat should, of course, be a lady. Pocket-sized telephones and other distractors must be put away. Reading is permitted at breakfast only."

He picked his knife up again and took to his bacon with it. The others waited for him to continue, none of them mustering the nerve to lift a finger. Mr Bouchier, in so far as such a thing was possible with a bonnet-style turban of blue and green taffeta, wide-rimmed in shirred silk and gathered velvet and adorned with any number of tiny bells, quietly removed his hat.

"The meal commences when a dish is served to the angriest person present. The dish—normally a small oval saucer of wilted greens—is then passed to the tallest person, followed by the most frequently jilted, the freckliest, the rudest and so on. The most sarcastic dinner guest should be the last served and should make a remark. Ideally, there would then follow a devotional sing-along."

At this point I fancied that Mr Lapel was looking rather fixedly at me.

"Neither food nor fellow diners should ever be touched with the palm of the hand. Candlesticks should be put away during daylight hours. Reaching is unacceptable. Spitting is—"

He broke off, eyes still on me. I glanced to either side but nobody would look back at me, so I put my cutlery down. Mr Lapel had done the same.

"You are from South Korea, perhaps, Mrs Harsykes?"

I told him that I most certainly was not and inquired as to what had put the idea in his head.

"In the Kyongsanbuk-do province in the south east of that country, I am told, it is considered perfectly benign to hold one's fork with the tines pointed at a fellow diner. Even," he said, resuming the slicing of his meat, "in what passes for polite society there."

Well. You can imagine. I was utterly besotted. Having emerged childless from two disastrous marriages, here, finally was a man to whom I might entrust the education of my offspring. As soon as was physically possible— about twenty minutes after pudding was served, around the corner from the Anthony cottage and behind the village well—I masturbated him. We were married within the month.

Having brought the gentleman and his encyclopedic grasp of seemliness back to live in the house, I very much looked forward to his impregnating me and was expecting that etiquette would continue to be a preoccupation for him in the matrimonial home. Finding this not to be the case, and that he had quite different interests, was the first of three disappointments which were to doom our union.

One evening very soon after the wedding, we were preparing to excuse ourselves from the dining table. Little Bridget had cleared everything away; she was so tiny then that it had taken her quite a while. Father never would join us for dinner and displayed an aversion to Silky—I suppose I ought to have paid more attention to that. As we stood, my husband addressed me.

"Tell me, Mrs Lapel, do you like knickers?"

I'll admit to a moment's hesitation before replying.

"I couldn't claim to have given the matter any thought," I said. "They serve a purpose. I like them better than I'd like their absence, I dare say."

He smiled that serious smile of his.

"*I* like them. I like them *very* much."

"Do you?"

Placing his hands on the table, knuckles down, he leaned towards me a little.

"Would you like to see *my* knickers?"

I was minded to decline, but he had already turned and gone to the sideboard, from which he retrieved a black leather portfolio. He came back to the table, opening it in my direction and revealing the contents—a sizable collection of ladies' underwear. Many different kinds, displayed side by side and pinned to the case as bugs might be to a board behind glass in a natural history exhibit.

"Since you are a lady," he said, "you may choose."

I looked from the portfolio to my husband.

"I'm not sure I have an opinion, Mr Lapel."

But he insisted and so I indicated a pair which, if I'm honest, had rather caught my eye with their zebra stripes and fine lace trimmings.

"*Very* good. An *excellent* choice," he said. "Please wait for me in the parlor."

Presuming his little game to have come to an end and in the habit of going to the parlor after dinner on most evenings, I had my knitwork to hand and went there. About ten minutes later, Mr Lapel joined me, silently entering the room and going to the arm of the sofa opposite my seat, over which he bent to rest his face on the upholstery. He wore nothing but the knickers I had selected.

"Tell me, wife," he said, his voice a little muffled, "can you see my testicles when I do this?"

I looked up from my latest project—a dishcloth for Bridget—and responded.

"Yes, I'm afraid I can."

"Good," he said. "I *want* you to see them. I want you to look *right at* them."

He remained in that posture for the rest of the evening, silent save for a kind of baby noise he made by chewing on a cushion, and that every once in a while he would ask me if I was still staring at his testicles. I would assure him that I was, although in truth I was concentrating on my zigzag stockinette.

The knicker scenario was to become a daily one.

"Can you see the tip?" he asked me the following evening, bent over the sofa and sporting the plain pair of white panties I had chosen for him. I looked.

"Yes, I can. It has popped out of the cotton, there at the side."

I very strongly suspected that he had popped it out himself.

"Good. I'm *glad*. I'm *glad* you can see the tip," he said and soon afterwards fell asleep.

One day, on Mr Lapel's return from the small office above the general store which he rented from Mr Lawter, he was not alone.

"Wife," he said to me in a decidedly formal tone, stepping aside and raising his hand to indicate his companion on the veranda, "this is Betsy."

Betsy was the second disappointment. Dressed in a billowing summer dress in a tropical print and a simple straw sun hat with a red ribbon round the rim, he was a tall, hirsute gentleman and quite astonishingly overweight. I couldn't tell you much about his face, concealed as it was behind an unkempt beard, and he said nothing, instead offering me the back of a hairy and meticulously manicured hand.

"Betsy and I are members of a club."

Without further explanation, the enormous man moved in and I soon enough grew accustomed to their sitting together on the chaise in the hallway with their portfolios, fondling one another's knickers and gasping with delight. In the evenings, Mr Lapel continued to exhibit himself and Betsy, though he never said a word, appeared to enjoy my husband's performances, giggling and applauding throughout. One small advantage, I suppose, of having him there was that I could get on with my knitting.

As that strange summer began to cool, Bridget came to me in the kitchen one morning before breakfast to tell me she wasn't sure if all was well with Mr Lapel. Once she'd rinsed her hands—the onions on the back patch were ready and she'd been out there for a few mornings digging them up—she took mine and led me into the hallway. There they were, side by side on the chaise and slumped over each other, Betsy's narcotical paraphernalia in his lap.

Very, very disappointing.

The Study

AT THE SIDE of the house, off a little passage behind the dining room. From it, a deep bay window gives out onto some rose bushes and a bird table, long left bare but lately tended once again by Noranbole, who leaves a fresh net of nuts and seeds hanging there whenever she remembers. The room is bright for an hour or two, depending on the time of year, in the midmorning and otherwise dim. Despite the locked door, the dust that Phinoola Quigg had once expunged has reclaimed the room. The smells of bee's wax and pipe tobacco linger, but the must of the heavy damask curtain predominates.

Behind the door is a bookcase with two glass doors that protect the pastor's most treasured tomes: Solomon Allport's *Fighting Fire With Fire in The Age Of Lust*, the much-thumbed *Illustrated Book of Trollops*, Gaspar Spurt's *Phrenology of the Minx* and so on. The hickory wood of the case is handsome against the vermilion wallpaper, still just visible behind a plethora of framed prints, proverbs and axioms that meanders from there to the window wall. In the far corner a reclining chair, low and deep with a single velveret cushion.

The window wall too is crowded with frames. Amid them hangs a very poor quality lithograph of Giorgione's Sleeping Venus. The beauty lies dormant on the robes she has removed, one hand covering a hairless vulva. On the frame below the picture a little brass plaque put there by the pastor himself and bearing the legend, "You Are Expected Not To Admire This".

The glare of the window on a sunny morning assaults. While Emma was growing up her father would sit in the light, undazzled where anyone else would have been dizzy and bewildered. He had had the desk and chair raised on a six inch dais so that he could enjoy a more commanding view from the window, over the rose bushes and down a short garden to where a treeline described the course of a stream overgrown with rushes. There is a plot of land that belongs to the house on the other side of that stream and Charles had plans for it.

The desk is a mahogany kneehole with a writing slope in the middle, covered in worked leather and flanked on either side by flat surfaces where he kept his various odds and ends—a spike for documents dealt with, some spare ink bottles, notebooks and a vase for his quills. On a raised shelf behind the work surface he kept a phrenology head and a craniometer, a few reference books and a figurine of Lot's wife, fashioned from rock salt. If the old Glenfield in the kitchen was Phinoola Quigg's flight deck, this was his.

The chair is made of walnut wood; a single, steam-bent piece forms both the convex backrest and the high arms. Four tiny castors made it easy for the pastor to push himself back, away from the desk along a short runway that stretches out into the center of the room. This is the position he would take up for periods of contemplation. In the light and long after it, when Phinoola Quigg had snuck in and lit the green glass lamp on the corner table, his chin would drop to his chest and his bony hands would droop from the arms, or find each other and lock fingers.

Eyes shut, he would fill the air above him with a motley procession of the debauched. A great spinning crowd in the dark around his head—till he could hear the whoosh of them passing—of the characters that populated his sermons. The Nell Gwyns and the Madame du Barry's, Polly Adler and the Empress of Byzantium, Cassandra, Su Xiaoxiao and Calamity Jane; they would swirl about him in a torment of chatter and mockery till, one by one, he had the better of them. A great storm-tamer, quelling the squall, subduing the disturbances, his lips rising at the corners of his mouth until such time as the housekeeper rapped him roughly on the shoulder to tell him his supper was getting cold.

❋

Following the encounter in the kitchen, Emma was not to speak to her mother again. There would be glimpses—the whip of a skirt in a doorway or a movement in the garden through the dining room window, as if Rose was a little less concerned, having endured the girl face to face, to render herself wholly invisible. That she might make an occasional and fleeting impression on Emma pleased the pastor's wife; it was another way to bequeath a little of herself to her daughter. But to speak to the girl or to be properly seen—these things would never be possible for her. Emma returned to the dry and sparse companionship of Phinoola Quigg and the odd proscriptive exchange with her father.

Charles Wakeling was quite another matter. He may have failed to stimulate a seemly relationship between his wife and daughter, but his reserves of patience for the extraordinary domestic circumstance in which he found himself a participant had been drained dry; he was therefore more resolute in his insistence that the lady of the house at least make herself available from time to time to her husband, even if only that brief connubial greetings could be exchanged and that, in the name of common decency, the flagellations which had petered out long before might be reinitiated. To this end, he applied various different kinds of pressure to Phinoola Quigg, with whose resulting assistance it became the case that, once in a while and with the assurance that Emma was out of the house and the hour of her return known with absolute certainty, Rose would show herself.

Thus it was that day. Charles sat motionless on the edge of his walnut chair—quill hovering above a sheet of paper that had remained blank for some time—ostensibly considering a sermon but poised in fact to intervene in the event of an escape attempt. It was not a flagellating occasion. The pastor had instead decided it would befit and uplift the process of his sermon writing to have his lady wife seated nearby, silent but supportive as he had imagined it in his youth. The wife in question was indeed sitting near him, beside herself in the distress that staying still caused her, never mind reclining in the only other chair available. She was making a show of leafing through her old gingham book but in fact her attention was entirely taken up by the business of regulating her shallow, panicked breaths. One of which escaped her as a squeak when Phinoola Quigg entered the room, unannounced and rather abruptly, and began to pace back and forth between the pastor (stock still) and the door she had left ajar.

"Well isn't this a fine thing?"

She had her bottom lip in her teeth and her hands were writhing all over one another.

"A pretty pickle, wouldn't you say?"

Out of a sense of duty, or perhaps to justify her presence, she would swerve to adjust the lamp on the corner table at each pass.

"I suppose it's my own fault, is it? Isn't it always?"

Charles Wakeling was a statue of himself, even as the housekeeper lurched at him repeatedly and came menacingly close before turning away towards the lamp.

"And what'll become of me, I ask you? How am I to live?"

If the quick-breathed Rose had been beside herself before Phinoola Quigg's explosive entrance, she was now a good two feet further to the left, and flirting with hyperventilation. A loose strand of her fine hair was lifted by the whoosh of skirt and her head swiveled tennis-style and wild-eyed as the other woman continued to accelerate.

"Sure don't we get what we deserve?" spat the housekeeper. "Isn't it only right that I'm to be punished?"

She had finally come to a halt, midway between the pastor and the lamp, but was swaying like a metronome, her hands still busy with each other. Rose had sat up straight and felt as though someone ought to say something. There was a pause, during which she realized it was going to be her.

"Well," she began, "I'm . . . it can't—"

"Oh, *can't* it?" said Phinoola Quigg. "*Can't* it indeed?" Her eyes were on the pastor.

"Well we could . . . oh I don't know. You see, the thing is . . . I'm afraid I'm in . . . you've rather lost me, you see . . . but I'm sure that whatever it is," Rose looked to the back of her husband's head for support that was unforthcoming, "we could . . ."

"Mother of God, ma'am, have you no cop on in that noggin of yours at all? Is it not as obvious as the hair on mine?" She was still wringing her hands and her eyes were squeezed shut.

"Amn't I only going to have a feckin *baby*?"

She sobbed.

"Oh my goodness!" said Rose, rising to her feet and, not knowing what to do when she got there, sitting again.

"My goodness! Surely we should . . . I mean, the *responsibility* . . . don't you think? Yes, we *must*. I can think of no other course . . . but who is it, Phinoola Quigg? You *must* be brave and tell us. Who is the father?"

There followed a fairly lengthy silence. Phinoola Quigg was the one to break it.

"Sure didn't he come in the night, ma'am?"

She looked from Rose to the pastor, who had picked up his craniometer and was using it to measure something on his phrenology head.

"And wasn't he gone in a flash?"

One of Rose's hands had instinctively gone to the neckline of her dress.

"Gracious!"

She blessed herself.

"What a thing! Oh, how awful for you! You poor dear! Charles, we must stand by our wretched housekeeper! Won't you sit awhile, Phinoola Quigg?"

She had risen again and gestured towards the chair in an apparent show of consideration. In fact, since there wasn't another, she had spotted a potential exit strategy.

"*Sit*, ma'am?"

The housekeeper was aghast.

"*Sit?* And it only an hour till teatime?"

She wiped the tears from her cheeks and straightened her perfectly straight apron.

"The leeks will wash themselves, will they? The dough is this very minute putting itself in the oven, I suppose? Chickens chop themselves and hop into pots of their own accord around here, is that it?"

She seemed to have regained her composure.

"Sitting? Is it sitting I came here to do, following . . . *him*," here she pointed at the back of Charles Wakeling, "halfway round the world? I traipsed across the grasslands and waded through the marshes, did I, to come here and sit?"

And she was gone, the door shut.

Disappointed by the turn of events, Rose sat back down and opened the gingham book. The pastor had replaced the craniometer and once again had a quill at the ready.

"I hope you don't . . . Charles . . . but I thought we should . . . in fact, I think we *must* . . . that is, if you don't . . ."

"Oh no," said the pastor, without looking up. "Yes. No, no."

"Because I really *do* think it's absolutely . . . the right . . ."

The nib above the page. The shoulders up.

"No. Yes, yes. Quite."

✳

"Neptunia House, Phinoola Quigg!"

Charles Wakeling smacked his hands together and rubbed them with the glee he felt whenever he talked of his pet project. He was at his desk and as he spoke his eyes were wide and on the line of trees which obscured the little plot of land behind them. Covering the desk, architectural drawings—the work of a fancy Small Town architect by the name of Mandakranta Schjødt—with scribbles wherever the churchman intended to propose adjustments. There were many; Neptunia House had become something of an obsession and the pastor was frequently inspired with ideas to improve it. He would sit up late into the night, formulating suggestions for the architect, and was often back at it before breakfast. Mr Schjødt, for his part, had recently taken up smoking.

"It's going to have it all, Phinoola Quigg! State of the art! No stone left unturned in our effort to purge those poor souls of their vampish hook-erisms!"

He drew his finger lovingly over the ground floor blueprint.

"The spacious dining room, the kitchen, a study for myself, a common room for approved gatherings, the sensory room . . ."

Here he turned to his housekeeper.

"Sensory therapies are fully endorsed by the National Federation of Tarts, Phinoola Quigg, so we must have as many of them as we can and they should be very sensory indeed!"

Returning to the diagram, he enumerated the remaining ground floor facilities:

"The Modulation Room—differently shaped lamps, Phinoola Quigg, that change color. That'll fix 'em! The Tickle Chamber—self-explanatory. The Plume Room—I'm going to fill that one with . . ." The pastor paused to catch his breath and take a sip from the glass of water on his desk, " . . . ostrich feathers."

It had been months since Phinoola Quigg's announcement and she was quite far gone now but still wouldn't brook the suggestion that she share her workload. She was by the bookcase, polishing the perfect panes of glass. Talk of Neptunia House never failed to invigorate and intensify her efforts.

"Sarah Twelves will live there, will she?"

"She will."

"And Martha Dewey?"

"Yes."

"And Fiona Withingham?"

"Yes."

"And Hillary Peck?

"Oh, definitely."

"And Fidelma Leete?"

"Ha! I can think of no better place for that little terrier, can you?"

"And Theodora Metcalfe?"

"I should think so."

"And Bernadette McGilvery?"

"Yes."

"And Dora Jude?"

The pastor slammed his fist down on the desk.

"Damnation! Blast it all to hell!"

He had also flung his quill away but, being a quill, it had merely fallen at his feet and he bent down now to retrieve it.

"My apologies for the outburst, Phinoola Quigg. You'll excuse me, I hope."

He substituted the ground floor plan for that of the upper floor, where the bedrooms were, and searched it for a place where he might make a change.

"I'd forgotten about Dora."

He took a ruler and penciled in a line, instantly creating a minuscule bedroom.

"Just think of it, Phinoola Quigg! All of 'em together under one roof, at the bottom of the garden!" He sat back in his chair and allowed himself a moment of self-satisfaction. "Insourcing. My ministrations will be ten times as effective under this new arrangement. Fortunate souls! A great day for them, when we turn the key in that door for the first time!"

"And for you?" said the housekeeper, wearing away at the glass.

"Oh yes. I can put that awful bicycle away for once and for all."

Phinoola Quigg put her duster down and folded her arms. She smiled broadly, her face a picture of good-natured amiability.

"Won't you only be in your *element*, father?" The grin expanding. "All those floozies, and you?"

"Indeed I will, Phinoola Quigg. I will tend to them as to new born lambs with all the love of a devoted shepherd. They are lost, but they are God's children and as much as you do, as much as anyone does," he joined his hands behind his head, "they need a pastor."

She was back at the glass.

"A rooster, did you say?" she mumbled.

"What was that?"

"Do you not know by now, pastor, that I talk nonsense to myself as I work?"

"Yes. I see."

"Should you not be getting back to your plans? For the hen house?"

"The hen . . . I think you mean Neptunia House, Phinoola Quigg?" Charles Wakeling was sitting up straighter.

"Was that the name? Sure what would I know? It wouldn't be my place, would it, as a domestic, to go calling a thing what it is?"

"Phinoola Quigg!" He was on his feet. "I'm sure I don't know what has come over you!"

"Or *who*, Pastor?" The hands were back in their most threatening position—on hips.

"Good gracious, woman! You are hormonal!" He indicated her belly. "You are not to blame, of course. I absolve you of this—"

"Absolve me? *Absolve* me? I'll absolve your feckin—"

But they were both interrupted by the sound of a snapping twig on the ground outside the window and a ripping noise as something pulled free of the rose bushes. Charles went to the window. He could see nothing but a sliver of gingham fluttering in the breeze.

"Someone was listening!"

"Really?" said the housekeeper, turning to go back to the kitchen.

"Now who could that have been?"

Emma Harsykes

Y MARRIAGE TO Edwyn Harsykes, coming in the wake of such tragedy, initially offered the promise of healing and of a fresh start for me and my new charge, but it was to be struck down with the same blight that rotted away at all of my subsequent marriages—bad feeling between my father and my husband. The absence of Phinoola Quigg and of my mother made the situation all the more claustrophobic.

Edwyn was the opposite of Selwyn in so many ways. I doubt the notion of stripping a hickory to make a long bow had ever occurred to him. He'd have been hard put to tell the difference between a bowie and a drop point and was not merely uninterested in, but actively opposed to, walking in the countryside.

"God intended that we should tread only where there are paths for our feet," he would intone whenever the subject came up, as if patiently correcting an idiot child. "That's the whole *point* of paths."

He didn't even like being in the garden and forbade all talk at the dinner table that made any reference to where the meat might have come from, above and beyond the kitchen. Not that this objection arose from any sympathy with animals in general. It was more a question of disgust.

"Hairy things!" he would exclaim at the merest mention of them. "Except for snakes," he would usually concede, "but I don't like snakes either."

He was an actuary and a dyed-in-the-wool indoors man and felt the need not just to declare the preference but regularly to argue the case.

"Have you ever had need of an umbrella in the spare bedroom?" he would reason. "Or been forced to take shelter from a gale in the kitchen? I think not. That's the whole *point* of spare bedrooms and kitchens."

He left himself open, I suppose, to allegations of dullness, but I found the contrast between him and my first husband a comfort and even took solace, initially, in the obvious and visceral hostility that arose between Edwyn and my father, since the latter's infatuation with Selwyn had had such catastrophic consequences. It must also be said that, despite not being a particularly empathetic gentleman, he was consistently kind and considerate with regard to my duties towards Bridget.

The child now found itself at the very center of my world. Though not mine, the burden of its guardianship weighed heavily on my young shoulders. Such a thing, to look into the blue emptiness of a baby's eyes and to know, to physically *feel*, that they do not merely look back but rather drink you in, or to run one's fingertips over the perfect softness of its skin and know that the peachy membrane is permeable, that it sucks up everything around it, including you, that it *takes* you, and that therefore you are present in the very bedrock of another person.

Cognitive, intellectual, moral—there was no escaping the imperative. I therefore embarked with utmost diligence on the most serious project of my life thus far: to guide the child, that wondrously open and receptive little creature, as safely and quickly as I could towards the competencies and philosophies that would equip her for a life—the life to which she was destined—of toil and drudgery.

The moment she was old enough to crawl I made knee pads for her, and mittens and shoes of chamois leather that she might be of some use in the polishing of the parquet floor, that she might glean a little pride from her work even at so young an age and, since she was wobbly, a little hat too. Mr Harsykes was a worthy accomplice—he bought Bridget a little pink carpet sweeper and a toy shovel that she might begin to familiarize herself with the necessary objects. I believe he was as proud as I was the day we heard, from the side of her cot—bedecked with a tinkling mobile of kitchen implements—the first word to come from her mouth.

Mop.

Who knows how it might have gone if Bridget had been the only one with whom we shared our home? But there was father too. Always father. I remember a day when Edwyn came to me, in the evening. I was keeping vigil by Bridget's work pen, playing an audio cassette to her—a recording of a lecture given by Colleen McObair to the Board of Indentured Minions on the correct inculcation of hireling spawn.

Mrs McObair's lecture was itemized and in alphabetical order and we had reached the letter 'm'—I recall it very clearly as I had just that moment been impressed with Bridget's pronunciation of *mangle*. Mr Harsykes entered without knocking—an omission he only ever made when agitated.

"Mrs Harsykes. You have locked the study, again."

"Good evening, Mr Harsykes," I said, rising to my feet and reminding him of the niceties. "I can assure you, as I have assured you on several past occasions, that I concern myself with neither the locking nor indeed the unlocking of the study door. You might consider the possibility of my father's having manipulated the lock as you describe, since both it and the key are his."

It was the same as ever; at the mention of my father, my husband became incensed. It was always either that or a look of total bewilderment, as if he simply could not accept the presence of my parent. Never mind that it was my father's house, and his roof under which we lived! On this particular occasion, my husband's face boiled a deep red and his eyes bulged.

"My God, woman! You're insufferable!" he said and left, slamming the door behind him.

I mention the incident merely to illustrate the toxicity to our marriage of Mr Harsyke's irrational hatred of my father and to point out a curious habit of his: that of attributing responsibility for whatever action or attitude of the pastor's he found offensive, directly to me. It was something which, I'm afraid to say, I found not quite respectable, or manly, in him. In any case, the question of the negative effect that their little feud may or may not have had on our domestic life in the long run became academic when, soon afterwards, our marriage came to a sudden end in a manner which, if I'm to be fair to Mr Harsykes, did rather validate the position he had taken so often on the shortcomings of the outdoors. He had only stepped outside the kitchen door to fetch a broom from the back porch and came off the worse in an unlikely but nevertheless fatal altercation between himself and a bad-tempered bobcat that had been napping there.

The Dining Room

"Isn't it my sad duty to inform you, Pastor, that the lady of the house is missing?"

Phinoola Quigg had pulled the weighty curtains to exclude the bulk of the early afternoon light, leaving enough of a gap to allow a single sunbeam to bathe the pastor's newspaper. He liked to be the first to seat himself for lunch—ostensibly to prepare that day's castigation for Emma; in fact he usually spent the time catching up on celebrity gossip. The portrait of his young, weeping grandfather hung where it still hangs, in the shadows on the wall behind him, and below it the dark wood sideboard was bare save for a trio of entirely unnecessary doilies which the housekeeper laundered every four days. The one in the middle had been graced on a couple of occasions by a green glass lamp—now in the attic—and the two at either side had supported heavy silver candlesticks that had been moved to the mantle over the fireplace on the opposite wall where they now share the space with an old, tambour style mantle clock.

The fireplace was unlit—it being the height of summer—and Phinoola Quigg had the cast iron and its detailing of floral motif polished to a near shine. She'd gotten a real sparkle from the two columns of ceramic tiling which flank the insert, depicting pastoral scenes of local life: corn threshing, boating on the lake, barn raising, bog racing, wolf running and so forth. Along the back wall, opposite the bay window with its unused seat, runs a second sideboard more utilitarian in appearance, where the housekeeper would place the serving dishes for each meal. It was here that she now stood, waiting to ladle out some fish soup, with a belly so alarmingly swollen the pastor wouldn't look at it for fear he might bring on the birth and be required to do something. On hearing the housekeeper's announcement, he lowered the newspaper.

"Good Heavens! Are you sure?"

Phinoola Quigg's smile was as broad and breezy as it was incongruous with the news she had just imparted but, coincident with it, her hands went to her hips, causing the hairs on the back of the pastor's neck to stand on end.

"The pastor detects a malodor from the soup I have made for him today, perhaps?"

"What? No, no, I—"

"Some deficiency in the state of his house? Dirty floors?"

"No. No there's nothing—"

"Perhaps he doesn't recognize me, who has slaved and toiled for his comfort all these years? Who is this woman standing next to the very good smelling soup in my spotless dining room? Is that what he's asking himself?"

"Phinoola Quigg, I assure you, I—"

"Standing there, bold as brass, as if she lived here? As if she worked, and scrubbed, and cooked and brushed and washed here? As if she had the tiniest right, the slightest hope of an expectation that she had any business even being here? Do I have the gist of your train of thought, pastor?"

"Absolutely not. I merely—"

The housekeeper had crossed her feet and leaned against the sideboard with the heel of her hand, tapping it slowly with her fingers.

"Are you sure? Because if I were you, wouldn't I be only apoplectic to find a total stranger serving my soup, and telling me things? Are you not perfectly entitled, as the tenant of this house, the head of the family and a man of the cloth, to confront intruders?"

"I never meant to—"

"Who is this person? Why has she made me soup? What does she want of me? Is she going to kill me? Is that it, pastor?"

"No! No, certainly—"

His palms turned up in supplication.

"Or is it a person at all? It looks like a person but might that not be a disguise? Couldn't it just as well be a monkey? A monkey in an apron? A stupid monkey?"

"Phinoola—"

"A stupid feckin monkey? A *monkey*, am I?"

"Phinoola Quigg, I do not think you are a monkey."

"Oh well isn't that lovely? He doesn't think I'm a monkey, does he not? Isn't that just the loveliest thing you ever heard? But then what could be the cause of his hesitation here today, since we have established that I am not a monkey? Is it my work? Have I not done enough?"

"Your work is *very*—"

"Or not for long enough? Have I not yet accrued the years of service I would need to have the audacity to address the pastor? Should I work twenty more? Or as few as ten? A single decade? Could I possibly be so blessed?"

Feeling the need to take control of the conversation, Charles gripped the arms of his chair.

"OK, enough—"

But it was too late.

"Would you ever answer me a question, Pastor?"

"Of course. Fire away."

"Do I look like a fool, to you?"

"No! No, absolutely—"

"A simpleton, perhaps?"

"No, definitely—"

"The recipient of a lobotomy? A gin-addled hooer?"

"Gracious, no! I merely asked—"

"If I was sure? If I was aware of the words that were coming out of my own mouth? Tell me, have I ever given you cause to regret employing me, father?"

"Not for a—"

"You have found me to be a sinful liar of a woman?"

"Well, sinful—yes, Phinoola Quigg. Aren't we all? But, you know, sinful in an acceptable sort of—"

"An idiot, then? You lie awake at night, perhaps, worrying that I, in my idiocy, will burn the house down?"

"What? I never—"

"That the dribble falling from my open mouth will stain the carpet? That my knuckles will leave unsightly tracks on the kitchen floor?"

"Nonsense, Phinoola Quigg! You are a very able housekeeper. Please be assured that I have the utmost respect for you."

"Respect? You mean to tell me that you hold me in some kind of esteem, is that it?"

"Absolutely I do!"

"So can we not reasonably assume then, Pastor, since I stand here before you, telling you with my own God-given tongue that your wife is missing," she had turned to stir the soup but had replaced the lid and faced him again now, ladle in hand, "that she is missing?"

❋

"Your mother is missing, Emma."

The young woman stood at the opposite end of the table to her father, waiting for permission to be seated. She was rather strikingly framed by the green wallpaper that still lines the room, from waist height where the dark wood paneling ends to the picture rail overhead, casting a submarine light upon the space and a touch of the exotic to an otherwise conservative scheme, with its motifs of scarab and cobra, vulture, serpent and stylized lotus flower. Flock patterns and graphics reveal themselves by subtle distinction—there must be eight shades of green to the design, or nine, or twelve: apple on jade, on parrot on bottle, on olive, on opal, on mint. The contrast between it and Emma was all the more notable as she was dressed from head to toe in black—the badge of her widowhood. That such a young woman should have reason to dress that way troubled even the stiff-backed churchman, but he had his own particular reasons for avoiding the subject.

"How do you know?" she asked.

"Never mind that now," said the pastor, his eye on Phinoola Quigg's ladle. "The point is she's gone. I think we should look for her."

He nodded to his daughter and she sat.

"Of course," she said. "Though I can't think where she would be. Or why she would leave. She has always managed so well to abscond within the confines of the house."

"Yes, it is puzzling."

"She seemed quite a contented soul, that time I met her. Has something happened, father?"

"Good gracious, child! How indiscreet of you! I can assure you that absolutely nothing of whatever kind has *happened*, as you put it. Goodness me, to be asked such a thing by one's own daughter!"

Phinoola Quigg hoisted an eyebrow as she filled the bowl in front of the pastor and then the one in front of Emma, who kept her eyes down and said nothing.

"Isn't she wriggly though? Hasn't she always been?"

"She is a bit nervy, all right," said Charles. "I had grown accustomed to it though, since it appeared to be a permanent state." He took a spoonful of his soup and inclined his head towards the housekeeper in approval. "Very nice. Perfectly astringent."

She stepped backwards into the gloom by the sideboard and Emma ventured another thought.

"Perhaps she'll come back?"

"And why would she do that?" said a voice from the shadows before the pastor could speak. "If it is her intention to come back, perhaps someone could explain to me why she left in the first place? Is it a little dance we're doing? Are we at a ball, then? Can you both forgive me, do you think, for being so disgracefully underdressed?"

"What can have gotten into her?" asked the pastor, apparently to himself. "I thought she was happy here, after a fashion. We left her alone for the most part. If I have been a little more insistent that she sit with me from time to time, so that I might enjoy a certain matrimoniality of *ambiance* in the pursuit of a good sermon, am I at fault for that?" He shifted in his seat uncomfortably and kept his eyes on the ceiling, since Rose's spells in the study had up till this point been kept a secret from her daughter. "I don't see how it could be that, and yet there isn't anything else I can think of."

"Isn't there now?" said Phinoola Quigg. "Nothing at all?"

"Not a thing. I am utterly baffled by this latest development. Completely flummoxed." He took another spoonful of soup and when he'd swallowed it, sat back in his chair and put the spoon down, unable to concentrate on his meal. "Totally bamboozled."

"That's interesting, isn't it? I suppose you'd be surprised to hear, then, that I've been expecting it?"

"Have you, Phinoola Quigg? How so?"

"Have I not said to you, Father, that I have found her changed these past few months?"

The pastor was bolt upright in his chair.

"You most certainly have not. How changed?"

"Would it be subversive of me to comment, as a mere domestic, that I have found her sullen and obstinate in the course of her habitual food preparation activities?"

"Have you indeed?!" He looked at his daughter. "So unlike her!"

"Or that, especially in the course of the mashing of potatoes, there has been a mentioning of names?"

"Names, you say? Well! Whose names, Phinoola Quigg?"

"Surely to God it would be insolence for me to tell you, Father? A lowly drudge, such as myself? Might the pastor not prefer to venture a guess, to spare me the indelicacy?"

The churchman blinked. He appeared pale now, as if in the wake of a realization.

"Well," he said, "I suppose she might have mentioned . . . oh, I don't now . . . I suppose she *could* have mentioned . . . Dora Jude?"

Phinoola Quigg lowered her head in beatific acquiescence.

"Though I don't see what the name should mean to her," he said with a quick look in his daughter's direction, "and might there have been a reference to Bernadette McGilvery, at any point?"

"There might, and would those be the only names the pastor would suggest?"

"Hm. Fidelma Leete?"

"And?"

"Hillary Peck?"

A graceful bow and an interrogative look.

"Fiona Withingham, perhaps?"

"And?"

"Martha Dewey?"

"Yes?"

Charles Wakeling's eyes were on his daughter as he spoke.

"Sarah Twelves."

He stood.

"Emma, please bring the gig round to the front door."

❋

There was sufficient commotion in Tiny Village for the pastor and his daughter to observe it from a way off. By the time they had pulled up outside the general store, where Charles had intended to make some inquiries, the gig was surrounded by a mob of angry villagers. The Champney twins—old men now—both carried fire torches, though it was broad day light, and Mrs Tuft had her pitchfork with her.

"You'll be looking for Mrs Wakeling, Father," said Mr Lawter.

The churchman was on his feet in the gig.

"What is all this? How do you know I'm looking for my wife?"

"She came through here, Pastor, a-ravin' and a-rantin'," said Jacob Natt. "I never seen the like. Had us whipped up into the frenzied mob you see before you in no time." He took a sandwich from Mrs Natt, who stood at his elbow with a basket of them.

"Where is she now?" asked the pastor of nobody in particular, looking over their heads.

"Gone up to the Twelves place," said Mr Lawter. "She only stopped in here for some paraffin and a packet of disposable lighters."

Taking up the reins again, Charles Wakeling prepared to set off for Sarah Twelves' house, but young Oldman Stodder put a hand on the pastor's forearm to stay him.

"Better watch out, Father," he said. "This is just a subsidiary mob. The main one has gone up there to rout the witch."

"Witch?" said the pastor.

"Sorry, I meant slut."

He looked the churchman right in the eye.

"Mrs Wakeling has put us in the picture, reverend. We know all about what that vile woman has done to you. Not to mention Theodora Metcalfe. Or Hillary Peck. Or Bernadette McGilvery. Or—"

"Yes, thank you, Oldman. Well, we'd better be off."

139

"Just saying, reverend. Mind your back. We'll be praying for you, but that other lot up there might not be so compassionate. They sure didn't look compassionate when they left."

"What is he talking about, Father? I don't understand," said Emma.

"Yes, if you could just try to remain calm, Emma. I think we'll wait till all the facts are in, if that's all right with you."

She had never seen her father so shaken as they pulled away from the general store. Around the corner they came to a stop again, stuck behind the wagon of Jebediah Grout, the village deputy, who was loading his personal belongings onto it and evidently leaving town.

"Gee, I wish he'd hurry," said Emma.

"I wouldn't be in such a hurry to see him go if I were you, my dear. With him goes the last semblance of law and order." A noise from behind them made them look around. Oldman and Darryl Horse had smashed the side window of the Mr Lawter's store and were running off with electrical goods.

"They didn't waste any time," said the pastor as the deputy's wagon finally pulled away. "Better get out of here, fast."

Two miles outside the village, the Twelves house and the adjacent farm buildings were aflame. Charles tried to bring the gig in between the barn and the chicken house at the back, since there was a sizable crowd out front, but the horse got spooked so close to the blaze and came to a stop in the narrow space, where they would burn if they lingered. The pastor got down and pulled on the bridle but the animal wouldn't budge.

"And what must we do to quiet the mind?"

Emma didn't know if she could hear or was imagining the words of Phinoola Quigg, but she understood.

"Here, take this," she shouted, throwing her shawl to the pastor, who used it to cover the horse's head. Pacified beneath it, the animal let itself be led until they were on the back lawn, looking up at the burning farmhouse. Somebody must have been keeping something apart from chickens in the chicken house because it exploded, showering them in soot. The pastor was on his knees on the grass—a broken, beaten man.

"Take a good look, my dear," he said. "A historic moment—you can tell your grandchildren how you watched the old morality disappear one night."

He couldn't look at his daughter. As one end of the house collapsed, there were cheers from the crowd out front.

"I could have cured them. All of them." He held his head in his hands. Emma knelt beside him and threw her arms around his neck.

"Oh, Father! If you've been a fool, you've been a gallant one!"

She held him and looked up at the crumbling upper floor.

"They make me sick! All those women! They got us into this, with their swaggering and their wily woman ways!"

"That's the way I used to feel about their swaggering and their wily woman ways," said Charles, but Emma barely heard him. She was on her feet now.

"I'm glad! Glad, I tell you! You said they would burn in hell fire and now look! You can be proud! Proud you were smarter than them!"

In the glow of the fire, the pastor's face was ashen. He shook his head slowly.

"I'm not so proud."

"Right, and nobody is going in to get Mrs Wakeling, is that it?" said Phinoola Quigg.

"Phinoola Quigg!"

The churchman had fallen off his knees in fright.

"*Where did you . . .? How did . . .?*"

"Sure isn't there a perfectly good handle on the back of the gig?" said the exceptionally pregnant housekeeper. "And didn't I hold on to it and run along behind?"

She passed between them, and stepping up onto the smoke filled veranda, disappeared into the inferno. The pastor wept on the lawn as the minutes passed. Emma looked from her father to the collapsing house; he was just a bag of bones on the grass, lifeless except for the sobbing.

"Stay here, father."

She dipped her shawl in the water trough and wrapped it round her head, then climbed onto the veranda and into the ferocious, billowing smoke, black and acrid, and the broiling heat. Inside, she could see little and kept her head low. Phinoola Quigg's voice could be heard from above so she made her way to the foot of the stairs and began to crawl up, eyes stinging and almost shut against the hot filth in the air. At the top she found the housekeeper prostrate on the landing.

"Have you seen mother?"

"Would I have just this minute called her an awful eejit if I hadn't? But sure how was I meant to get a hold of her with the feckin' baby coming?"

She was cradling a newborn girl, bloody and blue in the face.

"Would you take her?"

Emma wrapped the baby up in the shawl and looked around the landing for Rose, but it was a mass of blackness and flame. She turned to take the baby down and felt Phinola Quigg's hand on her.

"You'll take care of her?"

"I'll be back for you in a minute, Phinoola Quigg."

"But if you're not, you'll bring her up right? You wouldn't mollycoddle her, would you? You'd give her good, hard jobs to do?"

"Wait here."

She slid down the stairs, step by step, on her behind, holding the blue baby tight to her chest and smelling the fine hair singe on the arm she had around it. When she reached the bottom she made her way to the back door blindly, since she couldn't open her eyes now against the smoke; even on the threshold the daylight was cloaked, but she knew she was there by the up-ward tumbling of the fumes through the door frame. She was halfway across the lawn and had stumbled past her father by the time she had the courage to take a breath, but couldn't allow herself to collapse in the coughing fit that threatened to overwhelm her. Instead, she held the baby up by its legs and smacked it as hard as she dared, to get a breath or a cry from it.

"Father! What must I do?"

"It's dead, Emma." The pastor's eyes seemed to have sunk in his skull, his cheeks hollowed out in the course of an afternoon. "It's dead."

But it wasn't. In the very moment of her father's proclamation, the baby sputtered to life and cried and, remembering herself, Emma laid it down on the grass at his feet and ran back into the house. Muscle memory brought her to the bottom of the stairs, where she felt she was losing hold of con-sciousness. Her throat was inflamed and every breath was a lungful of poi-son; dizziness and delirium engulfed her with the fire.

"Is that you, Emma?"

Phinoola Quigg hadn't moved.

"What will we call the baby, Phinoola Quigg? It's breathing!"

"What kind of feckin' question is that? What are you doing back in here? Do I look to you like I'm going anywhere? Isn't your mother beyond all help?"

She pointed towards a narrow flight of stairs opposite which led up to what had been a garret but which was now a mass of charred debris. Emma could see sky through it and hear a howling from up there. Phinoola Quigg had dropped her head back to the floor and shut her eyes for the last time.

"Isn't Bridget as good a name as any other?" she said, and the stairs and landing collapsed.

Emma found herself on the floor below, head bleeding and pinned down by something, surrounded by fire. For some reason, she couldn't hear a thing; the blaze closed in on her in complete silence.

"Father!"

But she didn't even know if it had been a real cry or an imagined one; the difference didn't seem important. She rested her sore head and watched the fire come. Breathing was a little easier down here. She was tired. The baby was safe.

"Emma!"

Her father's voice, but still no other sound. She looked up and saw the pastor in the flames. He was burning in them, made of them, but his hand felt cool as it took hers. Whatever had been pinning her down was removed and she was lifted to her feet. He kept hold of her hand and put his other arm round her waist till they reached the edge of the fire, and there he released her.

"Father!"

She picked up the baby and turned to look for him but there was only the tumult of smoke and flame. Moments passed as the blood drained from her face and tears drenched it. She fell to the ground, resolving to lay the baby down and go back in, but before she could get to her feet, she saw him.

He walked from the blaze as if out for a Sunday stroll. No longer the broken man who had wept on the lawn, the pastor was bright with the flames that licked at him as he took his daughter's hand again and squeezed it. She couldn't remember so loving a smile on his face since . . . so open a smile on his face. She couldn't remember ever having been so grateful to him, so devoted to him, as she was in that moment.

Up onto the gig and off, reins in one hand and Bridget in the other, the crowd dancing round the house behind them, the horses rattling along and the bright, burning churchman mute and glowing beside her, the light from him guiding them, the plume of smoke that rose from him horizontal in the air, in the wake of their hurry, like a quill poised to trace the quick line home.

Emma Prentice

WHEN I WAS SEVENTEEN a suitor was appointed, since neither school dance nor annual fair had produced a lasting association between me and the kind of boy on whom my father might bestow his approval—let alone a candidate that could withstand the ferocious scrutiny of Phinoola Quigg. One by one, my motley classmates had been consigned to the litter basket of youthful experiment, either by my indifference or on the censure of the housekeeper for whatever their sin: moronism, incomprehensibility, suspected homosexuality, want of spine.

Selwyn Prentice was also a pastor's child—the eldest son of Walter Prentice who tended souls up Flats River way, out past the last outposts of civilization and any kind of comfort. His flock was comprised of gold panners, hermits and hard people, infinitely more given to bible quoting than any churchman I have ever met. There was little love lost between him and Charles Wakeling, on account of him considering the village pastor soft and somewhat lascivious, but despite the slight, my father considered Selwyn a safe bet and sent for him.

He joined us for lunch on a Saturday afternoon and delighted my father from the off, discussing the various different types of fish hook with ease and displaying a solid grasp of the characteristics of a wide range of reeds and soft woods. On declaring, just five minutes into that first interview, that he considered the raccoon to be the least susceptible of all animals to moral instruction, he sealed my fate. I have never seen my father so jubilant. He was practically ecstatic to observe the boy declining the bread and butter pudding that Phinoola Quigg had made, on account, he said, of its looking far too good and his not having done anything sufficiently odious that morning to have earned it.

"You are too hard on yourself, boy!" he scolded, though he was clearly entranced. "You could always offset it, you know, by subjecting yourself to something truly horrible later today."

But Selwyn, with the justification that he preferred not to experience pleasure on credit, took his leave and set out on the eighteen mile hike home in the rain. Hadn't looked at me once.

My father sat back in his chair with an air of blissful complacence and locked his fingers behind his head.

"You know," he said (to Phinoola Quigg, I assume, since no one had yet acknowledged my presence), "I'm not at all sure I could say, with any degree of certainty, that *exquisite* was too strong a word for that lad."

The lunches became a standing arrangement. Somewhere along the line, they began to plan the wedding, although I have no recollection of a proposal. Father and Selwyn would no doubt have thrashed it out between themselves on one of the hunting and fishing trips they undertook together. I very much doubt that Phinoola Quigg got involved since she never did forgive Selwyn for the pudding incident.

What happened on those trips was only ever related to me in grudging part, but over time they became longer in both distance and duration. The tales of daring deed they brought back with them got longer too, and richer in detail, and more ambitious in scope, as if they were driving each other to ever greater feats, the fatherly affection that the pastor continued to lavish on Selwyn edged with competition. Fish the size of ponies, eagles that could speak, wrestling on the muddy banks, bears that bowed in submission, salmon that leaped onto the fire, death-defying river rapids and the like. With the wedding out of the way—father managing, through a watery veil of tears, to officiate—I took the opportunity to assert my conjugal privilege and to insist that I come along.

"Emma!" cried my father. "Really! Absolutely—"

"No, pater!" Selwyn had raised his hand to pacify the pastor, with the familiarity that had come so easily to him those past months. "I've had this before, with my little sister. Far better to humor them, you know, the first time. A small sampling of the perils that a forest at night can throw up, or the demands of a high-spirited river, and she won't be fain to ask again!"

My father took a hold of his chin whiskers and nodded solemnly, and I went to fetch my boots.

For the next two days and nights I spoke to no birds. The most dangerous animal I saw was a rather sullen little squirrel that was losing fur. The men were no less sulky, stomping on ahead or—more often—behind and muttering amongst themselves. We headed up to the higher ground above Rangan's River and that first night I went down to the water and caught us a decent carp.

"I wouldn't have come back with anything so small, personally," observed my new husband as I gutted the beast, "but at least you've had your turn."

The following evening I had another, furnishing our little camp with a couple of trout. The other two were in foul mood and struggling with their tent, but once I'd gotten a fire going and we'd eaten, their spirits seemed to lift—largely, I suspect, because in the flickering light and the gloom of dusk it was easier to forget that I was there, listening to their daffy prattle, loosened with my father's hip-flask, which they passed conspiratorially between them as if I couldn't see.

"Oh, pastor! If I could have known or, for that matter, dared hope that I would one day be so honored by this association with you, and so edified by your condescendence, why, I would have rushed headlong here through time itself (were such a thing possible), skipping over the parts of my life softly and quickly which, in the light of what was to come after them— namely, your bolstering and educative patronage—would have appeared as mere obstacles to me or, at best, paltry stepping stones to touch but fleetingly with springéd toe as I leaped joyfully for that other shore (so bright and inviting!) which is to say, the soft sandy banks of your welcome, and the rich, abundant pastures of your guiding friendship which lay visible behind!"

Father kept his glazing eyes on the fire and poked it, chuckling indulgently.

"And if I, for my part, could have seen you coming, my lad, and known in the moment of doing so, with a swelling heart, that I had been a father, and found for my young girl that which, on her behalf, I prized above all else—a man up to whom she might contentedly look, wrapped in the embrace of his nurturing adoration and kept right by his straight back and his steady hand, I would have stood sentry on that shore, my boy, a lantern held aloft in my tireless arm by night, by day a fire kindled and tended carefully with dry tinder and wet leaves to send such a pillar of smoke aloft as would guide you from the other side of the world. You see that ditch over there?"

"You'll never make that. Ah, if only I could have espied the light from that lamp! Oh, how differently cast would have been the shadows of my early life! How brilliant the highlights! How nuanced the crepuscular interims!"

"I'm pretty sure I will, actually. It matters not, excellent young man. You are here! No, there was no lamp for you, no beacon in the night. Not for you did the sirens call, no maremind waving from her rock. It was your own character that brought you here, boy! Your unflagging industry and your steadfast piety have delivered you, at last, unto us."

Selwyn shrugged, eyes on the fire.

"Up to you."

The pastor stood.

"Right, let's do it then."

"Certainly. I might go first this time?"

"By all means."

They wandered off into the gloom, towards the ravine the churchman had pointed out. It was too dark now for Emma to see what they were up to. After a few minutes, her father returned. He was alone. Hands behind his back, he stood looking into the flames for a few minutes and then he spoke.

"Yes. Emma. There you are."

He kept his eyes on the fire.

"Yes. I'm afraid there's been a bit of a mishap."

The Parlor

ERE SHE IS.

Two pairs of heavy brocade curtains emit two razor-sharp slits of hard light into the cool, quiet gloom. One of these lines dissects the plum and bamboo motif of the upholstery on a cabriole sofa that sits in the middle of the room—laser-like as it cuts across the floorboards and splits the oriental design from floor to high, curved back.

A reading table is tucked behind the sofa and on it stands a lamp. From the lamp, a gas tube winds upward like a charmed cobra to a ceiling fixture overhead. None of the old fittings have been ripped out but there is no gas to flow from them now, nor any chair beside the table. Nobody reads in this room anymore, by any kind of light. Nobody sits on the sofa, which is turned away from the hearth.

Its back breaks the line of light. The old reading table and the rug it stands on cower in complete darkness and just a fragment of the luminous stripe curls along the brass stem and frosted glass of the lamp. Beyond that an absence till it hits the wall and divides the door to the hallway (always left ajar, so that the sounds of the house can be heard from here) from the fireplace. To the right of the hearth, an aspidistra on a walnut pedestal and to the left a set of black iron fireplace tools hang on a rack.

The mantel is of near black slate, two plump corbels bracing the molded shelf. The frieze and legs are marbled with muted, rusty colors and incised with golden geometries—a cross, a tree, a dragonfly—that barely glimmer in the dusty murk. The grate smells of metal and old wet ash and is unused. It smells of the want of fire.

On the wall above, for a dark room, a dark mirror, gilt-framed and starved of anything to reflect by the weighty drapes—just those two chinks glinting in the black glass and a lights-out-Mondrian array of faint shapes. On the far side of the fireplace, a second plant pedestal, vacant, and beyond that a recess with book shelving to chest height and a few decorative plates on top. Here, above them, hung from the picture rail, is a scene of the ten virgins of Matthew's parable—the five who got ready, ecstatically smug, and the five hard-done-by who didn't, and in front of the shelves, on an occasional table in the corner of the room, a bust of the pastor.

Here is the old room divider that was hastily gotten from Ms Pinch so that Rose Flimsy wouldn't be afraid and that never made it back to the schoolmistress' house—a triple-hinged, four panel set of silk depictions and contiguous design. At bottom right the tree of life in blossom, swallows and swifts in flight around it and at the base of its twisted trunk a peacock fanning and a stork, in combat—the one with a wound to its pavonaceous breast and the other with a bloodied beak. Above it lies the village, the rounded wooden bridges of the east, the allegorical progress of the lovers from right to left—the garden, the bedroom, the banquet, the temple, the promise, the betrayal, the revenge and the anguish. Beyond the last panel, a wicker chair and its worn, quilted cushion occupy an otherwise bare corner, not even a picture on the rail at this overlooked end of the window wall.

Here are those curtains: deniers of the day, double-lined with heavy flannel and a tan cotton sateen, great repositories of the dry dust that corrupts the white line thrown out across the floor from the narrow gap of their not quite meeting. And here another empty plant stand, and here the second set—taupe silk with gold brocade floral bouquets in rococo cartouche, fringed with burgundy silk cord. In other circumstances, they would emblazon the retina with red and green petals in stylized repetition, highlights glimmering with gilded thread. Here, they are black.

Against the last wall, a monstrous cabinet of some nine feet in height, in Rosewood, with two glass cases—one below and one above—and inlaid satinwood on the drawers and front panels. Old clothes are piled up behind the greasy panes in the bottom case, the top mirror-backed and empty and, to either side of it, the stepped, spindle-railed shelves are unornamented. The two cupboards at either side of the lower case are also bare.

And here is Emma, wedged between the cabinet and the door. She is dressed as darkly as the parlor in a belle epoque mourning gown—the only dress now, the last—of black wool poplin decorated with English crape. It is tight and so is the bun of hair that pulls at the forehead. The whole body is taut and tense, bent forward a little, the hands on the lap clenched, fidgeting with a napkin now and then but otherwise inactive, as are the eyes—wide open but vacant, attention turned inward. Rage on a stool—the same old stool that Phinoola Quigg, whose clothes are in the glass case, used to keep by the range in the kitchen—and rocking silently.

❊

Mostly inward. Every now and then the empty eyes seem to fill with recognition—to register, for a moment, the silk screens at which they are directed. They twinkle, sparkle with hate, then drain of life again beneath the puffy lids. The face is scrubbed clean but the skin is not clear; it is blotched with flushing resentments and huffy color, more bruise than blush. The lips are pursed, a blue taint to the edges, a mole and a hair in the philtrum, above which the nostrils flare athletically for one sitting so still, betraying the force that feeds the seething, that causes the body to rock rhythmically to an almost imperceptible degree, as much vibration as voluntary movement.

The one item of anatomy on constant, outward alert is the ear, listening at the open door for any household transgression, any fledgling domestic affront that might require intervention—this policing of the house her single care in the world, her only remaining justification. What else is left? Nothing of the girl (of the infant object of Penelope Rabbit's scrutiny, of the child who nursed old Sarah Twelves, of the waltzing adolescent) and nothing of the woman—nothing but a list of men, dead and disappeared, and grievances clenched like the napkin in her closed fist.

Has she not been dutiful? Appropriately demure and neat in her attire? Mindful of scripture? Sufficiently upright? Adequately contemptuous of fancy? Has she not been notably generous in her masturbations? *Singularly* generous? Paid regular visits to the cooperative, where the cheese boys would wait in line for her to attend them? Even, whenever marital status allowed, receiving the mayor of Small Town, Mr Bunbury, here at home each Tuesday evening to see to his own pent-up sac? Might that not have considerably eased the burden of his many grave responsibilities? Oiled the mechanisms of local governance? Could the Tiny Village Activated Sludge Processing Facility and Sustainable Construction Material Supply Project, then, ever have been brought to completion without her? The new tinted porch at the Mother & Baby unit? Is there not, consequently, a civic debt? Do they not, in fact, owe her something? *All* of them?

Has she not fed her elder daughter? Loved the younger? Did she not pay that man good money to guard them? Did she not school the orphan child well in her gruntwork as Phinoola Quigg asked? See to the maintenance of the tools in the shed? Participate wholeheartedly in the dissemination of village slander? Work tirelessly, year after year, collating the annual list of denunciations for the Ladies' Association? Borne her own burdens—the abandonments, the deceptions—with grace and fortitude?

And so on and so on, and on and on. The questions keep time with the beat of her cardiac organ. Her torment and her entertainment, she chews on their gristle with a grisly contentment. They surge with her lurching pulse and subside with it when the pitiless, punctuative silence takes over again, as it does now. Except for the sally to Big City to fetch the pair of delinquents, this is how it has been since Urine drowned.

An iris flicks. The body moves—takes a last look at the sofa that balks, the fireplace that baffles, the picture that swindles, the plant that disenchants, the curtains that vex. Gets up and crosses the room. Pulls at the room divider to reveal an arched bay and a brighter space behind it, unused till Noranbole set up an office for herself there last year, and where she now sits in the bay window at her desk, barefoot and lower lip bit in concentration. Apart from the desk there is just a musty armchair, piled with papers, and a few low bookshelves stuffed with box folders and files. The room is a roofscape of paper, a cock-eyed skyline of teetering folios, curling post-its and leaning towers of page and binder.

Noranbole's desk is just the opposite. A rectangular expression of perfect order, it is laid out with her tools: various foolscap notebooks, a pencil sharpener and an upright cylindrical container of pencils in various colors, a tablet with usb port, a geometry set consisting of protractor, rule and two set squares, various tubs of glitter, a stick of paper adhesive, stencils, ribbons and a very large set of felt tip pens. She works slowly and methodically, either unaware of or indifferent to her mother. At her feet, Spot sits looking at Emma.

"What is this?" A finger points at the marbled cardboard of a dark gray box.

Noranbole looks round.

"Proposed reforms to the Preferential Investment Pact. With a view to further liberalizing opportunities in the domestic market for overseas companies and the removal of unnecessary regulatory barriers to foreign investors, manticores and imps."

"And this?"

One hand is slapping dust from the dog-eared cover of a file that the other has picked up.

"Oh that. That's a treatise. Reflections on the Muqaddimah. Apropos of nothing, really, but y'know," she realizes she is muttering through a chewed pencil and takes it out of her mouth, "I was on a break."

"I see. You don't think your time would be better spent at the chores I continue to assign to you?"

"No."

She puts the pencil down and wields a magic marker.

"Bernard does them. I do this."

She glances out of the window, at her boyfriend in the yard, and frowns.

"He shouldn't be doing them either. He should be in Big City."

The skirt rustles as it approaches the desk, the eyes are on Bernard.

"I didn't kidnap him, Noranbole. Or you. You are here willingly. Your own guilt brought you back. The chores."

Noranbole's marker stops.

"It wasn't the chores I came back for, mother. It was you."

She's looking at Bernard again.

"I knew he'd come good," she said, "and he came good. And what did I do?"

She shakes her head.

"I won't do it again. I'll be better off back on the board at Terra Forma, making tough decisions that effect people's lives and generate economic growth. I'm good at it."

"Stupid girl."

The lop-sided curl of the upper lip is all derision, the head held haughty.

"You can barely scrape a carrot."

※

"You are lazy."

"I am loved."

"You have fat legs."

"My legs are fine."

"He will leave you."

"He will not."

Bernard still in view, carrying a whetstone down to the stream.

"I admire your confidence."

The eyes drop to the back of Noranbole's head, to the odd little double crown in her hair. There is a memory. A memory of a fear. Of holding the newborn head too tight, of rubbing it in that spot too often with a thumb and spoiling it. A guilt.

No. The shadow of a guilt. The echo.

She touches it and Noranbole bristles. Tenses. Waits. It won't last long, she knows—the action is mechanical, not tender. There is no heart left at her mother's dead center. The hand is taken away.

"He can't even speak."

"He can. He doesn't see the use."

He is returning to the shed and can't be heard through the window but from the distension in his cheeks and the puckered circularity of his lips is assumed to whistle as he goes.

"He may have a point."

No response from Noranbole.

"You think I'm joking?"

"No, mother." The tone is amiable enough. "I don't think anybody ever accused you of being funny."

There is a hesitation: in place of an answer, a new concentration in the eyes that look outside. A momentary confusion: a dropping of the lids in an attempt to retrieve something from the cold deep. The deep cold, inside.

"Somebody did. He thought so, at first. He said so."

"Who?"

Bernard with a bucket, bringing it to the well. Emma watching him.

"Your father."

Silence. Noranbole's only hope of hearing about him. If she says anything now, asks anything, her mother will change the subject.

She waits.

"We would sit out there," says the older woman, eventually, "just there beneath the window. The evenings were warm so we'd have a jug filled with cool water and cherries. There where the bench is now, we would sit on chairs," the eyes are dead to the world, inside out, "and say things."

Noranbole has turned to look and listen, one arm on the back of her chair.

"And he would laugh sometimes. Often, actually. Tell me I was a funny creature." She has moved to the window and has one hand on the pane. "I'm sure it was just sugar. They all have a bag of sugar in their pockets."

"You never tell me what happened to him."

"Because I don't know."

"Or care?" The younger woman has returned to her work. Head down, her tone is darker. "He must have had a reason. Something must have happened."

"He went away of his own volition. His own two feet took him. Ask *them* why."

"To extricate himself? Y'know, vis-à-vis your web."

The expected sharp reaction doesn't come. Instead, a pause and then, in a tone that puts an end to the topic, "Your father pursued me, Noranbole. I was the fly."

"Bernard has probably forgotten to have his sandwich again. I better go remind him."

"And for the pastor? We don't feed him anymore, I suppose?"

Noranbole stops in the bay. Her shoulders drop.

"Your father is dead, Mother," she says softly. "He died a long time ago, in the Twelves fire."

Unhearing, Emma continues to look out of the window, watching as her daughter crosses the yard with a turkey sandwich and a glass of milk, disappearing from sight where the barn door is obscured by the lean-to.

"Sit out there, we would," she mutters, "just there beneath the window. Until you dropped out of me, and then he belonged to you."

She looks at the desk, at the out-sized folder the girl has been working on so painstakingly. Thick and full of hand-drawn pictures and diagrams, photos pasted to the pages and magazine clipping collages. A ribbon tied in a bow round the cover. 'Book of Proposals' in bright crayon-color calligraphy on the front.

"Didn't stop him going though, did you? No more than I did."

She knows better than to touch her daughter's work. Knows the trouble there would be. And there is something about the idiot boy that makes her stop short of crossing him. Still, her forefinger travels to the edge of her daughter's writing pad and the corner of something that protrudes from beneath it. She presses gently and pulls it out a little. It's a stagecoach ticket, and another beneath it.

"Noranbole!"

The name screamed from beyond the lean to, wildly, hysterically. *That* voice. She is startled but nevertheless takes slow, steady steps towards the source. The outbursts continue as she goes. Somebody is beside himself. Crazed.

"Is it really you, Noranbole? Can it be possibly be you? I've only just been talking about you! Oh, that I should have lived to see this day! That I should stand once more within sight of your magnificence! In the divine light that shines from your unbelievably lovely visage! Really unbelievably lovely! That it should fall to me to be so favored! Just a humble man!"

She reaches the corner of the lean-to and sees them. Noranbole standing by the barn door and Bernard next to her with a milk mustache, tucking into his turkey sandwich. On the ground, prostrate and reaching out to touch Noranbole's foot—which she retracts—a man weeps. Leather hat, long leather greatcoat, spectacles in the mud as is much of his messy hair. He raises himself to his knees and uses the hem of his shirt to wipe the tears from his eyes.

"I just can't believe it! I really can't! Oh great day! Hello, Bernard."

Behind him, the arms cross and the lips purse, one eyebrow up—the body language of weary recognition.

"I'm surprised you have the nerve to show yourself here," the mouth is twisted and the voice wavers with a simmering fury, "Willem Seiler."

The man turns and rises to his feet, removes his hat and flourishes it to accompany an obsequiously low bow.

"What a wretch I am, and how just my banishment!" he says to the mud at his feet. "Seriously, I really did deserve it. But could you really expect me not to return—if not by design then by compunction, drawn here despite myself to walk once more the same sod of earth upon which you tread," staying down, he turns his head back to look up at her and grin, "Emma Wakeling?"

Part Four

Urine

THINGS HAVE CHANGED, up at the lake.

And in our homes:

Folks, for some reason, have taken to dining on the stairs. Occupants of single story dwellings, such as the Hucksteps, or the Grauntes who live in the bungalow out by Squire's Rindle, shuffle around at mealtimes in a state of confusion with their plates in their hands.

Visiting is different. A new etiquette requires that whenever a visitor comes by, the host should knock on the inside of the front door and wait for the caller's permission to open it. This approach obliges the homeowner to keep a constant lookout from a suitable window. The visit then takes place in the front yard. This happens in all sorts of weather and is definitely one of the more grating of the many changes that have occurred.

It isn't just manners. We have new laws. For example, while folks are still allowed to touch the furniture, they are prohibited from doing so with their fingers.

The tick tock of clocks has been fixed to a tock tick.

No pets.

Those are just a few of the big ones, but a thousand customs have been modified. You might credibly describe the changes as infinitesimal tweaks, of course. Nugatory rearrangements, nothing more. Trifling adjustments, you might say. Inconsequential modifications, you might also say. Picayune conformances, if you're going to be funny about it.

Whatever you want to call them, they add up: a coat on a hat hook, a cup in the glass cabinet, a newspaper on the dinner step, a ham on the bookshelf. An indoor plant on the patio. A bottle of vinegar in the wine rack. A sparrow taunting a caged cat. None of these things, perhaps, seem especially perturbing to you. Why do I take the trouble to mention them, you wonder. But consider the cumulative effect!

The fact is that amid these countless aberrations, and without anyone really being able to articulate the experience, nobody quite knows what anybody else is up to. Or *why*.

Things are strained, and getting ugly.

Picture it. A daughter at dinner. Looks askance at her father, inwardly rehearsing her retort to some anticipated slur.

The slur comes.

Brother in the coal bunker, dawn till dusk. Looking for mother's love notes, his heart blackened with the soot of suspicion.

Sister sneaking around the place, unpicking needlework and salting the marmalade.

That kind of thing.

Bedroom, bathroom, parlor, kitchen—every room in every house, every corner and cranny, suppurates with the greasy discharge of neurosis.

And all around the county:

Rumors abound. Nasty rumors spread by everyone, about everyone else. Ugly seeds sown that germinate, so that now we live in a bramble of back-bites and badmouthery. We sweat in the heat of calumny, swatting away the stingers as we trudge, slung mud sucking at our rubbers.

Byelaw 68. The penalty for sitting on a fence is fifty.

I haven't been up there yet to see for myself, but they say that Arlie Cotton has bred a duck that is over three foot tall, and mean.

Gideon Tupp is selling his horses. All of 'em. Says he can't stand the way they've been looking at him lately. Says he's unnerved.

Viola Dart, who runs the parish newsletter, has been going through our bins. I *know* this.

Gravity, down where the river takes a sharp turn and the crayfish boys keep their traps, has gotten a little twisty and I don't mind saying so.

The general store won't sell me string anymore—I've resorted to getting mine in from further afield and recycling old bits where I can.

And in the wider world:

Great big scary things. Such as the fact that, for a while now, compass readings everywhere have been edging incrementally clockwise, which is pretty huge if you ask me, but smaller things too—equally worrisome—such as the disappearance of cardamom and that black hasn't been recommended as a slimming choice in any of the fashion magazines for some time. You just don't see it anymore. It's as if it no longer has that quality.

Byelaw 27. The penalty for declining a reasonably timed sales call, where 'reasonably timed' is taken to mean that a meal has not been interrupted, or if a meal has been interrupted that the diners are either between courses, still at their aperitifs, or have already poured the liqueur, is a hundred.

On the face of it, individual empowerment appears to be accelerating wildly, facilitated by burgeoning access to non-state networks and communities and supported by the widespread use of new communication technologies and social media. Improved healthcare, enhanced educational achievement and the global growth of the middle class have all contributed to a decline in hegemonic power, simultaneously bringing about increased potential for demographic instability.

The great crises and upheavals have coalesced into something of a status quo. We lurch from trauma to trauma expectantly now, factoring shock and feint into our economic forecasts. We make hay while the sun shines. At night we hunker down. We are acclimated. During the first two weeks of last September, for example, nothing much happened and as a result there was widespread civil unrest. Mass suicides in Ampleton. In Middleton, dogs were thrown from windows. We ended up invading our neighbors to the north, at great cost, just to give people something to chew on.

Winters are unpredictable, summers swelter and storm, the humidity unbearable all year round. The skies constantly writhe with angry weather, darkening our world and seeming to slow it, so quick and furious are the clouds. We know we haven't been going crazy down where the river takes a sharp turn and the crayfish boys keep their traps, because further gravitational anomalies have been reported from every corner of the Earth and are now considered commonplace.

Yes, there certainly have been a lot of changes in our homes, all around the county and in the wider world.

But mainly up at the lake.

※

"I could call the President, I suppose," said Noranbole.

Noranbole!

Oh, Noranbole! Returned to me! She who I thought long dead! She whose ghostly doppelganger nestled unstirring in the cradle of my broken heart these years!

Noranbole!

Before my very eyes! On the little green bench where she sat, conscientiously—I can only assume—caregiving as that Maypole simpleton pottered around the back yard, performing menialities with the relish of all cretins for some nominally purposive assignment. Oh, kind heart! How her eyes shone with the compassion she evidently felt for her pitifully defective ward as he shuffled blankly from hammer to pump! What dedication in them! What devotion!

Seriously, she never looked at me once. I was on my knees at what I considered a respectful distance—say, eight or nine foot, which as well as underlining the great esteem in which I held her kept me safely away from Spot, who was tied to the bench and snarling—and had been bringing the wondrous creature up to date with all that had been happening in her (unendurable!) absence: the county-wide conspiracies, the simmering feuds, the bodily inversions I had experienced for myself down where the river takes a sharp turn and the crayfish boys keep their traps and of course, the unholy developments up at the lake.

Mainly the lamentable inadequacy of our response—that bungler, Bunbury, and his council of flunkies. The incessant legislations[1] they had wrought upon us. The byelaws, the edicts, the knots they had tied us up in till our civic life had asphyxiated.

I had (of course) peppered my reports generously with tributes to her unimpeachable divinity, her porcelain complexion, her overpowering (espe-

---

[1] For example:

In relation to the collection and disposal of household waste:

Extent ~

These byelaws apply to all waste resulting from activity in or of the domiciles (households) named in the schedule (all domiciles situated within the geographic limits of the county) and hereafter referred to as 'the domiciles' or 'the domicile'.

Interpretation ~

In these byelaws 'the Council' means Mayor Bunbury, Mr Squire, Mr Gallop, Mr Yeoman, Kelly, Mr Lawter, Mr Fry and Captain Le Gros.

For the purpose of these byelaws the owner (deed holder) of the domicile shall be considered in charge thereof unless at the time of refuse collection the domicile has been placed in the care of another person or let to another person under the terms of a rental agreement.

For the purpose of these byelaws the terms 'waste', 'refuse' and 'garbage' shall refer to any and all by-products arising from any and all activity taking place within or under the auspices of (picnics, for example, count) the domicile with the sole exceptions of poo (which is subject to separate legislation) and wee wee (in which the Council has no interest).

- Receipts for all consumables and goods intended for domestic use and purchased within the geographic limits of the county are mandatory and should be displayed on the notice boards that the Council has ordered attached to the front door of each domicile. Receipts for goods purchased outside the county will be issued by customs officials at the county line and are to be displayed in the same way.

- All receipts issued by vendors within the geographical limits of the county will be logged and an accurate record kept by the vendor and forwarded to the Council at weekly intervals to facilitate the weekly notice board inspections. Any discrepancies between the vendor's log and the notice board will be reported to the Council. Failure to display a receipt is a criminal offense.

- Waste arising from the use and consumption of receipted goods will be collected on a weekly basis, at which time the garbage yield will be reconciled with receipts which, where appropriate, will be stamped and removed by Council personnel. No other persons may remove receipts from the notice board.

Householders and any other persons present in the domicile at the time of refuse collection will place themselves indoors while the contents of the domicile's garbage tub are transferred to the armored vehicle by the guards (a special shout out here to Bradley Dawkins who has done such a marvelous job fitting out the old postal van with steel plate - Brad, you're a miracle worker).

Householders and any other persons present at the time of refuse collection will remain indoors until such time as payment has been deposited in the garbage tub's payment sleeve and the refuse carrier has been pulled away. Although payments may fluctuate in accordance with garbage yield and The Market, the Council undertakes to maintain levels of remuneration that fall at all times between pretty damn good and very handsome indeed.

cially in this heat) scent and so forth, and she had been her usual unflappable self in silent acceptance of my humble eulogies. Ms Emma was at a meeting of the Ladies' Association—I had watched her go from my hiding place in the Dogwood—and I was glad to have this time with Noranbole, to bask in the almost palpable caress of her resplendence of course but also, importantly, to outline my plan: the greatest plan of my life, perhaps of any life, certainly around here—the plan that, if only I could get someone to *listen*, would without the tiniest scintilla of doubt deliver us all from the perturbations with which we had lately been afflicted!

Noranbole's words surprised me. Stopped me mid-sentence, in fact. I was also momentarily occupied with a swarm of midges that had settled around me.

"Call the *President*?" If I hadn't been fending off the insects, my hands would almost certainly have been on my hips. "*The* President?"

She nodded.

"Yeah. I have a couple of numbers for him." She was twisting the cap from a bottle of milk, condensation on its white glass a promise of the deliciously cool contents. She used to bring me milk, but now it was this dungareed boob she superintended. Such is life.

A turkey sandwich too, in greased paper.

"But he's usually busy." She placed the bottle on the bench beside her and unwrapped the sandwich. "Mayor of Big City, on the other hand—if I call him, he'll hop to."

I played this back a couple of times, internally, before responding.

"The *Mayor of Big City*?"

The midges were fierce. I could barely keep my eyes open, despite the imperative of her incontrovertible visual appeal, and some of them were getting in my mouth.

"The Mayor of Big City will *hop to*?"

Oh Noranbole!

What spells had she woven out there on her travels? What great feats had she accomplished? And in what exalted circles? What stupefying adventures had been hers? What glory? What fame? Oh, but why should I be surprised? *Why?* Was this not the very paradigm of purity sitting here before me? The epitome of beneficence? The last word in winsome?

That it should be you, Noranbole! You, who returneth here to lift us from our squalor! That you should be the instrument through which my *magnificent* plan be realized! How right! How fitting!

"I'll do it later," she said, the imbecile having sat himself beside her on the bench with a nonchalance that bordered, if you ask me, on the cavalier, "because right now," and here her eyes met mine for the first time, "*I'm busy.*"

99 & 103. The penalties for crumpling receipts and for wearing mucky boots in the bank are a hundred and thirty, respectively.

※

The podium is painted glossy white, except for the handrail and the newels which are untreated oak, and the brass post caps. It goes everywhere with the Mayor of Big City. He is on it now, having stepped directly there from the stagecoach.

Mayor's wife also, and Shadow.

The Mayor of Big City grips the wooden rail to steady himself, Mayor's wife disdainful and precarious behind him. A retinue of local youths shoulder the whole thing along Main Street towards the Meeting House. Dick Netleton at front right is not as tall as John Polly on the left. Mayor of Big City and Mayor's wife struggling to maintain composure. Shadow appears unruffled.

"Two bit town," says the Mayor of Big City, taking a cigar from his breast pocket.

"One horse," says Mayor's wife.

"Where?" says the Mayor of Big City.

Mayor's wife rolls her eyes.

Seiler running alongside, waving for the Mayor's attention.

"Who's that guy?" says the Mayor

"Looks weird," says the Mayor's wife.

"Hey, who's that guy?" shouts the Mayor to Bunbury, who walks ahead in a cloud of incense, waving the Small Town Ceremonial Mace.

"Never mind him, sire! That person claims to have started all this— your benevolent intervention, I mean—but it was a local townsmaiden, as you know. We were unable to intercept his subsequent missals to you, I'm afraid."

"Those letters were weird," says the Mayor of Big City to the Mayor's wife. "I didn't like them."

"Guy keeps calling you sire," says the Mayor's wife.

"I know," says the Mayor.

Predawn.

Heat from a new sun yet to hit the water. Yesterday's still hovers, stale and dawdling low, not enough time in the short night to lift it.

Branches bare in high summer, black as the unreflecting lake.

Sky gunmetal.

No birdsong, no birds.

The breeze that sweeps over Swan Hill stops dead here, stilled by a rising stench in hanging strips of rank mist. In the fug, the surface should heave with insects. Teem with them. It should fizz with the flit of dragonfly and the whine of mosquito.

But it doesn't.

Meeting room.

Mr Lawter, Mr Gallop, Kelly, Mr Fry, Mr Yeoman, Mr Squire and Captain Le Gros.

"The Von Arx Haus in Zarn."

Kelly has his snakeskins on the table. Mr Yeoman is at the window. The others are in their seats. Nobody replies to Mr Gallop. Captain Le Gros consults his pocket watch and puts it back.

"The Blaverhasset mansion," he says.

"Yes, good one," says Kelly.

He leans back in his nebula of cigar smoke, carefully tapping a few flakes of ash into the pocket ashtray he holds in his other hand, and speaks again.

"Furtenburger's visitor center for the caves at Schmitzl."

Not a peep from anyone.

"The Mendes Stadium," says Mr Yeoman.

"She's a sweety all right," says the captain.

Mr Squire slaps the table.

"The Hondanooga Suspension Bridge," he says.

"Doesn't count," says Mr Gallop. "Try again."

"No, he misses a turn," says Mr Lawter. "It's my go."

He thinks for a moment.

"The George Tower."

"I decry it."

Mr Fry is examining his fingernails. Kelly snorts a plume of smoke and takes his boots off the table.

"You decry the George Tower, Mr Fry?" he asks, winking at Mr Lawter.

"Doubly so," says Mr Fry, not looking up.

Kelly incredulous. Sniffs victory.

"Really? Well, we're all ears, I'm sure. I censure your decrial!"

"As you wish."

Mr Fry stands, still intent on the backs of his hands.

"The elevator shafts on the north east corner of the George Tower, as some of you may know, were originally intended to reach the eighty-eighth floor, where the building so famously tapers. However, due solely to a miscalculation in the quantities of the differing steel beams (those for the upper shafts, originally intended to run from eighty-eight to a hundred-and-twelve, are more slender and lightweight), the sturdier beams of the lower shafts now only reach the eighty-second floor."

"Pfft," says Kelly and returns his snakeskins to their previous resting position.

Mr Fry begins to pace the length of the table, hands held behind his back.

"The decision was a pragmatic one, of course. New girders might have been commissioned but delivery would have taken weeks, if not months. Work simply went ahead with the surplus thinner beams. There was never any question of safety being compromised in any way, and the avoidance of delay meant that men whose families might otherwise have gone hungry were kept in work. I hardly need remind you all that the country was on its knees at the time, up to its neck in a terrible crisis."

Murmurs of assent around the table. Kelly looking uncomfortable.

"However, there *was* a knock-on effect. Nothing dramatic—it goes entirely unnoticed by most," says Mr Fry, taking his seat again and looking at Kelly for the first time. "But not by all, and certainly not by me."

He weaves his fingers and leans back.

"The substitution of the thinner units is betrayed by a recess that can be observed to the side of the elevator doors on each of those six floors. The owner of the building filled these recesses, at considerable expense, with ornate Greek amphorae of the archaic period. Despite the undoubted value and authenticity of the pieces, however, they in no way compliment the otherwise angular and metallic art deco symmetries of each lobby. The mismatch in fact led to a dispute with the man responsible for the interiors and for many of the building's external ornamentations, Emile Spüle. Spüle would not see the project through to completion and disassociated himself from the George Tower soon afterwards. He knew what I am telling you— that the decision, from a design point of view, had been a mistake."

"Oh, come on!" says Kelly, appealing to the others. "Six floors of a hundred-and-twelve story building! A few recesses—"

"Which brings me to my second decrial," says Mr Fry. He speaks softly but there is steel to his tone and his eyes are now fixed on Kelly. "I did say *doubly*.

"At the time of his departure, Spüle had not yet completed his sketches for the gargoyles that adorn the building at each corner of the hundred-and-eighth floor. With the project so close to completion, the owner, Carlton George, was reluctant to incur the cost of hiring another high profile designer. He gave the job instead to his son, Myron George—another pragmatic decision, no doubt, but the final product is a botched job, if you ask me. Myron was barely twenty-two years old and had little artistic talent. His gargoyles are a mess—not quite art deco, not quite gothic. Not fully realized, somehow. Not *convincing*."

He resumes the inspection of his hands.

"Of course, if *you're* convinced, that's entirely your affair—"

"Now just a minute!" Kelly is on his feet.

"He's very good at this, isn't he?" says Mr Gallop to Mr Squire.

"Ooh, they're here!" says Mr Yeoman at the window. "They're coming up the street."

Certain amount of commotion. Mayoral podium edged up to the Meeting House veranda. Mayor of Big City and the Mayor's wife unloaded, ushered inside by a fawning Bunbury. Introductions made. Seats taken.

"What . . . is that?" says Mr Fry.

"That's Shadow," says the Mayor's wife. "He's a Cogdat™."

Mr Gallop whispering in the Captain's ear.

"Hm, yes. Quite. I wonder if someone has been remiss, Mr Bunbury, in failing to advise his Excellency of this county's prohibition against pets?"

Everybody looks at Mr Bunbury. Mr Bunbury looks at the Mayor of Big City. The Mayor of Big City looks at the Mayor's wife.

"Shadow isn't a pet," she says.

She is retrieving a magazine from her bag.

"Because animals have souls? So you can't own them."

"What's that on its flank?" says Mr Yeoman. "Is it hurt?"

"Supposed to be a time and date display," says the Mayor of Big City, "but I think he's got some kind of mange."

"Well, and so the honor falls to me," says Bunbury, "as the mayor of this minuscule settlement, now that we find ourselves so commodiously ensconced here in our lovely Meeting House—one of the town's inaugural buildings, you know, and originally a chapel (you'll no doubt have noted the pulpit from which I now so gratefully address you)—to welcome your Excellency and your Excellency's wife. What a moment this is! Such optimism here today! Such hope, that one so eminent might be just the ticket, indeed, in helping us out of our current difficulties."

The Mayor of Big City takes another cigar from his pocket and lights it, keenly scrutinized by all except for the Mayor's wife who is reading her magazine.

"We can surely look forward now," continues Bunbury, eyeing the cigar, "to putting our troubles behind us. My colleague, if I might dare to use the word, from Big City has all the right connections—not to mention the wealth, depth, and breadth of his own personal experience—to take a proper look at the monstrous occurrences that have plagued us. Really get to grips with the situation, you know? And may I say how much I look forward to him doing so?"

"Where's Noranbole?" says the Mayor of Big City.

"The maiden who reached out to you so pitifully, sire? The angel among us who invoked your borderline divine presence here today? Why, I should imagine she is at her chores, sire, as befits a young woman of such virtuous simplicity."

"Right. I thought she would be here."

"Oh no, sire. Not here. In the Meeting House? Oh no. I must confess how surprised we all were, though absolutely delighted of course, that one so undoubtedly busy and critical to national life as yourself would have the time, inclination or indeed the boundless compassion to even respond to such a sweet but, and let's be honest here, rustic creature."

"Well," says the Mayor of Big City, "it was that, but also the complaints. Lot of complaints have been coming in, mainly from Provinceton. About the smell."

"Ah yes," Bunbury shrugs, "the neighbors. We've all had difficult neighbors from time to time, I dare say. You can no doubt relate."

"Provinceton is two hundred and forty miles away, Mr Burbury," says the Mayor of Big City, looking around. "Actually, I don't get it. Why can't I smell anything?"

"We're upwind, your Excellency. You'll smell it soon enough."

"Ew," says the Mayor's wife.

"Anybody got an ashtray?" says the Mayor of Big City.

Mr Yeoman, Captain Le Gros, Kelly and Mr Gallop leap from their seats and surround the Mayor of Big City, each of them producing portable ashtrays from their pockets.

"You can use mine, your Excellency," says Kelly. "I won't mind at all."

"Mine has a slightly larger aperture, sire, as you can see," says the captain, "and although it is my personal ashtray—I want to be very clear about that from the outset—it wouldn't bother me a bit if you were to use it for a little while."

"Would you like to hold mine for a moment, sire, while you decide?" says Mr Yeoman. "I find it sits in the palm like a warm peach."

"Gentlemen!" says Bunbury. "May I remind you that a council meeting is presently underway? Please return to your seats at once. Mr Gallop, fetch the communal ashtray from the cabinet and give it to his Excellency."

Mr Gallop, treasurer, walks the length of the table to the wall opposite the pulpit, an enormous bunch of heavy keys jangling at his waist. He uses one of them to undo the padlock on a steel cabinet and retrieves a glass ashtray which, on locking the cabinet again, he places in front of the Mayor of Big City.

"I was about to say, sire, that a tour of the town and environs has been meticulously arranged. As well as the lake, it will be our pleasure to present our state-of-the-art Garbage Heap to your excellence."

"I really just want to get to the part with the lake," says the Mayor of Big City, tapping a flake of ash into the ashtray.

Mr Squire jumps to his feet and points at the ash.

"I'll give you a five note for that!"

"I'll give you a twenty!" says Kelly.

"Gentlemen, gentlemen." Bunbury has descended from his pulpit and appeared suddenly at the side of the Mayor of Big City.

"Sire, I very much regret to inform you that my associates here are trying to mislead you. Why," he says, scowling at Kelly and Mr Squire, "you might almost conclude that they were nothing but a pair of common swindlers."

He takes a hold of the Mayor of Big City's ermine collar.

"If you would acquiesce, sire, to my taking that little flake of ash from your excellence, I am prepared to sit down right here, right now, and write out a check for a hundred."

His eyes are wild.

"What do you say?"

The Mayor of Big City is looking in the ashtray.

"For that?"

"And another hundred, sire, for every subsequent tap. Come on, what do you say?" says Bunbury. A blood vessel protrudes at his temple.

The Mayor of Big City turns to his wife.

"Wants to give me literally hundreds just for smoking this cigar."

The Mayor's wife doesn't look up from her magazine.

"Cool."

Mayor of Big City smokes furiously. Bunbury retrieves his check book and sits.

"So, your Excellency, we'll begin at the Garbage Heap and then move on to the lake."

"If we have to," says the Mayor of Big City. "Let's get on with it."

"I second that," says Mr Gallop, whose hair is sticking to his scalp. "It's so stuffy in here."

"Who are you telling?" says the captain, fanning himself with a note-book. "I have the full ceremonial regalia of the Middleton Fire Service on underneath this wedding dress, you know."

※

Black trees.

Water, etc.

I was there, the day they dragged Mark Fleming up to the lake. I'd soaked a tea towel in rose water and wrapped it round my head, braving the stink to take some measurements. How could I expect a man like the Mayor of Big City to entertain my plan if I didn't have it finely calibrated? How could I expect anyone to, if I couldn't map out its intricacies for them in simple terms they would understand?

My God, the *audacity* of it!

I knew the mood was ugly the moment I heard them so I gathered up my spool and my implements and retreated into the scrub.

"Pull his pants down!"

The Fleming boy had his back to me as Samuel Tibbs grabbed his britches and lowered them. The others gathered round him in a semicir-cle, staring at his member. Billy Hall and Simon Clarke held onto him at either side.

"What are we looking for?" said Samuel Tibbs, who was the closest.

"Any changes in color," said the Bennett boy. "I seen it myself, the day that madman drowned Urine. Bright green, so it was. That's how he be-witched the lake."

I checked an urge to show myself. To point out that the idiot Wakel-ing girl had only herself to blame. They were closing in on Fleming. Cora Munnings, the county midwife, picked up a sodden twig and prodded the boy's genitalia.

"It doesn't seem to be doing anyth . . . wait!"

The little mob leaped back a good four foot, in unison.

"It definitely twitched!" said the midwife.

Tucker Withingham was patting himself down.

"I feel different," he said. "Do I look different?"

"I want to let go of him now," said Simon Clarke. "I'm afraid."

"Wait," said Cora Munnings. "I think it's . . ." her voice trailed off, all eyes on the penis, " . . . no. Nothing."

"Throw him in the lake!" said Francis Bank.

"Yes, that's a good idea," said the Bennett boy. "It worked in the water last time."

They bundled Fleming into an old row boat and Billy Hall, the burliest of them, rowed him out onto the water.

"What if he just swims away?" he yelled back at the shore.

"Tie his hands!" said everybody.

Billy used his belt to tie the prisoner's hands and then dumped him in the lake, trousers still around the boy's ankles. The rippling, rancid water smoothed as they waited for him to resurface.

But he didn't.

✳

"I don't know what to say," says the Mayor of Big City. He looks to his wife for assistance but she's got her earphones in.

Mr Squire steps forward and smiles.

"I know exactly what you mean," he says. "It's astonishing, isn't it?"

The glass box is a perfect cube, lit from above and also from within, where four tiny halogen spotlights at each corner illuminate a central platform, to the base of which a small electronic data logger is attached that displays temperature and relative humidity readings, and upon which the exhibit sits.

Mr Squire has bent over and his nose almost touches the glass.

"Simply breathtaking."

Bunbury is cradling an elbow and stroking his chin.

"Possibly my favorite piece," he says, "though they're all incredible."

"What is it?" says the Mayor of Big City. So far the Garbage Heap isn't at all what he was expecting.[2]

The question seems to take the others by surprise.

---

[2] **Byelaw 1. In relation to the Municipal Garbage Heap:**
– Inspections and any necessary maintenance of the perimeter fence situated at a distance of one mile from the Municipal Garbage Heap will be daily, the current to be switched from continuous to pulse while repairs are carried out.

"I hadn't really thought about it, sire," says Bunbury. "It isn't easy to tell, actually, since it's obviously spent some time in a puddle. The water damage is, in and of itself, exquisite. My guess would be the bottom left hand corner of a ripped cigarette packet?"

"Yes," says Mr Fry, "or perhaps chewing gum? Family pack?"

They're in a dark salon with a row of banquettes down the middle and several display cases spotlit along either wall. The exhibition space is the only part of the Garbage Heap the armed guards have given the party access to. At the far end, a double door with a sign above it, also spotlit.

Municipal Garbage Heap Tearooms.

And beside it a blackboard on an easel:

Scones baked daily. Try our soup.

"It's absolutely marvelous, anyway," says Bunbury, "and also for sale, should your excellence wish to consider a purchase here today."

"Why would I—"

"At forty thousand, it's easily the keenest price tag in the exhibition."

"That's a thought," says Captain le Gros. "Perhaps it *is* a bit of a price tag."

"No, I don't think so," says Mr Squire. "Definitely part of a packet. You can see that it would have been three-dimensional before it got squished."

"Sorry," says the Mayor of Big City. "Did you say *forty thousand* . . .?"

"That's right, sire. Would you like to buy it?"

"No, I wouldn't. I don't like it."

"I see. What a pity. Well, there are other pieces, of course," says Bunbury, indicating a nearby case that contains a sodden ball of toilet paper, "but you're talking serious money."

"Can I have a scone?" says the Mayor of Big City.

They file into the tearooms where a shy-looking young woman more or less hides behind a tiered array of paper doilies on trays, piled high with scones.

"I'd like that one, please."

Wordlessly, the attendant puts the scone on a plate with some tongs, but she doesn't hand it over.

"That'll cost you four, sire," says Bunbury after a moment.

– During periods when the current has been switched to pulse, an extra guard will be posted to each of the perimeter towers to assist in the detection and disposal of any unauthorized persons present between the perimeter fence and the red warning line situated four hundred yards further out.

The Mayor of Big City retrieves some coins from his trouser pocket and hands them over, then sits at a table with Bunbury and the Mayor's wife. The others crowd round an adjacent table and lean in to listen.

"There's no butter."

"No, sire. Would your excellence like some? That would also cost you four."

"Oh," says the Mayor of Big City and takes a big dry bite from the scone that keeps him occupied for a good minute and a half.

"I don't get it," he says when he finally manages to swallow. "The deal with the rubbish. It's like you're all mad or something."

"Bizarre," says the Mayor's wife. She has removed one earphone and is texting.

"In what way, sire?"

The Mayor of Big City has a mouthful of scone again and it's a couple of minutes before he can speak.

"What do you mean, in what way? It's *rubbish*. We are literally falling over this stuff in Big City. People complain about it."

Chuckles from the next table. Bunbury smirks and shakes his head.

"So we understand, sire," he says with an air of indulgence. "Sometimes folks just don't know what they've got."

He shrugs.

"Just trying to find our way out of this awful crisis, sire. Conventional revenue streams have been appallingly sluggish. We haven't had a construction sector here since Kevin Arnold sold his van in March, and financial services—well, let's just say Mr Totman hasn't been very well lately and leave it at that, shall we?"

Kelly glances furtively at Mr Squire while Bunbury continues.

"Can I smoke in here?" says the Mayor of Big City, who has given up on the scone.

"You can smoke anywhere you please, sire," says Bunbury, placing his personal ashtray on the table between them and flipping the lid. "We encourage it."

Mayor of Big City lights up.

"When I think of how long we spent squandering our most valuable resource, I don't know whether to laugh or cry, sire. Instead of recycling—and therefore essentially destroying—our rubbish, we've rebranded it."

"As what, exactly?" says the Mayor of Big City.

"As art, sire."

For the first time, he takes a cigar of his own from his pocket, lights it, takes a pull and lets the smoke dawdle between his lips for a moment.

"And this is working?" says the Mayor of Big City.

"Too soon to tell," says Mr Yeoman.

"Early signs are not discouraging," says Kelly. "But they're not encouraging either."

"We're certainly very happy about all the shopping people are doing now we pay them for their waste," says Bunbury, "and we don't have to worry about the whole production versus consumption equation anymore since they're now the same thing," his eyes are on the abandoned scone, "which is neat."

Mr Gallop removes his snorkel and whispers something into Bunbury's ear.

"Yes, I was getting to that, Mr Gallop."

He clears his throat.

"There was something, sire, that we wanted to run by you. Little glitch in our economic model."

His eyes continue flicking to and from the scone.

"We were wondering if we might qualify for exemption from MARS?"[3]

---

[3] **Byelaw 99. In relation to the recycling of clothes under the Mandatory Apparel Recycling Scheme:**

Definitions –

In these byelaws, unless the context otherwise requires:

"Recycling center" means the single story, corrugated steel structure located on Old Man Stodder's land, just outside the red warning line on the track that heads up Sugar Bog way. You all know this.

"Outfit" means any garment or combination of garments – including headwear, footwear and accessories – coordinated or uncoordinated, or exhibiting any semblance of coordination, real or imagined – comprising one unit of the daily dress quota and is to be distinguished from separate outfits by being worn on the body while they (the other outfits) are stored safely in a designated wardrobe area, or through layering.

"Buy" means precisely what it has always meant. Do *not* dick with us.

Interpretation:

In these Bylaws, unless the context otherwise requires, the Mandatory Apparel Recycling Scheme applies. Nothing we can do about it.

Words importing the singular include the plural and vice versa; words importing gender include the masculine, feminine and neuter genders; and words importing persons include individuals, bodies corporate, partnerships, trusts and unincorporated associations, including the quiz team.

The headings used throughout these byelaws are inserted for reference purposes only and are not to be considered or taken into account in construing the terms or provisions of any article nor to be deemed in any way to qualify, modify or explain the effect of any such terms or provisions. We've pretty much had with the obfuscation, folks.

So here it is. Nobody wants to take their old clothes to the recycling center. We get it. Mrs Tuft, just so you all know, is very upset. She's been hanging around the Meeting House. Therefore:

– all citizens must report to Mrs Tuft's Modern Fashions and Costume Collectibles Emporium on a monthly basis to buy themselves an outfit. Failure to do so will result in a penalty – equivalent in value to the cost of one year's outfits – and the distinct possibility of Mrs Tuft coming round your house.

He smiles.

"Clothing is a bit of a spanner in the works, you see, as far as the garbage collection goes. Folks round here won't willingly buy anything they can't dump more or less immediately. They've gone rubbish mad! It was nearly the end of Mrs Tuft's Modern Fashions and Costume Collectibles Emporium. We had to legislate to keep the poor woman open."

"Legislate?" says the Mayor of Big City.

"Compulsory purchases, sire. Everybody, council included. Once a month."

He pulls at the constricting lace collar of his dress.

"I'd be the first to admit that things have taken an unusual turn, but nobody will leave old clothes at the recycling center now. They'd rather wear them out till they were just rags, and therefore not covered by MARS."

He pulls his hat to the back of his head and sighs.

"Wearing clothes out is a dreadfully slow business, sire. Hence the collectibles market. Our way of dealing with the glut. Swap meets and such. Some of us have become quite the hobbyists. On the upside it's been very liberating, emotionally. The captain seems a lot happier in himself, don't you, Captain?"

"Oh yes," says Captain le Gros. "Much happier."

"We'd never defy a National Decree so the Recycling Center remains, says Bunbury. "But nobody goes there. We just can't abide recycling."

Carefully balancing his cigar on the rim of his portable ashtray, he crosses his arms.

"In fact, we hate it."

"We hate it *so much*," says Kelly.

Mr Squire looks at his shoes (embroidered black silk, pink satin heels, 17th century) and shakes his head slowly.

"It just seems so *senseless*."

Bunbury picks up his cigar.

"So you see, we thought there might be scope for an exemption, and that you might be the very man to talk to since, as we understand it, all those collected clothes end up in those overpriced Big City stores."

He winks.

The Mayor of Big City arches an eyebrow.

– each (and every) domicile is to equip itself with a designated wardrobe area of no less than twenty feet squared and to make provision – an outhouse, for example or a building extension if and when Kevin is back up and running – for further increases.

– a compulsory daily dress quota is hereby set at a minimum of two (2) units and may at any subsequent time be raised at the discretion of the council.

And let that be an end of it.

"Why would I do that?" he says. "Sounds unpatriotic. Vintage Corp™ is a very important part of the wars effort, Mr Burbury. Somebody's got to pay for the wars," he says, tapping some ash into the ashtray. "It might as well be you."

"Right, well we thought we'd ask," says Bunbury, through his teeth, eyes on the scone.

"Are you going to finish that?"

※

"You weren't shitting me, were you," says the Mayor of Big City.

The podium has been set down at the lake's edge. It was a long trek up here and the boys are lying in the toxic muck—rubbing their knees and whining about the state of their backs and what have you. Shadow paddles, up to his belly in the foul water and sniffing cautiously at the surface. He puts the tip of his tongue to it and winces.

"It really does smell like wee wee," says the Mayor of Big City.

The heat doesn't help. Mr Gallop is very pale. The Mayor's wife presses a handkerchief to her nose.

"Old wee wee," she says.

A figure approaches along the shore, pushing a barrow. The wooden wheel sticks and slips in the mud. Both barrow and figure are laden with coiled lengths of twine.

"It's that guy again," says the Mayor of Big City.

※

When the lake began to fester I had to up sticks. I'd stayed put up there since the Urine thing, shunned and shunning, seeing no one, wandering away from the trailer only to forage and to measure a couple of winters.

Moved down to a patch of land at the back of Theodore Spalding's place that I'd never known anyone to occupy or tend. Lasted less than a year there; Spalding has never liked me and soon got antsy, producing a faded old deed of questionable provenance and making a big song and dance about it.

So I cleared out just enough thicket on the slope above the Wakeling compound, well away from the house but with a view of it—if I climbed up into the Dogwood—and dragged the trailer up there.

It was from the tree that I'd spied, that blessed morning months hence, the familiar and long-mourned outline (the curls of the nape and nose, the woozy swell of the hip) that could only be my beloved Noranbole.

Noranbole!

Oh Noranbole! You did it, my angel! Help was at hand, thanks to your blessed machinations! Your tireless efforts! Your astute networking!

But how could I have doubted you? *How?* Was it ire? Pique, perhaps? The bilious rancor I felt in the wake of your decampment? The rancorous bile that filled your every receding footprint?

But no! I thought you dead! I knew only grief!

It was upon your *return* that the huff rose within me.

Ingrate!

How is it that, finding myself once more in your hallowed presence, or proximity at any rate, I could feel anything but joy?

I am naught but a lowly dudgeon, my celestial queen. Unfit even to think of you.

Get out of my head!

Lest I soil you!

Oh, but it hurt, Noranbole, give me that! My goodness, it hurt. The pain! Left here in this fetid morass with all these muttonheads, only choler and umbrage for company! Flayed in the biting, stinging swarm of your mother's opprobrium, which up until the Urine incident I thought rather uncalled for but after which, to be fair, was partially justified!

Anyway.

On this particular afternoon I was in the little yard I'd cleared out behind the trailer, preparing my equipment. I intended to head up to the lake, knowing the Mayor of Big City would be there and reckoning it would be easier for me to get to him with only those effete council members to deal with and with the sludge making it all but impossible for him to back away. My attempt to intercept him on his arrival had been frustrated by the wobble of the mayoral podium and the surprising nippiness of its bearers.

I'd have time, at last, up at the lake, to explain—in all its sumptuousness—the delicacy, elegance and undeniable infallibility of my proposal. To make him *see*.

This was my moment!

I busied myself with my spools, filling my barrow and throwing a couple over my shoulders. My notes, pegs and instruments were in the pack on my back. It was almost a shame to set off—to sully the hitherto unblemished potentiality of the enterprise—but set off I did, down the narrow track in the thicket and then the wider path that led by the Wakeling compound where I had the great good fortune to spy Noranbole on the veranda.

"Noranbole!" I was powerless to stifle the scream that escaped from my breast as I fell to my knees.

"Noranbole!" I screamed again. "'Tis you, Noranbole!" 'Tis to you that I owe my eternal gratitude, Noranbole!" I couldn't stop screaming. "That we all do! Or should! 'Tis *you* that drew him here! But why should I be surprised? *Why?* Does not the sun draw the unfurling blossom? Do not the sweet, babbling waters draw the animals and the birds? Of course they do!"

Even in the fury of my unfettered passions the sight of her gave me strength—I mustered enough of it to get to my feet.

"But how?" I screamed. "How can I thank you? Properly, I mean? As you deserve to be thanked? *How?* By saving you, that's how! By saving us all, which is exactly what I'm off to the lake to do!"

I waved my hat at her as I turned to go.

"Thanks again."

She didn't reply. My God, the poise of the girl!

But she did pick up her shawl from the bench beside her and disappear around the corner of the house, returning almost immediately with the May-pole dullard, who with uncharacteristic speed and dexterity donned his hob-nails, took her by the arm (presumption!) and accompanied her to the garden gate and onto the road behind me. They both had a deeply engaged look about them—wrinkled brows and an urgency in their bearing that an uneducated person might have mistaken for concern.

To have excited the interest of the one you adore! Can there be a better feeling in the world?

Oh Noranbole!

With my chest close to rupturing with pride and a renewed sense of the nobility and magnitude of my quest, I carried on. A few moments later I heard that heavenly voice behind me and, turning to reply, saw that it wasn't me she addressed, but her mother who leaned from one of the upstairs windows. In no time at all the older woman was shawled and bonneted and on the road behind us and, observing that she was gaining ground and in the company of Spot, I instinctively hastened.

Under the cherry tree as we passed, a despondent John Polley in a huddle with Paul Bennett and Samuel Tibbs. Up to no good I didn't doubt—the local lads had grown surly since the mishap with Urine and, inexplicably, the return of Noranbole hadn't seemed to cheer them up any. For this I held them in contempt, but was glad to see them take an interest and follow, putting themselves between me and Ms Emma, moreover, who had been getting closer.

"Here we go again," says Bunbury. "I'm terribly sorry about this, sire. He's persistent, I'll say that for him."

They can hear the mud squelch beneath the wheels of the barrow and see the others now, straggling behind.

"Breach of security, if you ask me," says the Mayor of Big City.

"Amateurs," says the Mayor's wife.

The figure drops the barrow handle at the base of the podium, falls to its knees, raises its arms towards the sky and screams.

"Your Holiness!"

But the Mayor of Big City is looking past it and has cheered up.

"Hey, Noranbole."

"Hey, Mayor."

"How are you?"

"Very well, thank you. And you?"

"Oh, you know."

※

"Your Holiness!" I screamed again, a little surprised that I'd been interrupted, if I'm honest. "'Tis I!"

He looked down at me. What a fine figure! Urbanity and class evident in every fold of his velvet smock, in every pomaded hair that glistened beneath the brim of his Homburg. Here at last was a sounding board worthy of my design! It had surely fallen on deaf ears for the last time!

He did seem a bit young.

"'Tis I, your Holiness! He whose inspired plan—whether you're aware of it or not and I completely understand that you may not be—brought your majesty here today!"

"Plan?"

"My letters, your Holiness." I lowered my arms "The diagrams? The schematics? The color coding and lengthy—but elucidating—footnotes? If you don't read the footnotes you can't—"

Removing my hat, I clutched it to my breast.

"You didn't read them, did you?"

"Not really," he said, leaning over the rail of the podium to tap his cigar on the rim of a little ashtray the Bunbury fool held aloft. "I didn't like them."

"I didn't like them either," said his wife. "They were strange."

I'd gotten to my feet.

"Right. Well, to be honest . . . it would have been helpful if you'd . . ."

I put an index finger to my lips.

"No. This is good. Yes. It's *better* this way," I said, doing my best to pace to and fro in the sludge. "It'll be fresh."

I pulled the pack from my back so that I might consult my notes.

"Right—"

"So how's it going, Noranbole?" said the Mayor of Big City.

"Not too bad, Mayor," said Noranbole. "It's been a bit unpleasant here lately."

Ms Emma was scowling at me but this was no time to be put off. I'd found my place in the notes.

"Right, your Holiness—"

"I'll say. Why don't you come back to Big City then? Bernard could be champion of the thing again and you'd be very rich and everything."

"Yeah," said Noranbole.

I looked from one to the other. This seemed to be a natural pause.

"OK. You may be aware, your Holiness, of the Swan Hill quarry, which lies just beyond those trees and which was dug in order to—"

"And you had that great job and all that," said the Mayor of Big City.

"Yeah," said Noranbole.

"You may also be aware," I might have raised my voice a notch or two, "of the Principle of Capillarity. A scientific phenomenon first observed by Da Vinci himself! What I propose, your Holiness, is—"

"You could probably get it back," said the Mayor of Big City, "because apparently they don't really know what they're doing."

"Well, on that," said Noranbole. "I've actually—"

"To clarify," I enunciated slowly, "by employing the capillary qualities of my—"

"No, I get it," said the Mayor of Big City, and this time he was looking at me. "Run a string from the horrible lake to the quarry and slowly drain the horrible lake. Right?"

"Well, basically . . . I mean we haven't discussed my elaborate system of pulleys yet, so it's a gross over-simplification, if your Holiness will forgive me for saying so, but essentially *yes* . . ."

"Because what I'm thinking is that then you would have an empty lake and a horrible quarry. I don't get it. The water would still be disgusting."

Now I had him.

"Not, your Holiness," I said, my voice thick with impending triumph, "if we filter it!"

179

He took a drag on his cigar, looked over towards the trees that hid the quarry and seemed to consider for a moment.

"Filter it how?"

I couldn't help myself. My hands went to my hips and I threw my head back.

"With string!" I screamed.

My triumph was complete. This was almost *too* exquisite.

"Great coils of it, your Holiness! We'll attach—"

"That won't work."

Startled, all turned as one at the sound of this new voice.

Unseen by anyone, a small boat had traversed the lake and neared the shore by which we all stood or, in the case of the boys, lay. In it sat a tiny, hooded figure, arms folded and face hidden in a deep cowl.

"This water can't be cleaned," it said. "It's enchanted."

It rose from its seat, fluorescent yellow and reflective silver in its water-proofs.

"I enchanted it."

There was a charisma to the figure in the boat that kept us all quiet. Even Spot. All we could do was watch as it raised its little arms above its head and bowed in apparent concentration. We waited. Nothing happened.

At first.

Paul Bennett saw it before anyone else did.

"Look! It's like before!"

All eyes followed his outstretched finger. Deep below the surface, something glowed green. It rose—a pulsating dome in the dark depth. At first the ascent seemed slow, but from what great profundity did it come, green glow widening as it climbed? As it neared we could see the velocity. We could *feel* it rushing upward.

I was transfixed. We all were, though the Bennett boy and I had seen this before. I had a feeling I wasn't going to like whatever happened next and just enough time to feel aggrieved about the timing of it all before, behind the figure in the boat, the water at the center of the lake bubbled. And broiled.

And broke.

❁

A welling of the rancid lake. A heaving hump on the surface.

It bursts!

Something shoots into the air, trailing great cascades—a deluge of ammoniac water. The boat is rocked, the occupant drenched. The thing hovers, then glides towards the shore, coming to a stop above the onlookers and showering them with the warm, evil-smelling fluid. It inclines, looks down upon them, stretches out its awful arms.

It is appalling! Its gaze harrows! Its odor queases. Putrescent, pungent piss angel, arch and cruciform!

One of its eyes is all white!

The other is all black!

Between its distended lips a row of teeth, worn and jagged and between those an over-sized tongue, flapping like a landed fish and bleeding from any number of cuts. It is dreadfully, mercilessly naked. Strips of scaly skin hang from its thighs, revealing red raw tissue. Pustules cover the soles of its feet. It gurgles and discolored spittle falls from its mouth.

"Wow," says Samuel Tibbs.

"She's still got it, hasn't she?" says Paul Bennett.

"I would," says John Polley.

The boys are on their knees in the mud, faces upturned. Putrid droplets speckle their blissful expressions.

Seiler aghast—looks from them to the monster.

"I've got a semi," says Samuel Tibbs.

"I actually thought it was going to be Mark Fleming," says Paul Bennett. "I'd have put money on it."

"My beautiful, beautiful girl," cries Emma Wakeling. "Is it you?"

Unintelligible vocalization from the levitating creature.

The boat has approached and the figure steps ashore. Its cumbersome waterproofs are removed to reveal a very well turned out and petite woman in her early thirties, a navy blue pencil skirt and modest heels which struggle in the mud. She produces a tablet from somewhere and holds it clipboard-style, beaming at Noranbole.

"Hi Norrie!"

Noranbole beams back.

"Hi Vacuity!"

"Vacuity Blanc?" says the Mayor of Big City. "The marketing witch?"

Seiler aghast again. At the word 'witch', he raises an arm instinctively, as if to protect himself. Vacuity takes a step towards him but, thinking better of it in her heels, instead raises a finger in his direction. She appears jovial and upbeat as his feet leave the ground and his breathing stops. He rises slowly, gagging as he goes. Eventually, he comes face to face with the creature. Both of them excruciated in the air, Seiler's arms are racked like its, his lungs crushed, his face purpling as the creature licks it happily. He tries to speak, but can't. His eyes boggle and glaze. Then they close. As the veins in his neck swell, it seems to be they that strangle him. Finally, they recede. He isn't making the choking noises any more. She lowers her finger.

His body drops to the mud.

The throat opens. Gulping air and on his way back from the edge of consciousness, he props himself on one elbow and, stretching out a hand to ward her off as best he can, cowers before Vacuity.

She tilts her head and beams at the Mayor of Big City.

"*Branding*, actually."

The creature has dropped with Seiler and pants contentedly at his side, not taking its hideous eyes off him for a second as they fill up with tears of devotion.

"Mother of . . ." he says. "For heaven's *sake*."

He looks from Vacuity to Emma.

"Could somebody—"

"They make a nice couple, don't they?" says Vacuity.

The lads are incensed.

"I don't know what she sees in him," says Phil Polley.

"No one will ever love her as I do," says Paul Bennett.

"That's a filthy lie," says Samuel Tibbs.

They brood.

"So, Vacuity," says Noranbole. She has taken her old friend by the hand. "It was you who enchanted the lake."

"Yup," says Vacuity, all smiles.

"Why did you do that?" says Noranbole.

"Well," says Vacuity, "I thought that if Mrs Wakeling had her other daughter back she might let you off your chores and you could come back to Big City and we could guidance the corporation together again. It's a big mess."

"Oh, OK. I kind of had that," says Noranbole, beaming. "But this is also good."

"The smell," says Bunbury, "has been absolutely *horrible*. Why did you make it smell so bad?"

"Oh, that," says Vacuity. "It's all got to do with the magic I used."

She tilts her head.

"I can't really disclosure it," she says to Noranbole, "for ethical reasons, but I basically had to undecompose your sister."

Noranbole looks at the creature.

"Pretty decent effort," she says.

"So what about it, Mrs Wakeling?" says Vacuity. "Can Norrie come back to Big City?"

Emma is on her knees, straightening the few strands of lank hair on the creature's head.

"Hm? Yes, yes, whatever you like," she says.

"Can we go home now, Gerome?" says the Mayor's wife. "I'm not enjoying myself."

"Sure," says the Mayor of Big City. "Burbury, please have your boys pick up the podium and carry us away from all of this."

Seiler leaps forward.

"But wait, your Holiness! What about my plan? The lake? My string?"

"Oh, none of that will be necessary," says Vacuity. "It should all clear up now. Couple of days, tops."

The boys hobble off with the podium on their shoulders, the council mooching along behind them. Shadow coughs up a hairball and barks at it before trotting along after them.

Despite the return of his doting mistress, Spot is nowhere to be seen.

"I am aghast," says Seiler, trying to release his wrist from the creature's iron grip. "There's just no other word for it. Who's going to push my barrow back?"

"Never mind that now," says Emma. She is smiling but doesn't look at all friendly.

"We have a wedding to prepare."

❋

"Please make it let go of me," says Seiler. "*Please.*"

They are in the parlor. Emma Wakeling is on her stool and Seiler is on the sofa. The creature sits beside him and has pretty much ruined the silk brocade upholstery.

"I need to go to the bathroom."

It hasn't released its grip on his wrist in two days.

"Go to the bathroom, by all means," says Emma. "Urine can help. Since you are to be married, there should be no secrets between you."

The return of her daughter seems to have awakened something in Emma and she is at her needlework for the first time in years, spectacles hanging from one ear and tilted on the tip of her nose. Her pipe is propped on the little table at her side. Still no sign of Spot.

"Urine, dear. Please take Mr Seiler to the bathroom."

He is dragged from the sofa and hauled along the floor to the downstairs toilet.

✳

Outside the general store. The old Concord that runs between here and Provinceton has pulled in. The horses are in their nosebags and the coach has emptied out.

There's a huddle—a few touts and self-appointed porters annoying the new arrivals, only some of whom will have come from Provinceton. Others will merely have changed there, having come from further away—maybe as far as Big City itself—on the overnight Diligence.

One of the latter category stands apart from the others, replacing a pair of long leather gloves and taking in her surroundings with an air of mild disgust. A heavy-looking leather shoulder bag sits at her feet. Hendley Flint, the youngest of the porter boys, breaks away from the others to offer his services. She looks down at him in a way that makes him think he must be very dirty, though he isn't.

"Because I have no arms, is that it?" she says. "What can it be that fills these gloves, then?"

She waves them in the boy's face.

"Should we call a paranormal investigator, do you think?"

Hendley meant no harm. Merely wanted to help, for as little as a penny or a perhaps a bit more if the lady was agreeable, since he is hungry and a penny doesn't get you much nowadays. Might he help the lady find her way?

"Ah, you've spotted the complete absence of eyes in my head, have you? Tell me, how is it possible that such a clever young man as yourself is portering and not using your obvious talents for the local police as a forensic scientist?"

Hendley would definitely give that some thought as it sounded like a very good idea and he didn't enjoy the portering, so much. Where is the lady headed this morning?

"Aren't you the curious one? It'll make your day, will it, to know I'm going up to the Wakeling place?"

She picks up her bag and without another word sets off in the right direction with such an easy confidence that Hendley concludes she's been here before, though he doesn't recognize her. In fact, he's never met anyone quite like her. She has only taken a few steps when she stops and turns round to look back at him.

"Sorry, boy," she says. She is shaking her head and prying her purse open.

"The older I get, the more I talk like that. I've no idea why."

She snaps the purse shut, flips him a tuppenny bit and goes on her way.

✳

The creature likes to pull Seiler out to the gazebo in the back yard of a morning and sit with him there, slobbering over his face. That's where they are now. Seiler puts up with it. He is taken to the bathroom whenever he requests it; nevertheless, his trousers are stained and he stinks.

His eyes, as it sucks on one of his ears, are on something in the middle distance that probably doesn't exist. On the other side of her, Spot, who she found cowering in the food safe yesterday, whimpers beneath her other hand.

Seiler is meek. Impassive. Vacant, even. Been like this for a few days. Not a word. Silent resignation. Today, though, is the day Noranbole leaves for Big City with her ninny-hammer. Emma Wakeling has been talking to the creature about it.

He clears his throat.

"OK, listen."

The creature stops sucking.

"Look . . . my dear."

It sits up a little.

"The thing is. I know I might have been a touch . . . resistant at first. I acknowledge that."

It nods.

"But I must say, and I think you'll be pleased about this—I've had a complete change of heart!"

Silence.

"That's right! I'm really looking forward to the wedding now! I could *not* be more excited about it!"

It tilts its head and, to the extent that such a thing can be ascertained by looking into its lolling, iris-less eyes, scrutinizes him.

"And that's why I wanted to have this little chat with you . . . my . . . love."

Nothing.

He clears his throat a second time.

"I think it's very important that we get this thing off on a sound footing, don't you?" he says, daring to look at it for the first time.

It nods twice, eagerly.

"Marriage is a very serious undertaking, after all. We are talking here about embarking upon a life together," he says, attempting a smile. "Teaming up, you know? And so on. We are talking about nothing less than *love*, my dear! The universal lifeblood. Eternal, undying love!"

His attention is back on the invisible thing in the middle distance. The creature tears up a little.

"Ah, but love itself is not enough."

He sighs.

"So fragile! So fleeting if left untended. I'm sure you'd agree, my dear, that we must never take this love of ours for granted?"

The creature does agree.

"It must be nurtured. Cultivated. Tell me, do you feel the same way?"

It does. A single, rust colored tear carves out a path over the rugged and somewhat jaundiced terrain of its cheek.

"And with what shall we nurture it, my dear? Hm? How to give it the strength it will need to thrive?"

It doesn't know. A belch from its lips releases a cloud of gas that makes Seiler's vision blur. He takes a moment to steady himself.

"With trust, my dear! We must have complete trust in one another!"

He gently places a hand over the one of hers which is clamped around his wrist.

"This will never do, my dear. It simply won't do."

He gives another smile a go.

"For how could you settle, my sweet thing, for *dragging* me down the aisle? Knowing, as you now do, how I long to *stride* down it! Boldly, as a free man, with you at my side? You think I lie, my dear? Oh, how sad! What a stain on our love! I do not lie. I cannot. It simply isn't in me."

The creature lowers its head. It looks at his hand on hers, then back at his face. For what seems, to him, a very long time indeed, it does nothing. A few more dirty tears streak its unevenly toned combination skin. Then, slowly, and without taking those terrible eyes from his, it releases its grip.

He bolts.

※

Noranbole and Bernard on the track that runs along the upslope boundary of the Wakeling compound.

Vacuity.

"There's no way my car is going to capacity all of this," she says.

Piles of luggage. It's taken them the whole afternoon to sort it all out.

Two big hat boxes for both of Noranbole's bonnets. She doesn't especially want them but Emma has taken the opportunity to have a clear out.

A stiff leather trunk for her frocks.

Her banjo.

A presentation case containing a finely decorated dinner set of speckled olive green and chartreuse floral motif with hand-painted gold trim and a bag of cutlery.

A decanter.

Two disassembled rods and a kit basket of fishing tackle.

A minidisc player.

Eleven large cartons containing the Book of Proposals and other documents.

An enormous clock.

A normal-sized clock.

A rocking chair.

The old bicycle.

Her flute.

An assortment of blankets.

"Psst!"

Noranbole looks at Vacuity.

The escritoire.

Vacuity looks at Bernard. He has wrapped his belongings up in a towel and tied it to the handle of his pick.

He looks at Noranbole.

Emma hasn't come out to say goodbye. She is in the parlor, presumably, planning for the wedding.

"Psst!"

They look up. Someone in the Dogwood.

"Mr Seiler?" says Noranbole.

"Shh!" says Seiler with a finger to his mouth. He clambers down and creeps off in the direction of his trailer.

"That was odd," says Vacuity.

Noranbole has her hands on her hips.

Bernard scratches his head.

"I can take the documents," says Vacuity, "and maybe the chair."

They hear footfall and look up to see Seiler return, a spool of string slung over his shoulder, Lepidopter in tow. He signals for them to be quiet.

"You recognize it, of course?" he whispers to Noranbole, dropping the spool at her feet.

"Not immediately—"

"Shh!" says Seiler. "Please! We *must* keep our voices down!"

He picks it up again and holds it out.

"See?"

All eagerness.

"It's the original!"

He thumbs the frayed end of it lovingly.

"My very best. The Winter String!"

"Right—"

"It's yours!" he whispers. "How could I begrudge you that? Hm? *How?* Are you not the empress of my breast? My animating principle? Am I not devoted to you? To the very *idea* of you? Am I not indentured to your tiniest whim? Compelled to obey the slightest little caprice that might cross your delightfully feminine mind? The mule is yours, too, if you want it."

Overcome, he falls to the ground and rolls around, weeping as quietly as he can. He reaches out with one hand and lays it gently on Noranbole's shoe. As politely as possible, she kicks it off.

He gets up, wipes his eyes and takes the string. Passing it under Lepidopter's belly, he throws it over the mule's back and repeats the action till there are three loops round the barrel of the animal, from croup to withers, into which he tucks the folded blankets on the back and along both flanks to create a level platform. Then he pulls the string tight and, turning to Noranbole, nods at Bernard and whispers.

"Could he put his finger here?"

"Could you put your finger there, Bernard?" says Noranbole.

Bernard puts his finger there.

Seiler takes the chair around to the other side and trusses it up. Then he lashes the dinner set to it and the clocks to that. The banjo and flute he bundles and wedges between the chair legs. The rods he assembles and binds one to each side of the mule, vertically so that they will act as braces.

One by one, Noranbole's things are lashed to Lepidopter with the Winter String. Seiler knots it as he goes. He is in his element, intent on this final application of his science. He is calm, now, and nods at Bernard again.

"Could he give me a hand with the trunk?"

"Could you give Mr Seiler a hand with the trunk, Bernard?"

Bernard picks up the trunk and has to climb up to get it to the top of the pile, which is now at least twice as tall as the animal. Lepidopter doesn't seem to mind; unusually, for a mule, he is smiling.

The decanter and the minidisc player and some of the cartons are left for Vacuity, who takes Bernard's face in her hands.

"Bernard, listen to me, sweetie," she says, beaming at him. "I want you to take these and put them in the back of my car, OK? Can you do that for me?"

Bernard nods and does it.

"Oh Noranbole!" whispers Seiler.

He's losing it again a little. On his knees.

"You'll think of poor old Seiler every now and then, won't you?"

"Yes, OK," says Noranbole.

He grabs her hem.

"I came here to escape with you, you know! Oh, the life we'd have! I'm sure we could have gotten Bernard a placement somewhere," he whispers.

More tears.

"But this must be enough. To see you off. To, if I might dare suggest such a thing, be of some assistance."

He looks back towards the house and his shoulders slump.

"My destiny lies here," he says. "'I will marry your sister. I know that now. 'Tis my lot. My comeuppance."

He puts the back of a hand to his brow.

"You must go."

"OK," says Noranbole and they do.

She and Bernard walk either side of Lepidopter, who has quite the spring in his step for one so laden, and Vacuity purrs alongside slowly in the car. Seiler watches them go till they disappear from of his sight. He stays as he is, on his knees, for a moment.

Then he stands and turns towards the garden gate.

❈

Emma isn't in the parlor, as presumed. She's in the attic at the window with her telescope, watching as the little company leaves.

It's late in the day and a reddening sun descends on the quartet as they go, threading through the village on the only road that heads west before looping back over the river, towards Small Town, Provinceton and the rest of the country.

Who was that figure, who had seen them off? She couldn't make it out through the hedge. She takes her eye from the glass and listens to the house.

Nothing.

"Urine?"

There is much to be done. She crosses the wooden floorboards and closes the attic door behind her, descending the few steps to the landing.

189

Opposite her is the room that used to be her nursery. With her ear to the door she can hear nothing.

"Urine?"

She waits a moment and then opens the door enough to stick her head around it. Urine's pen is unoccupied, as is the straw bedding she's had Seiler put down beside it for himself. The overnight manacles are exactly where she hung them herself this morning. She closes the door again and goes downstairs, into the parlor.

"Urine?"

She opens the curtains. They're not there. Neither are they in the kitchen where Urine sometimes goes to stick her tongue in the salt box.

"Urine?"

Emma is in the garden. The gazebo is empty. She has checked all the places; her daughter doesn't go anywhere else.

Then it occurs to her.

❊

"Urine?"

Seiler is in the garden. The gazebo is empty. She won't be at the roses as she's already eaten them all. He goes into the house, rehearsing an explanatory speech. She isn't at the salt box.

"Urine?"

He is half-calling, half-whispering as he opens the parlor curtains, sees that she isn't there, and draws them again. He doesn't want an encounter with Emma until he's had the chance to appease the creature and takes each step of the stairs timidly.

"Urine?"

He can hear the floorboards in the attic creaking and knows it must be Emma. He daren't call again and opens the door gently. The room is empty.

Something is wrong. He has looked in all the places.

A slow dread fills him.

What has he done?

What has *she* done?

The moment the question formulates itself, the dread becomes an idea. A terrible idea.

He tiptoes back down the stairs and closes the front door behind him quietly and when he gets to the garden gate and the path, he breaks into a run.

The stench has gone.

The lake is its old self.

Black.

Silent.

"Urine?"

He has done a circuit, looking out over the water and calling for her. It is a dark mirror. The moment he saw the undisturbed surface, he thought he was too late.

Now he knows he is.

"Urine?"

The voice he dreads. Emma appears from the bushes and sees him.

"You!"

She hitches her skirt and makes a beeline for him. He backs up till his boots are in the water.

"Didn't I tell you?" she shouts back over her shoulder. A few of the boys have followed her up here—Samuel Tibbs, Paul Bennett, Lance Holcroft and Timothy Spencer.

"I told you, didn't I?"

She grabs Seiler by his collar.

"What have you done with her? You've murdered her, haven't you?"

"What? No! No, I—"

He whimpers. His lips wobble.

"Then where is she? Why isn't she with you?"

"I . . . I don't know. I came up here to look for her . . ."

"Why has she released you? Why would she come here?"

He feels the flush of shame, and serious trouble.

"I think she may have been a little . . . I *may* have upset her—"

"Upset her?"

"It's *possible*. I didn't—"

"You lie!" says Emma. Her eyes are on the lake now; she lets go of Seiler and wades to knee height.

"If you've harmed her, I'll harm you," she says, calm as the dead. The water is at her waist.

"Urine?"

She surveys the surface, moving slowly so as not to disturb it. Her eyes search for bubbles, for the green light, for anything.

"Urine?"

Seiler and the boys watch her as she makes her way out. The water is at her chest. They are mesmerized by her descent. No green glow. No movement except hers.

"Urine?"

The lake laps at her chin.

Then at her lips.

They sink from view.

The nose.

Eyes right on the surface, reptilian, scanning.

Then they sink too.

Water closes in a tightening circle over the bun of hair, like a wound in the lake, healing.

One ripple.

By the time it reaches the shore, there is nothing at its point of origin.

Seiler and the lads wait for breath bubbles. None come. A full minute passes. And another. A third.

Nothing.

Seiler takes off his hat.

"Well," he says, "I didn't see that coming." He turns to face the boys. "I suppose someone ought to—"

He sees how they look at him.

"Now, now, lads. Let's not—"

"He's drowned her," says Paul Bennett.

"Again," says Timothy Spencer.

Lance Holcroft points to a birch.

"Let's use that."

Samuel Tibbs has a spool of string over his shoulder. The end of it swings from his hand. It's been fashioned into a noose.

"Hang on a second," says Seiler. His boots are back in the water. "Isn't that one of mine?"

✳

There is no answer.

The woman's heels are noisy on the wooden boards. Her steps communicate, in their quickening, an insistence that someone must be at home. At either end of the veranda, as she turns, she leans out a little and checks the grounds—the barn and outhouses on one side, the bay window and rosebush on the other.

She knocks a third time.

"Mrs Wakeling?"

She puts her ear to the door.

"Mrs *Wakeling*?"

Something creaks. A step on the stairs. Another. Very, very slowly, some-one is coming down. Fearful, the woman listens. At the bottom of the stairs (she knows them well and has counted the steps) a shoe hits the wooden floor and the same slow footsteps, syncopating with the metal tip of a walk-ing stick, approach the inside of the front door till the woman knows that she is only inches from their owner and there is silence again.

"Mrs Wakeling?"

"Yes?"

The voice surprises her. She doesn't know it. It is very faint. If her ear wasn't pressed to the wood she wouldn't have heard it.

"Excuse me," she says, "I'm looking for Mrs Wakeling. Is she here? She can't be at the Ladies' Association. It's Tuesday."

She has removed her gloves and fans herself with them. Her hands are clammy.

"Has something happened? Do you know where I can find her?"

"I am she," says the voice.

But something isn't right. If that is Mrs Wakeling, she must be terribly ill.

"It's you, Mrs Wakeling?"

Something prompts her to use the name she would never have dared use in the old days.

"Emma?"

The cattle egrets' chorus threatens to drown out the tiny voice so the woman puts her ear back to the door.

"Ah!" it says.

Then nothing.

And then the slow sliding of a low latch. The visitor steps back. A key is turned and another latch, higher up, is lifted from its notch. The door opens slowly, revealing little since the hallway is unlit. When the owner of the voice takes a step forward, into the sunlight, the young woman puts a hand to her mouth.

There she is. Mrs Wakeling. She stands—if it can be called standing—no more than four feet in height, due in large part to her implausibly gnarled, hunched bearing.

She has one eye, which in her downturned head is unable to direct it-self towards the visitor's face, one serviceable arm and one misshapen ear. Everything on her left hand side, from head to toe, and much on the right, is encrusted in scar tissue. She supports herself with a stick to compensate for a useless-looking left leg and carries a little leather bound book, tucked under a withered arm.

"You mean my daughter," she says.

"Your daught . . ."

The visitor leans forward and down, giving the old creature a chance to look back at her.

"You are *Rose* Wakeling?" She shakes her head. "But I thought you were dead?"

Rose is shuffling slowly around to face back into the gloomy house.

"Dear me, no dear! I'm very well indeed, I assure you."

Her diction is made unclear by the disfigurement of her mouth.

"Yes, *extremely* well, I should say."

She takes a shaky step.

"Won't you come in?"

The bewildered visitor finds herself curtseying, though the old lady continues on her faltering way down the hall and no longer faces her.

"I haven't introduced myself. I used to work here for the other Mrs Wakeling? My name—"

"Oh don't be such a silly, Bridget," says the receding Rose. She totters and takes a moment to steady herself, tucking the padded top of her stick more tightly into her armpit.

"Do you think I don't remember you? It's very nice to see you again. Now close the door and wait for me in the parlor, there's a dear. I'll bring some tea and you can tell me why you're here."

✳

As they cross the river on the old truss bridge, Pa Maypole is waiting for them.

The rim of his hat covers his eyes and he holds a match to the bowl of his pipe, his back to the trunk of an old willow on the grass verge. He isn't getting any younger himself, and anyway was a weather beaten man by the time he was twenty; these days he is every bit as knobbly as the tree. The hair that hangs from the hat is dirty silver and uncombed, the gray beard yellowed with tobacco. His eyes, when he has the pipe lit and looks up, are narrow slits nearly lost among deep, leathery lines.

They stop and wait for him to speak.

"Well looky here," he says, peering at the trio on foot and at Vacuity too, who stays in the car, engine running.

"If it ain't another mahogany ampertation."

He pulls himself up and puts himself in front of Bernard, toe to toe.

Looks up at his boy for a long time.

Spits at the ground without breaking eye contact.

"Ain't no surprise," he says. "Nuthin round here but bosh and burrow milk."

Pulls on the pipe and snorts smoke.

"Buncha tin horns!"

As he speaks, he retrieves a hundred note and a slip of paper from his wallet. Bernard doesn't dare refuse the money, raises an eyebrow as he takes the paper.

"Big City address," says the old man. "Where I gotcha from, boy. Some big city angelica—most partickler you be raised round here. I was morn happy to plank up but she wasn't having it. You give her a look see, if you want to."

He pockets his wallet and Bernard does the same with the money and the note.

"You accrue a certain tally o'summers," he says, to nobody in particular, "and life ain't nuthin but afterclaps."

He looks at Noranbole.

"You are a trat and a piece a puddin'. No argufyin' nutherwise. Tie to this boy, you hear? He may be a yack but you can ride the river with'im."

"Certainly," says Noranbole.

"I ain't no cackle head, neither." he says and his eyes drop to her belly for a moment. "That's no table muscle. That's a bay winda or I ain't never seen a winda."

She blushes.

Pa juts his head towards Lepidopter.

"Don't bake that mule," he says to Bernard.

The younger man nods, says nothing.

"And go easy on the base burners. Nobody respects a painted nose."

Bernard bites his lip.

"Keep your sand."

The old man clears his throat. The boy is tearing up a little.

"Watch out for bunko ropers," says Pa, kicking a stone. They can't look at each other.

"And don't be a slink."

He smacks the boy hard on his chest and Bernard punches him in the face, just the way he likes.

"All right, at this point we're just obnubulatin' the distincture of it. Pull foot," he says, taking a seat on the verge again and waving them off.

And they do.

※

It takes Rose a long time to return to the parlor. Bridget's instinct is to go and help but she is so taken aback by events that she sits still and waits, casting her eyes over all the little things she used to polish, the drapery she used to beat.

When the old lady does appear she is pushing a little trolley—one step at a time since she also needs her arm to wield the walking stick. She seems blissfully content and unaware of the time she's taking, humming a happy little tune as she goes. When she reaches the sofa, she places her leather book on a little side table and leans the stick on the trolley to give the tome a pat.

"Gingham," she says.

Bridget can no longer contain herself.

"Do you know when your daughter will be back, Mrs Wakeling?"

It is astonishing to her that the little woman would attempt to lift such an enormous teapot.

"Oh, she won't be back, dear."

It *is* lifted, though, in a trembling hand, and tea is poured shakily into cups and saucers.

"As you so rightly point out, dear, it's Tuesday. If it were Thursday and she was at the Ladies' Association, why, I would expect her any minute now," says Rose, her head and one eye swiveling to consult the wall clock, "but as it's Tuesday and she isn't, then I'm afraid I don't."

"What, *never*? But why not? What has happened?"

The old lady takes a seat beside her and offers the sugar bowl.

"Something most extraordinary, I would have thought, wouldn't you? Would you like a lump?"

She smiles apologetically.

"You'll have to take it with your fingers, I'm afraid. I've only got one arm, you know."

Bridget takes a lump of sugar and stirs her tea, unsure of how to proceed. In the event, Rose breaks the silence.

"Why are you here, Bridget? Are you looking for work? I might—"

"I have a boy," says Bridget, eyes down. "I'm looking for him."

"Oh, how lovely!"

"A young man by now, I should say. Sent him back here when he was born, less than a year after I went to Big City. I thought he'd be better cared for in the country—it was obvious to me I was unfit to look after even myself!"

She takes a handkerchief from her sleeve and dabs an eye.

"But I am now. I *am* fit now. I want to meet him. He's been with Patrice Maypole these years. I don't even know his name."

"It's Bernard."

"I don't know what I'll say to him. He probably—"

She looks at Rose.

"Did you say *Bernard*?"

"Yes, dear. A lovely boy."

"My son is *Bernard Maypole?*"

"Well yes, dear. That would follow."

Bridget's hand is shaking. She puts her tea on the trolley.

"And he lives with Pa Maypole?"

"Why no, dear. He's been living here," says Rose and takes a sip. "But he won't be back either."

"Won't be back? Where's he gone?"

"Elsewhere. With Noranbole."

"Little Noranbole? They're—"

"Yes, dear."

Rose pats the younger woman's hand.

"Quite a lot of news, isn't it? Would you like a biscuit?"

Moments pass before Bridget can speak.

"Well," she says, straightening her back and replacing her handkerchief, "isn't that just lovely? Isn't that just the loveliest thing you ever heard?"

She gets to her feet and puts a hand on the trolley, in part to steady herself and in part to push it back to the kitchen, which she has a hankering to see.

"You might allocate me some appropriate scutwork, Mrs Wakeling?"

"Me?"

Roses's one hand is at her chest.

"Who else? Aren't you the lady of the house?"

※

In the attic. The green glass lamp in its spot. Telescope at the window. The bicycle is gone, strapped to a mule's back, and the clear expanse of wall that was behind it is now a cinema screen—through the telescope and onto it, the red dome of a half sunk sun casts a simulacrum, cut straight at its midriff where the road crests Waldo's Rise, out at the county limit. The wall fades to black around the luminous half circle, a silent solar movie.

And now the clean diameter line is breached. A shape, irregular and a little lopsided, bleeds upwards into the fiery cupola—pointed, widening as it rises, till it sets four hoofs on the border that divides the blaze of light above from the void below. At either side of it, two human figures, a third its height. And now, off to the left, the unmistakable contours of a '72 Hillman Hunter GLS.

As slowly as they grew out of it, the four bobbling outlines dissolve again into the darkness. Soon there is just one melting bump—the tip of Lepidopter's burden. Then that too is gone. Only the red arch remains, itself sinking.

Out on Waldo's Rise the foursome take the slow descent into open country. A gentle gradient nudges them onward. The heat has relented; the long-shadowed evening is fresh and full of grassy musk as they look out over all the little farmsteads. The last rays of the day ignite the corn tips that swing and sway, as if the world itself is waving at them. A lark trills its song of contentment.

Oh, happy lark!

Sleepy cows loll about in their pasture, their big brown eyes on the travelers, seeming to wish them well as they go. Horses, happy-tired from a day's labor, peer over gates and flick their ears in greeting.

Delightful sights, scents and sounds abound in the air about them; here the summery buzzing of bumble bees, borne on the breeze that blows round the wheelwright's shed, there a troop of tiny blue birds that swoop and perch on the mule's rump.

Pigs unearth acorns with rummaging snouts; their monotonous grumbles syncopate the melodious peal of tong and hammer from the blacksmith's forge. A trio of chirping sparrows circle, little wildflowers held in their beaks to pin behind the pilgrims' ears. A single butterfly flits from nose to nose, then rises high above—a flickering airborne kiss.

"This is brilliant," says Bernard.

He has taken off his hobnails to feel the fine, cool sand on the soles of his feet and pad the soft moss that grows here and there between the wheel ruts. With each breath, he fills his lungs right up with the day's perfume, breathes out slowly and in again, deeply. He has joined Noranbole on her side of Lepidopter and holds her hand. A smile plays over her face as she walks and he knows exactly what it's doing there. Why she's practically skipping. She's happy because she thinks she's saving him. He doesn't have the heart to tell her she isn't.

Might kill the moment.

Instead, he lets his own mind wander back to when she really did save him—up in Pa's attic, a long time ago now. Vacuity taps a jaunty rhythm on the steering wheel and spies on them affectionately. The mule too casts fond, furtive glances.

Everything is going extremely well. Morale is off the scale. They knock out a verse of "She'll Be Coming Round The Mountain", then two of "I'll Be Home For Christmas".

As they near the county line where the road will begin its long loop around Swan Hill and the bogs, Noranbole stops to take a last look back, but Waldo's Rise obscures the Wakeling compound.

Bernard gives her a squeeze and is on the point of saying something else. No nonsense this time though, and no jokes. He wants to make it count, to say something that means something, something he's wanted to say since forever. Something that couldn't be simpler. He opens his mouth to say it, but before he can speak they hear a ping.

Seiler's string has come undone where he has fastened it poorly at the top of Lepidopter's load. Noranbole rolls her eyes. Bernard picks the loose end from the ground and pulls it tight, to steady the cargo. At the top, the lid of the leather trunk is thrown open.

"Spot!"

The little dog scampers down and cowers beneath the hem of Noranbole's dress. She bends down to pet him but retracts her hand immediately.

"You're all wet," she says, rubbing two fingertips against her thumb. Spot's fur is matted in some kind of yellowish mucous. He trembles a little, looking back up at the trunk in a way that suggests he hasn't enjoyed being in it.

They all follow his line of sight, except for Lepidopter, who can't. He keeps his eyes on Noranbole's, ready to buck if things look like they're getting out of hand. Something else is emerging from the trunk. The top of a head, an iris-less eye that, as far as any of them can tell, looks down at them. Dirty fingernails at the rim, more of the yellow ooze dripping from them.

"Looks like we have a stowaway," says Noranbole. "So much for my frocks."

She's the only one of them who shows no surprise. She does her best, though, to look disapproving. She feels she ought to. One hand goes to her hip and she raises the other to wag a finger. But her frown won't stick. Neither will an attempted pout. It unravels into a grin. Then a giggle.

"Urine!"

END.

Guillermo Stitch is the author of the award-winning novella, *Literature*™.
He lives in Spain.

If you enjoyed *Lake of Urine*, please tell your friends and your bookseller, and consider leaving a review on Amazon, Goodreads or your website of choice.